Templar, Cathar, Soldier, King.

Jeremy Ottewell

ALSO BY JEREMY OTTEWELL

The Catalan Knight
The Curse of Constantinople

Text copyright © 2017 Jeremy Ottewell
All rights reserved

To Lisa

Table of contents

Genealogy of King Peter the Great, of the Royal House of the Counts of Barcelona, Kings of Catalonia Aragon.

Genealogy of King Pere "The Great," of the Royal House of the Counts of Barcelona, Kings of Catalonia Aragon.

King Jaume I
(b.1208 reigned 1213-1276) m. Queen Iolanda of Hungary (1215-1251)
Issue:
(in addition to Jaume de Mallorca, Isabel de France and others) King Pere El Gran (b.1239 reigned 1276-1285) m. Queen Constança de Hohenstaufen, Queen of Sicily (1249-1302)
Issue:
Alfons (1265-1291) Jaume (1267-1327) Elisabet (1371-1336)
Frederick (1272-1337) Iolanda (1273-1303) Pere (1275-1296)

Map of Iberia by Ortelius, © Institut Cartogràfic i Geològic de Catalunya

Josep Goodman's Map of Catalunya, Aragón, València, Isles Balears, English Guyenne in France. Copyright Lisa Girling.

Note on travel. A journey to Barcelona from Sant Pere de Ribes by carriage would take a day; to La Puebla de Castro by carriage, four days.

CHAPTER 1. THE BLACK CAVE

October, 1274, Sitges, near Barcelona.

"It's stormy out there," Catarina said, looking out over the sea. "It makes me queasy." She glanced at Josep, tall for his twelve years, tanned and brown-haired, looking intensely at the approaching boat.

"The boats are rocking," he said. "The sailors must be soaked."

Catarina frowned and bit her lip.

"I'll give you a treat if you see Jacques' boat first," she said.

From the hill into Sitges, you could see boats approaching Platja Sant Sebastià, Saint Sebastian beach, from a good way off. A strong wind was blowing from the southwest, the local name was the Garbí, a harsh, hot wind typical for late summer. Catarina squinted into the wind, her rich, brown hair blown back from her face. She was still beautiful for her forty years.

"I think I can see it," Josep said.

The boat, a lleny, a sloop with a single mast used for transport and longer than a fishing boat, was approaching fast, its delta-shaped lateen sail full to bursting.

"It looks low in the water," said Josep.

Catarina groaned and grabbed Josep.

"Someone's standing at the front," shouted Josep. "Is that him? What does he look like, Mama?"

He was so excited he didn't notice his mother's fear as she watched her best friend approaching. He was breaking his journey back to Barcelona from the vineyards of the monastery of Escala Dei, inland from Tarragona, stocking up for winter.

"It makes me so nervous to see people standing up like that in boats," she said. "They always fall in in the end."

They scurried down the rocks onto Sant Sebastià beach from the bluff next to the old castle wall where they had been observing.

Jacques' boat anchored and Catarina and Josep watched as he was rowed in.

He stood up at the front of the small boat, brow knitted in concentration, looking calm and stable as if the rolling motion had no effect on him at all. It was as if he were impelling the boat on through a force of will. He seemed a man at ease with his physical ability, even his stillness was charged. In long white cassock with the red cross pattée blazoned across his barrel chest, sword swinging at his side, Jacques de Molay cut a strange figure, half monk, half soldier, and Josep, who had seen both many times but never in one man, was awe-struck.

"Is that what a Templar knight looks like, Mama?" Josep asked.

"Yes, Joe," Catarina said, her knuckles white as she clutched Josep's overcoat.

Jacques jumped ashore, pushed the mop of thick dark hair back from his forehead, then in one motion grabbed both his dear ones round the waist and pressed them hard to him. They gasped and laughed and all three started talking in Catalan, English and French. The keels and sails of the fishing boats hauled up on the beach were white on the golden sand. The three walked to the top of the beach to their carriage next to the sandstone church, pink in the late afternoon light, where the Moorish castle had once stood. As Josep clambered up, Catarina turned to Jacques.

"There's something I must talk to you about concerning Joseph," she said quietly in English, using her son's English name. Josep of course heard her. Jacques' face fell, his eyes widened, preparing for the worst.

"My dear Catharine," Jacques replied in kind using the English form of her name reserved only for the closest intimates. "Is he ill?"

Catarina tensed and coughed.

"So be it," she said. "We'll have the conversation now if you would prefer. What am I to do about Joseph's education, Jacques?"

Jacques tried to answer but she continued.

"He's outgrowing my ability as a teacher. He's getting a little bored and wild."

"I see I shall have to tell the boat captain to return to Barcelona without me," Jacques said, realizing the afternoon he had meant to stay would not be long enough and he would have to stay the night.

He went back to the rowing boat, spoke to the sailor and returned soon with two wineskins of the rich red wine he had just purchased and they rode the carriage pulled by the matxo back to Sant Pere de Ribes, crossing the low pine-clad ridge separating the two towns. Jacques feasted his eyes on the vast blue reach of the sea to his left and the dusty green maritime pines ahead as they went from the beach up the long gentle hill. They passed late summer vineyards, the leaves turning copper and crimson, the surrounding hedgerow green again for the first time in six months after the first of the autumn rains. Evening sunlight dripped over the hills to the southwest drenching the horizon with orange patchwork quilts of cloud against the intense blue sky.

At the foot of the other side of the hill stood Can Baró de la Cabrera, the masia, the square, whitewashed Catalan farmhouse, where Catarina and Josep lived. Clara Mir, the owner, came out to meet them as they came up the track, not surprised to find Jacques with them. At fifty, she still had her thick copper-coloured hair with a touch of grey around the temples and penetrating blue eyes. She was strong and broad-shouldered from a life of farm work.

"Hola Catarina, hola Pep," she said, using the Catalan abbreviation for Josep. "Hola Jacques! Quants anys? Quina sorpresa més agradable," she said in Catalan, "How many years has it been? What a pleasant surprise."

Jacques gave her one kiss on the right cheek, a practice normally reserved for family members, less intimate friends giving one on each cheek. She laughed and blushed.

"Paseu, si us plau. Benvingut, Jacques," she said, welcoming Jacques and inviting them inside.

The evening meal was simple but good, served in the ample terracotta-floored kitchen. They ate gilt-head bream with a salad made with fresh onion, aromatic olives and fire-grilled red peppers. This was served with moist, springy pà pagès, rustic loaf, toasted on the huge open fire that occupied half the kitchen, then rubbed with garlic and olive oil, a simple classic. They also had goat's cheese and drank red and white wine from the masia's own vineyard. Everything except for the fish had come from Clara's land, including the olive and carob wood used on the fire. The room smelled lightly of woodsmoke and the atmosphere was conducive to talking.

"How do you know my mother?" Josep asked Jacques without preamble.

Jacques sought Catarina's eyes before answering.

"I met your mother when she worked in beautiful Bordeaux, in Guyenne."

"Where is Guyenne?" Josep asked.

"It's an English part of France," Jacques said. "She was working for Lady Isabel, the wife of the Governor of Bordeaux, Sir John de Grailly. Wasn't it your father who…?" he started saying to Catarina.

"An English governor in France?" Josep interrupted.

"Yes," said Jacques. "He's like the representative of King Edward of England there. I believe it was your father's connections that secured the job in the first place, was it not, Catarina? Your grandfather, nen, was a commander in the Duke of Cornwall's army."

"Was he?" Josep asked.

"Això mateix, nen," Jacques said in Catalan, "that's right, lad. The Governor wanted more English staff and women like your mother to attend his wife in English to help her learn the language."

"Didn't she speak English?" Josep asked.

"Well, she did, but she wanted to speak it like her husband, who is English. She struggles a little, like me, no?"

"A little," Josep replied.

"Merci beacuoup, Josep, tres gentil!" Jacques said in his native French. "As she was usually surrounded by her own people, who were French-speaking Aquitaines from over the border, she usually spoke French at home."

"Is that why you speak French, because you are also from over the border?" Josep asked.

"It is, Pep," Catarina said in Catalan. They were in Clara's house and out of courtesy to her, Catarina wanted to speak Catalan. She cleared her throat quietly. "They do speak French in Bordeaux but they don't like to so much because they want the English to stay and the French king to leave them alone. But I was there for four happy years and that's when I met Jacques."

"Why? What was he doing there?" Josep asked his mother. Catarina glanced apologetically at Jacques.

"Josep, so many questions!" she said.

"It is not a problem, my dear," Jacques said to her. "I was the Templar representative at the court of Sir John de Grailly," he said turning to Josep.

"I regularly tavelled from Larzac to Bordeaux all the way along the Pyrenees on an old Roman road called the Domitian Way, a beautiful journey."

"Why don't we still live in Bordeaux?" Josep asked his mother, cutting Jacques off.

"We were in Barcelona with the Graillys when your father died, Josep." Catarina said. "It was Jacques who found someone to help me give birth to you."

"Did you know my father, Jacques?" Josep asked the templar.

Jacques shot a glance at Catarina, who went pale.

"Indeed I did, nen, and a fine, good man he was."

There was a lull in the conversation.

"Vaig conèixer en Jacques sis anys abans que naixessis, Pep," Clara said. "I met Jacques six years before you were born." She got the boy's attention while Catarina glanced at Jacques as if to say, "Do you see what I mean?"

"He happened to be passing Sant Pere de Ribes in the company of my brothers on their way back from the war in Murcia," Clara continued, hoping to divert Josep's attention a moment longer.

"I delivered a baby the evening my brothers returned. Like your mother, the woman had nowhere else to go. She spent the night here then went on her way with her newborn. I never saw her again."

She paused, a little emotional. "I often wonder what happened to her and her little girl, so when Catarina came bearing a note from you, Jacques," Clara turned to Jacques. Their ploy had worked, Josep was listening carefully.

"I thought, I'm not going to let Catarina and her child go till I know they'll be safe."

"And twelve years thence, to my great joy, here we remain," said Catarina, looking relieved the topic had changed from Josep's father.

"Lady de Grailly never warmed to me," Catarina continued. "Of course, I could not return when I discovered I was with child. I contacted Jacques and he organised my journey to Clara."

"So much killing in the world, I do what I can as a midwife for the living!" Clara said.

They all smelt the fetid odor of an unwashed human body at the same moment. Bru Miret, Clara's second cousin, had entered the masia. He staggered into the kitchen, following the sound of voices. Jacques knew who he was but his appearance was atrocious. His ginger hair had formed into matted pads and his dirty beard covered his chest, making him look half human, half wolf. He was drinking from one of the wineskins Jacques had brought for Clara. She leapt to her feet and ushered him from their presence.

When she returned, Jacques and Catarina were talking about him.

"He is an abomination to civilisation, he spends most of his time in the hills living among the creatures of the wild," Catarina said.

Josep was more interested in Bru than following the conversation. He had heard all this before but had not seen Bru for some time. He got down from the table and slipped out of the room without anyone noticing.

"He is an almogaver, Catarina," Jacques was saying. "They were once shepherds driving wolves from the flocks in the hills. They developed into shock troops that could fight anywhere over the centuries of the Islamic occupation of Catalunya."

"Yet once the reconquest of Catalunya was complete, I fail to see what need for them remained," Clara said.

"The almogavers were left to "mop up" my dear," Jacques replied.

"Or, to speak plainly," Clara said, "slaughter the isolated pockets of Morisc Muslims that hid in terror deep in the hills and woods of Catalunya." She wiped her hands on her apron once and again as if she could not clean them.

"The Moriscs who have not relocated to the cities take their lives in their hands by living in the hills," said Jacques. "They have the king's protection in the cities. As for the almogavers, The Catalan Aragonese Crown still uses them in their wars in Murcia. They are horrifying butchers but their efficiency is legendary."

"Which is why Bru's influence over Joseph worries me," Catarina said. "Joseph?" she said in alarm. "Has anyone seen Josep?"

They made a thorough search of the house, which, though not huge, was labyrinthine as new parts had been added to older ones over the centuries. Clara's old joke, that there were more windows visible from outside the house than you could account for from inside, was no longer amusing. Josep was nowhere to be found.

"He'll be with Bru," Jacques said trying to sound as relaxed as he could. "Mirets and ferrets have the same nature: they burrow down where you least expect them, then shoot out and tear out the throat of their prey!" The blood drained from Catarina's face.

"My God, where has he taken him?"

"Not to worry, he'll be safe enough," Clara said.

"I'm sure you're right" said Catarina, "but I think he's still a little young to be tearing anyone's throat out, or even seeing it happen."

"Jacques," Clara said, "do you remember where the Cova Negra is? Maybe they have gone there. Didn't my brothers take you there once? It's along the Jafra river bank, about two miles from here, you can't miss it."

"Yes, my dear, of course!" Jacques answered and set off immediately.

†

"One of these nights I'll take you up to the Cova Negra down the Riera de Jafra and we'll see if we can't catch ourselves a rabbit or two!" Bru Miret had said to Josep weeks before. That evening at Can Baró, Josep had been easy to persuade.

"We'll be back before they miss you," was Bru's clinching argument, as they headed off.

By the light of the moon, the trip to the Cova Negra, the Black Cave, was magical and phantasmagorical. Along the dry riverbed, maritime pines scented the path as the sap of the trees oozed in the bark with the heat. They waded through thickets of reeds, bamboo and tall grass but finally they stopped. The sounds of small animals scurrying away were all around them as Bru struck his fire stone expertly, catching the spark in the ball of rolled up dry grass he had ready in his hands. The flame leapt up in his cupped hands, which he then used to light a torch. The red eyes of a larger creature, maybe a fox or a stoat, appeared for a moment before it darted away.

The next instant Bru had disappeared into the ink-dark cave. Josep followed, the ground cool and soft underfoot, stinking of cat musk. Then he heard a muffled cough from the back of the cave. Bru sprang forward, his left hand holding the torch, his right hand drawing his coltell, his almogaver cleaver. He had the blade to the neck of a man. From the flickering light of the torch, he appeared to Josep to be a Morisc of fifty or so.

"What have we here?" Bru said with a laugh. "Better than a couple of rabbits, eh Josep?"

Another voice echoed through the cave. "Drop the knife, Bru!"

Bru whirled round to see Jacques. Bru's eyes shone like a wild animal's in the torchlight. He was like a cat caught with a bird in its teeth.

"Harm anyone and I shall scramble your kidneys with my own knife," Jacques whispered holding up his blade. Bru blinked, stepped back from the Morisc and ran off into the woods.

"Josep, you owe your mother an explanation," Jacques muttered as they started trudging back to the masia.

When they got home, Josep was severely scolded and sent upstairs to bed. He listened at the door for some minutes but could make out only muffled words from the conversation Jacques, Clara and his mother were having downstairs. Then he heard Jacques saying goodbye, quietly closing the front door behind him and marching briskly down the road.

The moist, warm air of the summer night enveloped Josep, making it difficult to breathe, almost like drowning. Josep strove to control himself. His heart was beating wildly. He could not get the image out of his mind of what he had seen in the cave, he could not forget Jacques' warning to Bru, the look of agony and panic on the face of the Morisc, on the floor at the back of the cave. Was he injured? Surely, otherwise why would he not have tried to escape or at least hide when he heard Josep and Bru coming? But had he been there for long, had he accidentally found the cave or was he prey that Bru was keeping there?

The moon began its descent to the southeast over the hill that separated them from the sea and which they had crossed twice that day. Josep strained to hear anything but the house was silent. Outside, the lonely sounds of the night, owls hooting, dogs barking, the beating of wings were all Josep could hear. Where had Jacques gone? Josep wondered. Had he gone to get the man from the cave? Josep mulled over the events of the day, felt invisible in the darkness, could barely sense himself breathing. He dozed off. He dreamt he was underwater and the blood was ringing in his ears.

Josep awoke to the sound of Jacques' footsteps at the end of the road. From his bedroom window, he watched him approach the house. He was moving slowly, carrying something over his shoulder. He paused under Josep's window and Josep tiptoed into the shadows, then cautiously inched forward so he could see without being seen. His mother and Clara hurried out of the front door and opened up a barn opposite and Jacques took whatever he was carrying into it. Josep had time to see a human body wrapped in white sheets with dark patches on the sides and glimpsed the face of a man, pale in the moonlight. He seemed to weigh little.

"It must be the man in the cave," Josep thought to himself. "But is he still alive?"

After some minutes, Clara, Catarina and Jacques rushed out of the barn into the main house with the body and Josep could hear furniture being moved around in the kitchen.

"The Morisc must be cold and there is no fire in the barn," he thought. They were building up the fire for him in the kitchen even though it was late summer and still so hot.

"The man must be alive but dying," thought Josep, "they're trying to keep him warm, maybe as comfortable as they could while he...while he dies," he struggled to finish the thought. Josep heard Clara's voice downstairs.

"If Bru finds him, he won't live till morning. I'll stay with him. You two go to bed."

Long after all had gone quiet in the house, Josep still stood at his door straining to catch any sound. He crept downstairs into the kitchen. The fire was hot and next to it lay the man on a bed of rushes and long grass. Clara, head on her chest, sat next to him dozing. Tiptoeing forward, Josep saw a ripple of movement on the sheet wrapped round the man.

"So," he thought, "he is still alive." Looking more closely, he saw it was indeed the man from the cave. But who he was or what had happened Josep could not even guess. "Is Bru to blame for this?" he thought. "How could he do a thing like that? Bru is dangerous, as Mother has always told me. I should have listened to her."

Josep returned to bed and slept deeply. The following day, when he woke, the man had gone, the makeshift bed had vanished but there was still a damp patch where the area next to the fire place had been washed down.

Jacques soon appeared, looking grave and tired.

"Jacques, I saw you bring back the man from upstairs. Has he died?"

"Yes, Josep," Jacques replied. "He died at sunrise as he knelt praying to Allah facing east as all Muslims do, with these beads in his hand." He pulled a simple string of beads from his pocket.

"It took him all his strength to pray. He woke Clara when he passed away and fell to his side. I've taken him up the hillside and given him as decent a burial as I could. He wore a ring on his finger, so perhaps his wife is somewhere out there, perhaps also children."

They hadn't had time to talk about Josep's future the night before but it was soon evident to Jacques that Josep was more than Catarina could handle, as she had said. Moreover, Josep's intelligence shone through to Jacques.

"Catarina," Jacques said after lunch that second day, "you wanted my opinion about Josep's education. The boy needs to go to a formal school with other boys. Will you allow me to see what I can arrange?"

"His place is with his mother, Jacques. How could I contemplate being parted from my son?"

"My dear, he will grow wayward here, you said so yourself. This is why you wanted me to come here, is it not, to talk this matter through with you and Clara? He might be influenced by Bru and others like him as he grows up. Besides, he is talented and needs the right instruction to grow. With your permission, I could take him to La Puebla de Castro, to Cavallers."

"Where is that?" Catarina asked.

"It is in the Aragonese Pyrenees, four days' ride from here. It is the best School for Pages and Squires in the kingdom," Jacques replied.

Josep bolted down the stairs. "I don't want to go away to school!"

Catarina's face showed her fear and sadness.

"But Joseph, you trust Jacques, don't you? Jacques, do you promise me that this is best?" Catarina asked, searching his eyes. Clara felt responsible for the predicament Catarina was in though circumstances had taken their own course. She saw the poor mother torn between her bond with her child and anxiety for his future.

"Can I come back often and see you and Mother?" Josep asked her later that day as he packed his bags to leave.

"As often as you wish!" Clara replied, smiling broadly and hugging Josep. But she knew this would depend on factors beyond Josep's control.

CHAPTER 2 CLASS WAR

Two days later, Catarina, Josep and Jacques set out for Cavallers, in the town of La Puebla de Castro, in the north of Aragón, a long journey. They headed for Claramunt as Jacques had official Templar business there.

Their carriage, drawn by two horses, all of which Jacques had acquired, was comfortable enough and the road followed the River Llobregat towards Castellbisbal. Jacques seemed to know something interesting about everything and was good company. He pointed out the Templar castle of Castellciuró near Molins de Rei and as they approached Castellbisbal, the hills behind the town, where the Comte de Sert's lands lie, much of it rocky crags and steep, hidden valleys.

"They say there are still secret pockets of Muslims living there" he said, "people who never leave their little valleys that still continue their way of life almost unchanged for centuries now."

Inevitably, this reminded Catarina and Josep of Sant Pere de Ribes and their reasons for leaving. To lighten the mood, Jacques then explained the aquatic life of the river, how good the mute ducks that swam upon it were roasted in pears and wine, whether and when the Llobregat was navigable or not in its different sections, even why it was called the Llobregat, meaning, he said, lugubrious.

"There are pools further up the river where the river has cut deep gorges into the rocks quite different from the wide alluvial plain we see here. In these deep pools dwells the Lady of the Wells. She was thrown into the pool by her wicked husband and drowned when her hair tangled itself in the underwater reeds. So they say she is still caught in the reeds there, her hair has now become the reeds and she cries out her accusation against her husband day and night bemoaning her fate for all eternity."

"What a cheerful tale," said Catarina, shuddering suddenly. "Can't you tell us something about what Josep can expect at his new school?"

"Yes, I want to know what a page is and what I will have to do," Josep said.

"A page is like an apprentice knight, Josep," said Jacques. "You will attend your knight and live and breathe his way of life."

"Who will he be?" Josep asked.

"He will be a young unmarried man probably," said Jacques, "someone who still does not have his own household and company of soldiers so needs someone to help with his horse, to run errands, to look after his weapons."

"What weapons will he have?" asked Josep. "Will he have the same weapons as a Knight Templar"

"We will have to wait and see, but yes, I think so," Jacques said.

"I suppose the school will have the things I need and I can borrow them," Josep said.

"No, indeed, Josep, you will have your own things but I must organise that with the school when we arrive there," Jacques said.

"Jacques, where shall I find the money to pay for those necessities?" asked Catarina.

"God will provide, my dear, do not fear!" Jacques said.

This made Josep laugh and Catarina reached out and pulled Josep closer to her.

"What will they teach me at the school?" Josep asked.

"The first thing will be how to ride!" said Jacques.

"I know how to ride, don't I, Mother?" Josep said. "I'll show you how well I can ride when we arrive in Cavallers."

Jacques laughed. "You'll also have to learn how to look after the horses," he said.

"Horses? How many horses?" Josep asked.

"Your knight will probably have three or four and you will also have your own, so maybe as many as five," Jacques said.

"I will have my own horse?" Josep shouted, standing up in the carriage. Catarina pulled him down quickly.

"You will have to accompany your knight at all times he requires you, Josep," said Jacques, "so your horse and your knight's horses will have to be ready at all times."

Josep's mind span with these ideas. "I want to start already!" he said.

"They will keep you busy, nen!" said Jacques. "When you are not with your knight, you will have to study all the subjects a page needs to know."

"Will we be able to go out of the school?" Josep asked.

"I'm sure the teachers will take you out to train you in horse-riding and perhaps other activities, I do not know for sure, Josep. But they will toughen you up. You will be near the mountains and rivers so you will have to learn to swim well and be fit and tireless. But you will also need to know what your knight has to do so you will need to know where places are and what the knight has to do to serve his king."

"Will they be in dangerous situations?" asked Catarina.

"The life of a knight is an active one and they are soldiers," said Jacques. "But they are trained in their work and like all soldiers, put the safety of their pages and other companions before their own."

Catarina did not seem convinced by this but changed the subject.

"Look, I think I can see Montserrat already," she said.

The Catalan holy mountain was to their north, its south side illuminated in the afternoon sun, its saw-tooth ridges slanting at steep angles. It seemed denuded of trees or any vegetation from a distance, like a remnant of an underworld battle thrust out into our world, mysterious and sobering.

"We won't be welcome at the table of those overfed Benedictines at the monastery of Montserrat!" said Jacques, trying to dispel the strange atmosphere that had settled on them again. "A Cistercian convent like Vallbona would welcome the Poor Knights of the Temple of Solomon and has not forgotten its oath of abstinence and poverty."

"I didn't see much evidence of abstinence or poverty in the dinner you had yesterday, all that rich food and wine!" said Catharine, snapping out of her gloomy mood and enervated by the mention of food.

"I'm hungry," said Josep. "When will we be there?"

"We will be in Claramunt in an hour or so," Jacques said.

As Jacques bore good news to the Senyors of Claramunt, they supped on roast quail and excellent Anoia wine and slept well. From the hill-top castle, a spectacular sunrise over Montserrat to the east awaited them the following morning and they soon put distance between themselves and the jagged peaks. The road opened up to the plain beyond the line of hills along the coast of Catalunya to the scattered hamlets and towns, which lie like a gem-studded cloak across the undulating hills of the pre-Pyrenees. They were surrounded by vineyards and fields of hazel, almond and olive trees, the produce of which Catalunya's rural economy depended on.

They stayed the second night in a tavern in lovely porticoed Agramunt and in full view of the Pyrenees all the next day managed to cross the Aragonese border to Monzón before nightfall on the third day, its huge castle visible from twenty miles away.

Once they had mounted the steep cobbled street that led to the castle, the Templar, Berenguer de Belvís, the commander of the castle and friend of Jacques, came out to meet them.

"Do you want to know why Monzón is so important to the Templars?" the commander asked Josep. "This is where the story started for the Templars in the Kingdom of Aragón," he said. " Ramón Berenguer the Fourth died and left our order this huge castle and some of his money every year."

"Why?" asked Josep. "Did he have no children or family?"

"He had family and children, jove," the commander laughed, "but he wanted us to continue his Christian work in the kingdom. Rei Jaume, our king, was educated here as a boy."

Josep wondered if his school would be as huge as this castle. It seemed an enormous place for one boy.

"Is my school as big as this?" he asked. "Will there be other boys there?"

"Your school is much smaller, Josep," replied Jacques, "and full of boys like you."

"Will there be Templars there?" Josep asked.

"Not as far as I know!" the commander laughed, putting a hand on Josep's shoulder, "but we have people working for us everywhere."

"Good," said Josep, "I like Templars." He smiled up at the commander.

Berenguer de Belvís showed Catharine and Josep to their rooms and Jacques left them there and went with the commander.

"My dear Jacques!" he said once they were in his own quarters, clasping him by the shoulders. "We have not seen each other for too long." Both men were tall and bearded but Berenguer de Belvís was completely grey-haired already. "What brings you to these parts?" he asked.

"My Lord de Belvís," Jacques began, bowing his head. "I must ask you for your earnest opinion on a matter of utmost urgency and sensitivity. What is your impression of the boy?"

"Well, Jacques, he seems a fine young lad, pleasant and well-mannered. His mother is English, is she not? How many languages does he speak?"

"Catalan, Castillian and English as a native, my Lord, and he has basic French but forgive me, that is not the purpose of my question. I mean to ask your opinion of the boy as a future novitiate."

There was a pause as Berenguer de Belvís suppressed a sharp intake of breath.

"He seems a very able young boy," began de Belvís carefully, "but you know the Order is against the entry of boys, preferring young men who have experience and can tolerate the hardships of monastic and military life."

"Yes indeed, my Lord, you have perceived one very worrying part of the problem. The boy is wild and needs training, he is beyond the control of his mother and..."

"Who is his father in fact, Jacques?" said Berenguer, quickly getting to the heart of the matter.

"That is the most worrying part, my Lord, as you are quick to see," Jacques replied. "So far as I know, the mother has never revealed the father's identity to the boy. He was a diplomat from the Emirate of Granada based at the time in Bordeau. She came to me when we both happened to be in Barcelona and she felt she could no longer continue as a maid in the household of Sir John de Grailly of Bordeaux."

"You mean, when she was several months with child?" Berenguer asked. "Why did she not simply return to her family?"

"Apart from the distance, my Lord, I do not think she could face her family." There was a pause.

Berenguer nodded. "Am I coming to the right conclusions, Jacques?"

"I'm afraid so, my Lord. There was never even mention of an engagement. I feel I would have heard about it if there had been one as I considered myself her friend and had accompanied the de Grailly household from Bordeaux to Barcelona and back a dozen times over the four years between 1261 and 1265 and had always had the privilege of her company."

"That is all very well, Jacques, but what bearing does it have on the young boy's entry into the order?" the Templar commander asked.

"My Lord, if it were possible, I would adopt him and he would become a Templar when he came of age."

"But Jacques, you would need the permission of his mother first, which I doubt she'd be prepared to grant, then you would need to show that you are the person most appropriate to adopt him. You need to reconcile that charge with your responsibility as a Templar, which to my mind is far from easy and then there is the matter of service in the Holy Land: when are you due to be posted abroad?"

"Imminently," Jacques replied, unable to look the commander of the castle in the eye.

"In other words, you would not be able to act even as guardian to the boy let alone adoptive parent, Jacques. Forgive me for being so blunt but it seems something has obscured your reasoning in this matter."

"Highly likely, my Lord."

"Is it the mother herself, Jacques? Are you in love with her yourself?" He did not wait for a reply. "Then I urge you to consider your position very carefully."

He moved away into the shadow momentarily, bowed his head then drew the curtain over the window that looked out over Monzón from the castle. Here he always came when he had a difficult decision to make that involved him personally.

"Jacques, I will tell you what I advise. You can be his benefactor, which requires you only to provide for his financial upkeep. It is the most discrete arrangement in my opinion in these circumstances. If you wish, I shall administer his affairs from here..."

Jacques grasped his hand and bowed his head. He knew immediately this would be the perfect solution and also acceptable to Josep's mother.

"My Lord, that is very generous of you. It is more than I dared to hope for."

"And I will keep an eye on him for you, too," the commander continued. "But your heart has overruled your head here, Jacques. I advise you to extricate yourself as cleanly as you can. I hear that you are heading for Ferran Sanchis' academy. Keep your affairs carefully in order, Jacques, Sanchis is a manipulative and ambitious character. Keep your guard up."

†

The following day, Jacques, Josep and Catarina set out mid-morning. Their route was a practically straight line across the undulating Pyrenean foothills of Osca, the higher peaks visible to the north, the wild scrub of the plain ahead to the west, the hot sun arcing over them to the south.

"The sky is so bright blue, it almost hurts my eyes," Josep said.

"Yet does it not also make you want to praise God to experience it?" asked Jacques.

Before long, they passed Barbastro and entered La Puebla de Castro.

"This town is part of the fief of Feran Sanchis, the illegitimate son of King Jaume," Jacques said. "Ferran's name is on everyone's lips at present as he foments revolt among the Aragonese barons against his father."

Yet as they entered La Puebla de Castro under the Portal de Oliveras and went into the Plaza Mayor, the first thing they noticed was that, unlike in Monzón, Catalan was not being spoken but rather a language that sounded like Catalan but was full of other strange sounds. Jacques told them it was Aragonese. Josep and Catarina spent time acclimatising themselves to this ancient mountain language.

Jacques located the school and Josep and Catarina noticed what a beautiful old farmhouse the main building was. It was a whitewashed, Mudejar construction with a perimeter wall all the way round it in about three acres of land and had access to the river Essera from the property five minutes' walk away. In the distance behind the farmhouse one could see the peak of Monte Perdido on the left to the west, Posets straight ahead and Aneto to the right to the east, behind Monte Turbón in the foreground. It was a dramatic location.

The Principal explained that Josep had been assigned as page to Lord Pedro de Ayerbe.

"However, Ferran Sanchis is our Lord and Master here, young man," the Principal went on, "as this school belongs to him, as does this whole village."

Catarina didn't get a chance to ask any questions as at that moment, Dalmau Rocabertí, eldest son of Viscount Jofre Rocabertí arrived together with a young lad of about Josep's age, called Ramón Muntaner. Short, muscular and dark, it was his second year there training as page to a knight called Dalmau Rocabertí. Jacques and Dalmau greeted each other like old friends.

"My best wishes to you and your father, Lord Rocabertí," Jacques said.

"I am pleased to see you well, sir!" replied Dalmau Rocabertí.

"If only I had been able to avail of your father's hospitality at Perelada when I last crossed into Catalunya!" Jacques said smiling broadly. "But I was unable to as I sailed down to Barcelona from Marseille. I look forward to being able to stay the next time I cross the Pyrenees. It is a long journey from Larzac and though I love the rolling hills of the Languedoc, it is always a relief to arrive in the Alt Empordà with its beautiful, wild coast and have the Pyrenees behind me."

"You are always welcome at Castle Recasens, sir," replied Dalmau courteously.

That evening, Josep, Catarina, Jacques and Ramón dined together.

"Leaving Josep tomorrow will not be easy," Catarina said to Ramón before retiring.

"My mother felt the same way last year when I was new here. I will try to be a good friend to him," he said.

Next morning, Josep was up early and went down to the stables. There he found Jacques preparing their horses for the journey back to Sant Pere de Ribes. He helped and they finished by giving them something to eat.

"I'm starving!" said Josep.

"Me too!" Jacques replied. "I want some hot, fresh bread, with warm cow's milk!"

"Race you to the kitchen! I'll show you how I can ride!" said Josep, jumping to his feet.

In one motion, they both mounted their horses at a leap and seconds later careered through the open gate of the courtyard. They had to veer sharply to the left in order to follow the curve of the perimeter wall of the courtyard and Josep and his horse, being lighter, managed to cut inside Jacques just in the last paces before the kitchen. Josep dismounted and brought his horse under control in a couple of steps. A fraction of a second later, Jacques did exactly the same and they both stood panting slightly with the exertion. Jacques for a forty-year-old man was still very agile. Jacques was astonished at the speed and grace of the boy and was delighted. They went together into the warm kitchen. The cook could see immediately an early breakfast was required.

"I have rarely seen anyone so naturally able with a horse" Jacques commented later to Catharine. "Where on earth did he learn to ride like that?"

"He'll fall off, I know he will!" Catarina said, fighting back the tears, "and when he does, where will I be? I need to be around him, he's only a small child, he needs his mother," she said.

Suddenly, Jacques saw Catarina at home without her boy, missing him terribly. He desperately wanted to reassure her and started off on another tack.

"I've seen youths and men try for months to get that move right and he picks it up in seconds. He's a natural, Catharine, he's not a danger to himself!"

"His confidence is far too high!" said Catarina. "Who knows what he'll dare to do when I'm not around to look after him or to smack him into some sort of understanding of personal danger to himself? He's always been a nightmare. Remember that night with Bru! And that's not all. He's always been a danger to himself."

"That is precisely why we have brought him here, my dear," Jacques replied. "Firstly because he has to learn what his limitations are and how to behave safely in the situations a young page is going to find himself in. But mark my words, Catharine, this boy is a natural."

†

The time for Catarina and Jacques to leave arrived later that morning. Catarina and Josep held each other close.

"Your equipment will be here soon, Josep," Jacques said.

"I love you, Josep," Catarina said. "Please take care and enjoy yourself here." Jacques helped her up into the carriage and before Josep knew it, she and Jacques were fifty paces gone.

Josep turned and walked, tears in his eyes but resolute back across the cobbles from the gate to the main door. As he came into the wood-panelled refectory, nobody paid him the slightest notice; they had all been through that moment and one had to go through it alone. He would survive. They made room for him on the simple wooden bench without stopping their conversation. He sat next to Ramón and in moments had immersed himself in their company. The smell of the refectory comforted him: freshly baked bread and bacon.

He was so busy that he had no time to himself. His equipment arrived later that week and he had to sign for it personally, which meant he had to check it carefully in the presence of the school's draper. Much of it seemed to him superfluous and extremely uncomfortable or cumbersome. His habit, which was woollen and fitted over his head, came down to his ankles, tripping him up several times at first. He wasn't used to wearing long garments, having spent his entire childhood in a short tunic. He had expected it to be white and had secretly hoped it would bear the cross pattée of the Knights Templar on the shoulder. Of course, it was not white but brown, like the habits of the lower ranking friars in the school who worked as servants, nor did it have the cross on the shoulder, yet it was an important moment. It made him realise that he had imagined himself as a diminutive Jacques, a thought that amused but saddened him. He realised with a pang he felt about him as he imagined he would his father.

The item of clothing that was most bothersome for Josep, however, was the gorget, which went over the hood of the habit, fitted tightly across his shoulders and upper chest and up his neck to below the chin. Made of coarser wool than the habit, it itched. He went around the first few days with his chin up and his head rigid to avoid the itching, which all the boys teased him about as they remembered themselves what it was like to get used to it. He also had to wear a heavy mantel, also of wool, the weight of which was carried on the shoulders but fastened around the neck, making it difficult for him to breathe and swallow. Gone were the light clothes of home. Whereas before he was used to light clothing to keep off the chill, here the mountain cold demanded something heavier. He couldn't imagine moving quickly as he always had and wondered how he'd ever be able even to mount a horse with all this weight. He could scarcely even run. His boots, which laced up to his calves, were like lead weights. He'd scarcely ever worn anything more than the lightest espardenyes, light Catalan espadrilles.

That was the clothing. Though not obligatory uniform, he also received: three daggers, a sword, a lance, a shield, a coat of mail (made to measure) and two helmets, as well as a full harness and saddle for his horse. When that day he saw the total bill, he was shocked. It had all cost about a thousand Barcelona sous, about three years' salary for an ordinary tradesman according to the draper, keen to point out also that that did not include the cost of his palfrey, which could well come to a hundred sous more. Yet there was nothing to pay. All this Jacques was paying for! He felt a huge lump in his throat. He would put up with the itching, he vowed to himself, and get used to the weight, he would have to get stronger and he would do his level best to make Jacques and his mother proud of him. He fought off tears with an indignant fury he hadn't felt before.

"If that is all, Master Draper, may I be excused?" he asked as brusquely as he could.

"Of course, jove."

The school was called Cavallers Marches Academy, Marches referring aptly to the borders between Catalunya, Aragón and France, always notoriously difficult to control and close to La Puebla de Castro. Much of Catalunya Aragón was a kingdom of mountain borders. It was terrain in which the almogavers and the Templars were experts. Josep had expected his education to take place in the open air, up in the mountains with Templars as teachers.

Memorisation had meant nothing to Josep before he started his education at Cavallers. Memorisation, however, was the order of the day in the classes of Chivalric Arts given by Fray Arnaldo el Zurdo. He had narrow, pale blue eyes that never registered emotion. The boys were scared stiff of him. He always sat bolt upright at his desk, his arms hanging limply at his side. Josep was in class with Ramón Muntaner and the other boys he had met the night before, Mateu de Villalba,

Guillem de Queralt, Bertrán de Solsona and Albert de Balaguer. Guillem de Queralt was standing next to the master's desk, on his right-hand side facing the other five boys, began his hesitant response. He was not the brightest boy in the class. He was dwarfed by his cloak and his gorget was crooked.

"What is the purpose of the gorget, Master de Queralt? Fray Arnaldo de Zurdo asked.

"The gorget is there to protect the neck and shoulders in battle," Guillem ventured.

"That is a partial answer, Master de Queralt," said the master of Chivalric Arts. Silence. Poor Guillem didn't understand this prompt for him to continue and instead obediently kept silent.

"Master de Queralt, do you know that silence is the devil's consent?" continued the master in a wheedling tone.

"No, sir, I did not know that silence is the devil's consent and I do not know what I am to answer," replied Guillem, his colour rising above the line of his gorget. He was plump, always a little sweaty.

Fray Arnaldo el Zurdo smiled his cold smile.

"That is, shall we say, frank of you, Master de Queralt and we know that to be too frank could involve you in acts of disloyalty and disobedience to the crown of this country, do we not?"

It was a poor pun on frank and being French.

"It is so, Fray Arnaldo, sir!" he stammered, at a loss as to what to say or do. Mateu de Villalba, taller than the others so he always stood out, was silently mouthing something at Guillem. Fray Arnaldo el Zurdo noticed. Then, as quick as a flash, his left arm shot out and the open hand swiped across the all-too-near face of Mateu de Villalba catching him full on the open mouth with such force that the twelve-year-old boy let out a shriek of pain and surprise and clattered off his stool onto the floor.

"That is the punishment for putting false words into the mouths of fools," whispered Fray Arnaldo el Zurdo registering nothing on his face, though the blow was delivered with such force that it must have hurt him, too. He flexed the fingers of his left hand gently, then returned his attention to Guillem, whose eyes were riveted to the floor in front of him. Mateu managed to pick himself up and attempted to stem the bleeding from his bitten tongue.

Beads of sweat formed on Guillem's forehead but Fray Arnaldo el Zurdo looked coolly ahead and returned to his question.

"What is the purpose of the gorget, I ask you again, Master Guillem de Queralt, not where it is but what its purpose is."

Clearly Guillem had absolutely no idea what the answer was. With a slight clearing of the throat and a grimace that could have been interpreted as a smile, Fray Arnaldo el Zurdo placed his right hand under the poor boy's habit about knee height and proceeded to stroke the backs of his legs. Guillem's face flushed darker and the sweat ran down his forehead and into his eyes, turning them red.

"The gorget, as I have been at pains for the past hour to explain to you, has a dual significance for those wishing to embark on full realisation of the mystery and sanctity of the knight's station. Its location is clearly to protect the organs of the heart and the lungs as well as the shoulders. For without the heart, we cannot love God, without the lungs, we cannot praise God and without shoulders we cannot adopt the pose of the crucified Christ when he died to free us all."

There was absolute silence as he said this.

"This includes wretches such as yourself and your accomplice, Master Mateu de Villalba, from eternal damnation. It is therefore the allegorical equivalent of obedience when worn by the holy military orders. I explain this at length in my edition of the most venerable Ramón Llull's Treatise on Chivalry, a copy of which will be issued to you today. You may thereby refresh your memory in case demons enter your unprotected skull, Master de Queralt, what do you say, sir? Address me as your reverence!" His voice rose from the measured clearly pronounced monotone to a shout.

"It is as you say, your reverence!" stammered Guillem, his knees trembling.

"You may repeat to me exactly the purpose of the gorget before those demons get a chance to mine the fleshy catacombs of your mind!" said Fray Arnaldo smiling weekly.

"I beg your pardon, your reverence. I do not understand what it is that you would have me say."

Then it came, this time like two sharp cracks. The rippling motion under Guillem's habit stopped and Fray Arnaldo's bony fingers rapped hard on the back of Guillem's sensitised legs. The next moment the rustling motion, up down, up down, was resumed. Fray Arnaldo el Zurdo coughed quietly and there was momentary rippling of his jaw muscles. Selecting his new victim, he switched his attention to Josep.

"What is your name, young Master?"

"Josep Goodman, your reverence" Josep replied.

"And are you?" continued Fray Arnaldo el Zurdo, as the other boys looked on in confusion.

Josep understood and knew he was trapped already. All the boys were in his power, of course, as they were his pupils. Yet this master felt the need to demonstrate his power. Josep understood this intuitively and hated him for it but struggled to disguise his thoughts, trying to look as confused as the other boys.

"Perhaps you would like to come to the front of the class and explain how good a man you are, Master Josep Goodman. I remember why I don't remember your name. It is because you bear no coat of arms. Where did you come by such a name?" he whined, as if Josep had committed an error of politeness in having the name that was given to him.

"Master Guillem de Queralt, you may return to your place but remain standing, adopting the cruciform position."

The hand beneath the habit stopped its stroking of the back of his legs which had continued all this time. Guillem in his consternation took three steps forward, reached his stool, turned around and threw his arms straight up above his head.

"Adopt the cruciform position, you imbecile! Do you mock Christ because he was crucified naked? You look as though you are about to take off your habit!"

He flew at him and striking him across the face as he had done to Mateu, sent him crashing into Josep who had risen and taken a step forward to the front of the class. It was too much for Guillem, who collapsed on his back and started to shake uncontrollably, his arms bent at the elbow above his face to ward off any more blows that might come.

Fray Arnaldo el Zurdo stood over him calmly.

"Go and get Fray Blas from the infirmary immediately, Master Ramón," he said to Muntaner as if the situation were perfectly normal.

"Tell him we also need the offices of a priest as demons need to be cast out of this child urgently."

Muntaner sprinted from the classroom and could be heard across the courtyard shouting Fray Blas' name. Josep looked anxiously at Guillem fearing he was having some kind of attack. Guillem's eyes were wider and he had turned scarlet. Perhaps noticing this change, Fray Arnaldo el Zurdo turned his back on the boy and walked to his desk, where he sat down and started making some notes. The other boys rushed to Guillem, supporting his head and getting him into a more comfortable position.

"Check he's not swallowing his tongue" said Mateu de Villalba.

Guillem's colour normalised, he was breathing more regularly but he still looked terrified, his gaze transfixed on Fray Arnaldo el Zurdo.

Presently, Fray Blas appeared together with several other brothers and a priest Josep didn't recognise who had happened to be around. Guillem was taken to the infirmary and Fray Arnaldo el Zurdo was heard repeating what he'd said about needing to cast devils out, to which nobody seemed to pay any attention. The boys took the opportunity to run into the inner courtyard and play, as children will if kept inside too long. They ran off the stress both of the class and the situation that had developed there. Josep re-enacted the scene in his mind then and many times in his life. It made him hate tyrannical authority for life.

"Surely people like Fray Arnaldo el Zurdo come to a bad end!" he said to Ramón.

"Not without claiming a few victims!" Ramón replied.

That night Josep made sure to go and check on Guillem in the infirmary. He must have been out of danger because Fray Blas was not there and the infirmary door was not locked.

Josep went in and saw he was alone but for the one figure occupying a bed in the corner of the room. The child was sleeping on his side, facing the wall. He was whimpering in his sleep. Josep didn't want to awaken him but was relieved to find him still alive. What Mateu de Villalba had said about people having seizures swallowing their tongue had disturbed him. Guillem was not in danger from that. He retraced his steps and left the infirmary as quietly as he could but was angrier than he had ever felt and wished he could hurt Fray Arnaldo el Zurdo badly.

"That would teach him a lesson. He is not a teacher, he is just a bully," he said to Ramón.

"Maybe that's why he became a teacher," Ramón said.

The next day Josep shadowed Guillem. He felt otherwise it would be like abandoning him to his fate, somehow like the Muslim in the cave. The days of hard slog continued. Not only did the use of each piece of equipment that the boys owned need to be understood but also its allegorical importance had to be learned. The system of education in this respect could be summed up with the phrase: "Con sangre entra" or in other words, "The information will only go in if you draw blood." However, Josep considered himself lucky in several respects. His own copy of Fray Arnaldo el Zurdo's edition of Ramón Llull's treatise on chivalry that had been handed out that first day was already dog-eared. Expensive though it no doubt had been, Josep had sweated getting into his head the allegories it contained and the effort showed on the tatty book. Some of the explanations were fascinating, such as what it said about the lance. For a start, it was made of ash. Ash was known as excellent material for the lance as it was light but also strong. This was important for a tool that greatly extended the reach of the bearer as too heavy and it would have become unwieldy, too weak and it would have snapped. Yet its strength was also to be found in another attribute: its flexibility. It was capable of absorbing great shocks without splintering so when thrust at an opponent at high speed for example from horseback it did not shatter on impact. According to Fray Arnaldo el Zurdo, this was because it had spiritual properties as demonstrated by the reverence in which it was held by agricultural folk, who used it for making sickle and scythe handles. The ash tree was easily identified in the country as its seeds were the spinning flying keys.

Josep reserved judgement on Fray Arnaldo el Zurdo's explanations but found Llull's text itself fascinating. Alder also had special properties. The fact that it was water-resistant made it ideal for boat-making and cart wheels. It thrived in wet conditions yet rotted quickly if kept away from water. It was easier to cut than wood from bigger trees like oak or beach, hence was ideal for small water craft. He further learned ash also made excellent arrows and the heavier hand-held dards, or short spears, used by the almogavers.

By showing aptitude for learning information, Josep avoided the pedagogical "assistance" employed by Fray Arnaldo el Zurdo and started enjoying studying. This was so as the applications of this information were given not by Fray Arnaldo el Zurdo but by Fray Francesc, who trained the boys in weapons use, horsemanship, medicine and survival. Fray Francesc was a natural teacher. By nature gentle with a fascination for his subject, though sometimes stern, he also had great humour and took pleasure in educating the boys. Many classes were spent in the woods around the Academy in La Puebla de Castro training the boys in the identification of raw materials and then in fashioning weapons and their appropriate care. Josep thought at last he was learning what he had expected.

"These tools are extensions of the body," the monk teacher said once, "they make you taller in the case of the sword and the lance, faster in the case of the arrow, heavier in the case of the sword and axe. However, as the correct use is important, so too do we need to ensure the correct care of the instruments necessary to carry out God's purpose."

As the weeks passed, Josep found himself better able to deal with the mystical elements of his lessons with Fray Arnaldo el Zurdo as he was able to equate the figurative with the practical. This, as Josep knew from the first day and the explanation of the gorget, went far beyond the obvious. The case of the cruciform shape of the sword hilt representing Christ was clear, even the fact that the lance as it was straight represented truth but Fray Francesc had a special way of interpreting "the truth" of the lance, its particular "virtue" which linked it with "hope."

"The lance shivers as it delivers its blows for it does not know if the blow it delivers will be the last one and therefore it shakes off the blow and prepares for the next one. We must try to match its flexibility and not put all our hope in circumstance, occasion or person but be gentle as far as possible in our expectations of all things including ourselves. For only if God accompanies us can we succeed and we live in hope that we deserve his assistance."

It struck Josep that Fray Arnaldo could learn a lot from Fray Francesc. The latter was the perfect antidote and complement to Fray Arnaldo el Zurdo's regime of fear. Josep realised he could think and reason more clearly and quickly than before. His personality was changing for though he feared and hated Fray Arnaldo el Zurdo, he was always polite, attentive and obedient to him despite his revulsion towards him. He was also never servile. Physically, he was also growing stronger. The deep sleep he'd needed at first was lightening. He could be active from dawn till dusk and be woken in the middle of the night without complaint and with a high degree of efficiency and courtesy at all times.

"You are shaping up well, jove, and I shall be delighted to report this to Berenguer de Belvís in Monzón, who has frequent contact with Jacques de Molay," Pedro de Ayerbe said to him one night. He had woken him to help him shoe a horse in the middle of the night.

"Thank you, my Lord."

"Go back to bed and rest a little more before dawn," his knight said.

Sometimes he was woken to attend his knight at meetings in the dead of knight with various other knights. Though he never understood the purpose of these clandestine gatherings, he never asked any questions and enjoyed just being involved in them. He was often too excited to get back to sleep quickly afterwards but would lie there in the dark looking up at the stars from the window above his bed, dreaming his dreams, accompanied by the wild sounds of the night. He no longer dreaded fatigue or stiffness in his muscles, he accepted the discomfort as it made him feel he was growing stronger. Yet he also knew from his peers that these were things you didn't talk about at length for fear of seeming to brag. You had to keep your head down, accept praise when given but also laugh and joke as much as possible. He was also learning how to make people like him.

CHAPTER 3 THE RIVER EXPEDITION

By early November, with Fray Francesc, they were practising mountain and river horsemanship in the ravines and fast sections of the River Essera. They had travelled two leagues or twelve miles north of the college, where the river leaves the plain and starts to snake through high ridges towards Benasque.

"Stop!" shouted Fray Francesc to the group of six.

"We shall descend in an orderly fashion, using the undergrowth for footholds for the horses," he said. "Follow closely. We will then attempt to cross the river."

From the limestone escarpment where Josep held his horse, it seemed impossible to cross a river in such conditions. The rains had reinvigorated the deep green forest and the river was turbulent. Whisps of cloud obscured the mountain ridges, while, lower, mist rose from the trees as the day warmed and black clouds threatened above the higher mountains in the distance. Josep's mouth went dry. Far below, three lines of trees beneath, raged the river. One false move and horse and rider would tumble into the seething torrent.

To their right, the escarpment fell vertically to the river as it changed course, sweeping round to their left. There was practically no tree cover here. Ahead, Fray Francesc was descending on a narrow, stony path hidden by brambles, myrtle, holme oak and rosemary. Picking their path slowly behind him, the boys dislodged boulders that went hurtling down the ridge into the churning river. The horses whinnied and stamped as the six kept them firmly reigned in. The sweat dripped into the eyes of the boys but they could not wipe it away as they were holding the reigns so tightly. By criss-crossing the slope, going ten metres one way, then ten metres the other, Fray Francesc led them expertly down the ravine. When finally down, they paused to look up the almost vertical slope and couldn't believe they had negotiated it safely.

Allowed to dismount and being close to the water, they freshened up and watered their horses. There was a narrow strip of woodland here five metres wide between the river and the slope, containing many different types of tree. Fray Francesc got the boys to identify the types: chopo, poplar, abedúl, birch, fresno, ash and wettest of all edging the water, alisos, alders.

The six boys tried to guess what Fray Francesc intended for them. Eyeing the leafless lower branches of the alders, they saw thirty metres across the river and fifty metres downstream a narrow inlet where reeds were growing, leading to a grotto overhung by the sheer limestone face of the opposite bank.

"I want you to build a raft that is strong enough to carry two of you across the river to that grotto on the other side. We will leave the horses tethered here for the time being."

The boys set to with excitement. It was practical, challenging and useful. They split into pairs, Josep making sure he partnered Guillem de Queralt. Ramón Muntaner partnered Mateu Villalba while Bertrán de Solsona paired up with Albert de Balaguer.

"We should work together and talk about how to do things," he said to Guillem.

Climbing the trees that lined the riverbank, hanging off branches until they snapped, then taking out knives to strip the branches, the boys had soon piled up a great deal of wood and were sweating from exertion. Finally, it occurred to Ramón Muntaner to enquire how they were going to lash the wood together. He asked Fray Francesc if he had any rope.

"I was wondering when someone would ask!" he replied with a hint of sarcasm, producing a saddlebag with rope. The six boys returned to their task with renewed vigour. The next question was exactly how the lashing was to be done.

"We've got a lot of wood and we could choose the best pieces..." Josep was saying when he was interrupted by Bertrán de Solsona.

"You mean you can take your pick of the best of the pieces, we help you make your raft and then you get to try it out first, right?" drawled the young noble. He was fair and had blue eyes and an upturned nose. Josep thought he looked like a girl.

"I was thinking we could..." Josep answered trying to control himself and not get angry.

"Well, don't think for me, thank you!" Bertrán de Solsona said with a sneer on his face.

The two other boys next to him laughed. Luckily, Ramón still seemed to be on Josep's side.

"Have it your own way," Josep said, "but don't take all the best wood for yourself, either!"

The boys scrambled for the wood. Josep had mentally picked out his wood already and dived for some of the longer pieces of alder but in the mayhem, quantity was paramount rather than quality and some boys ended up with more than others. Guillem de Queralt was left with little more than a jumble nobody else wanted. Josep felt a stab of anger. His cheeks started burning and his ears ringing. He wanted to grab Bertrán de Solsona by the throat and ask whether that was an equal share but controlled himself. Bertrán de Solsona and Albert de Balaguer laughed smugly.

A kind of calm then settled over them, in competing pairs, Ramón Muntaner working with Mateu de Villalba. Josep still angry with Bertrán de Solsona had to breathe deeply to concentrate as he thought he was going to have to do the thinking for his pair.

"Such a shame!" he said to himself as he contemplated the situation. He had been open-minded about the other boys in his class when they had started but was learning quickly he was regarded an outsider by Bertrán de Solsona, who tried to ridicule him and make him feel small whenever possible. Josep found him petty, competitive and secretive.

Sometimes he wanted to shout, "It's not a competition you know, we can learn from each other!" but that was obviously not Bertrán de Solsona's way though he was happy to sneak a glance at Josep's work in class. He strained to hear what Josep was saying to Guillem.

"The secret is to make it long and thin so it goes faster, then you can get to the other side more quickly!" Josep said loudly enough for Bertrán de Solsona to hear. He had decided to teach Bertrán a lesson and have some fun.

Bertrán and partner, Albert de Balaguer, were the first to finish. Bertrán de Solsona was so convinced he was right having heard Josep that he'd bossed his partner about. Albert stooped and awkward was always daydreaming and easy for Bertrán to dominate.

"Fray Francesc," Betrán drawled in his aristocratic accent, "Don't you think as we seem to have finished first, before the others," he paused for dramatic effect, "don't you think it would be fair for us to be allowed to demonstrate the qualities of our craft first?" He had that sneer on his face again.

"Anyone would think it was a prize-winning galley, the way he boasts about it!" Josep said to Ramón Muntaner making sure he avoided Bertrán de Solsona's glance to check everyone was paying attention.

"By all means!" replied Fray Francesc. "Strip off, then!"

"I beg your pardon?" answered Bertrán de Solsona. "I mean, I beg your pardon, Fray Francesc, but that won't be necessary. Our craft, our craft will bear us over the river safe and sound in a trice!"

Josep cringed at the pretentious, bragging tone in which he said and repeated the word "craft" as if it was obviously better than anyone else's.

"You'll regret…" Fray Francesc began to say but before he could finish, Bertrán de Solsona had edged the flimsy vessel into the water. He neglected to attach a rope, completely forgot about his horse and left his partner Albert standing on the river's edge looking more confused than usual. He proceeded to sit down in the middle of the raft, just wide enough to take him and stay afloat, then let go of the low branches he had been holding to steady himself. The raft immediately lurched forward with the current, nearly knocking Bertrán off balance though for the moment he managed to read the motion of the river. All seemed to go well for half a minute as the raft picked up speed. The look of mild apprehension even Bertrán de Solsona couldn't disguise disappeared from his face and he affected a look of nonchalance, putting his chin up. The raft was dragged into the middle of the river at its most turbulent and scudded to the left as the strong current bore it downstream like driftwood. Seconds later, the front end hit the near bank thirty metres downstream.

This was lucky for Bertrán because, as Josep could see, his raft was so narrow it couldn't possibly stay afloat for long and Josep even in his angriest moment hadn't thought Bertrán would be so foolhardy as to make something so ill-suited for the water. Clearly he'd taken what Josep had said completely to heart. Josep was gratified and laughed out loud as the raft embedded itself in reeds, coming to a sudden stop. Bertrán wasn't expecting this and it pitched him head first into the water. One branch slipped out from the loose lashing and floated downstream on its own as the boy emerged dripping from the water. His blond hair was darker when wet and his blue eyes flashed cold with anger. Much to Josep's relief, all the boys laughed at Bertrán, which concealed his own mirth that his ruse had worked out so well.

"Lucky you didn't come off in the middle of the river!" shouted Fray Francesc, taken by surprise by Bertrán de Solsona's impetuousness. Josep realised he was relieved from his tone.

"The young fool!" Josep heard the monk say to himself as he ran to the pack horse and undoing another saddlebag from it, unpacked some warm woollen blankets.

"Am I to undress in public?" Bertrán de Solsona asked, fighting for a little dignity.

"For heaven's sake boy, disappear then but get on with it!" replied Fray Francesc. "If you'd stripped when I told you to, you'd have dry clothes to get into!"

No sooner had he gone than Fray Francesc produced from inside his habit a firestone and a flint. From next to the well-stacked kindling, he picked up a small ball of dry scrub for tinder and using his body and habit as a wind block, knelt down and struck a spark into the tinder, then another, then another. A wisp of smoke emerged. Scooping up the smoking ball, he cupped it in his hands and blew softly. All of a sudden a flame sprang up and he dropped the crackling burning ball into the kindling, which immediately started smoking. Within minutes, flames were licking up the sides of the firewood.

"I think we should pause to review what we have achieved so far," said the monk teacher. "However, first, some lunch."

The boys put their hands forward to warm them by the fire. It was November after all and several hundred metres up in the mountains. Yet Fray Francesc had come well prepared. The boys skinned four rabbits the monk provided and spitted them on green sticks, which they roasted over the fire. While waiting for these to do, they tucked into a loaf each of fresh bread with rosemary, sage and garlic. They were having a good time and nobody noticed when Bertrán de Solsona's hunger got the better of his pride and he surreptitiously rejoined the group. Josep when he noticed him again couldn't believe the arrogance of the boy. Used to being the centre of attention, he waited to be passed some food. Rather than asking, he finally sullenly got to his feet and got himself some bread. This he did rather self-consciously as his manner of dress became apparent: he had put the woollen blanket on his thin frame like a Roman toga. He was dry but clearly cold and uncomfortable.

After they had finished lunch and were clearing everything away, kicking over the fire and burying the rabbit bones, Fray Francesc invited them to comment on the rafts nearing completion. Josep and Guillem had spent time on their lashing and their raft looked robust.

"There's little point in looking at Queralt and Goodman's," began Bertrán de Solsona condescendingly. He always used people's last names as if it gave him authority over them though annoyingly he was the only one to do so.

"Anything Queralt is involved in always ends in disaster," he said looking at Guillem as if he had been washed up by the river.

Guillem had had a bad time since starting at the academy but it didn't mean he lacked character. Growing in confidence that day, he calmly walked over to Bertrán de Solsona and tugged at the knot that held together his toga on his shoulder.

"You should take more care with your public image, Lady Bertrana," he said. The knot untied and the boy, with his small nose and fine features, was left next to naked. Everyone laughed.

"I think you'll find we've done a better job with our knots!" Guillem said.

"You little....just you wait!" was all Bertrán de Solsona could say before Fray Francesc cut in.

"That's enough boys! Ramón and Mateu, explain your design?"

"Of course, Fray Francesc," started Ramón politely, exchanging a quick glance with Mateu to check he could go ahead. That was the thing about Ramón, Josep reflected: he was polite to everyone and never lost his cool. He knew how to handle a situation, was organised and had common sense and humour, Josep thought.

"We wanted something big and wide to stay afloat so we used the thicker logs at the front and the back and tried to make the whole thing as square as possible."

He and Mateu, both short and stocky, then lifted the raft and put it in the water. There was something wrong with it.

"It's a good idea but with the two long branches at front and rear, it would have moved sluggishly in the water. It's a good idea to make the craft solid but you're launching in the water the wrong way. The heavy logs need to be along the sides not going across the raft." Fray Francesc said.

"Steering would also be a problem, wouldn't it?" said Guillem de Queralt.

"Since when were you an expert?" Bertrán de Solsona said with an exaggerated look of surprise.

"Indeed it would," said Fray Francesc, ignoring Solsona's sarcasm. "Otherwise, it would be swept down the river like your own, Bertrán," he said, catching his eye to drive the message home. Bertrán sullenly stared back at him rather than nodding his agreement. Ignoring the boy's rudeness, Fray Francesc carried on.

"So what do you propose to steer it with?"

"Well, we were going to use a long stick but all the other long sticks went down with Bertrán de Solsona" Ramón said pointedly to jeers from the other boys, clearly exasperated by Bertrán de Solsona's moodiness and trying to snap him out of it.

"Pardon me, Fray Francesc, but wouldn't the stick be snatched out of your hands by the current?" Guillem de Queralt asked.

"Good point, Guillem. Why don't we try it out?"

There was a shout of assent and much hurrying to and fro looking for appropriate branches. Josep came back a minute later dragging two long but light branches behind him.

"They're from Bertrán de Solsona's blighted adventure," Josep muttered loud enough for Bertrán de Solsona to hear him.

"I'm surprised you're man enough to be able to lift them," Bertrán de Solsona said through his nose, his head thrown back.

"More than you could do right now, Madame!" Josep replied swiftly. Bertrán de Solsona's colour rose again.

"May you die in the attempt!" he replied.

"Death by drowning, what an unpleasant death," Josep said mocking his accent and pompous way of speaking. "More your style, wouldn't you say, based on present evidence?"

Again everyone laughed at Bertrán de Solsona who this time had had enough. He harrumphed off and sat down on a rock about ten metres from the group. The incident stuck in Josep's mind for years to come. "Death by drowning..." he repeated to himself. It seemed to resound in his mind, expand into spaces he didn't even know existed, producing in him fear and nausea. He snapped out of his daydream.

"Come on, Mateu!" said Ramón. "Help me launch this thing the other way round!"

The raft was solidly made as two big extra logs, also rescued from Bertrán de Solsona and Albert's raft, had been fitted to the sides. It slid easily into the water. Ramón and Mateu jumped on.

"Don't forget the steering oar!" Josep shouted to Mateu but it was too late. It remained on the river's edge as the raft sped away from everyone too fast for anyone to be able to pass it to them. Ramón and Mateu hunched down as low as they could to stay on. The raft headed out of sight as the river swerved round to the right. The raft disappeared from view but luckily embedded itself into the left bank about three hundred metres downstream. Miraculously the two returned a quarter of an hour later "a bit damp", as Mateu put it, bearing the raft, which now looked completely unfit for the water.

"That would have worked if you had paid attention to the last details," said Fray Francesc. There was an eruption of suggestions as everyone realised there was only time for one more try and Josep and Guillem's raft remained.

"Wait!" Fray Francesc cut in. "What went wrong? What did they do wrong?"

"They didn't fasten their raft to the shore," said Guillem before anyone else could point out their error.

"Exactly, Guillem but let's call things by their proper names." Fray Francesc said. "The cuer or rudder oar as the Aragonese and Catalan raiers or raftsmen on the River Noguera Pallaresa call it. They forgot to take the cuer with them."

Everyone laughed. The last raft was carefully checked and Fray Francesc started tightening each loop of the lashing on each pole as hard as he could. Guillem had had the inspirational idea of of making shallow incisions on the end of each pole and the ends of the lashing ropes were tied all the more tightly as they cut into these grooves.

"The raiers do exactly the same," fray Francesc shouted as he helped cut more grooves. "But they use strips of birch bark that retain their shape and grip better and act like a kind of external frame to the raft."

"But their rafts bang into things all the time and go over rapids and waterfalls, don't they?" observed Guillem.

"That's right, Master Guillem!" said the teacher, pleased Guillem seemed to know and understand these details.

"Remember, the cuer is going to be a devil to hold onto," he said to Guillem and Josep. "Make sure you keep as low as possible and let it go if you feel you're being pulled in! We'll drag you back whether you get to the other side or not."

Josep checked the mooring rope connecting the raft with the land was secure. Then the two boys edged the raft into the water and scrambled into the middle of it. Having found their balance, Josep held on tight to the mooring rope while Guillem pulled the long cuer from the land onto the boat and then carefully pushed it over the rear end one foot at a time until all of its full five metres except for what he held in his arms were submerged behind the raft. They were ready.

"Keep low and take it slow!" Fray Francesc shouted over the roar of the river. The other boys were rooting for the last two to succeed and get to the other side and back in one piece. Despite himself, even Bertrán de Solsona was watching.

"I hope they make it," Mateu said

"Then at least we can say someone did," Ramón replied.

"That's the way, Guillem, ease the rope off," said Fray Francesc.

The raft lurched as it picked up the current.

"Guillem, don't let go of the cuer. The current will push it this way and that but you must try to angle it towards the opposite bank."

Guillem made a slight adjustment to the rudder in the water as the raft slipped downstream thirty metres or so then started gracefully to glide across the river as he held the cuer in his arms with all his might. He was the right shape for the task, short and strong.

"I can't hold on to it!" he shouted. "Josep, get down, I'm going to have to let it go. Don't let go of the rope!"

No sooner had he spoken than there was a loud clunking from under the raft as the cuer was sucked under by the bottom current and the raft lurched to the left.

"Hold on," he shouted, "we're still heading in the right direction, even though we're spinning!"

A cheer from the boys on the near bank was followed by a loud crack as one of the front logs glanced against a rock and threw the two boys off the raft and face down onto the muddy river bank opposite. The raft was stuck in the mud but the ropes attached to the near side stopped it being swept downstream.

"Pull us back, pull us back!" the two boys shouted and all hands took up the rope and started hauling the raft back to the near side. Ten minutes of pulling on the rope and the boys were back where they'd started. Bertrán de Solsona was the only one not joining in, apparently helping Fray Francesc start preparing to leave.

"If we do it again, I'm mounting the rudder properly!" said Josep to Fray Francesc. "It's impossible to hold it with the river like this. It nearly had Guillem in!"

Packing up their belongings, they left for Cavallers as dusk fell and carefully picked their way up the steep slope in zig-zag fashion behind Fray Francesc. As they reached the main road, a group of twenty horses galloped past them. Nobody recognized the riders in the dying light of day and Guillem and Josep's horses shied away and slipped back onto the dangerous path they had come up and they struggled to control them. Fray Francesc shouted more in dismay than anger and his shouts were heard. The party stopped, turned and rode back.

"Identify yourselves!" the leader demanded.

"I am Fray Francesc from Cavallers School of Pages," Fray Francesc shouted back from the end of the line of horses and boys. He had immediately gone to the end to help Guillem and Josep.

There was a pause.

"I think you'd better go to him, master," said Ramón to Fray Francesc, taking the reigns of Guillem and Josep's horses from him.

Fray Francesc looked up and in the twilight recognised the leader of the group.

"Lord Sanchis!" he said, spurring his horse to a trot and stopping in front of him. He bowed from the saddle.

"Do you not recognize your betters when you meet them on the open road?"

"My lord, we have come up a dangerous stretch from the river, it is getting dark and the boys are tired. We need to get back to Cavallers as soon as we can."

"That is no excuse for discourtesy. I am Prince Sanchis to you, Fray Francesc, and you will have a report on your activities for me first thing in the morning." Several of the knights accompanying him laughed at Fray Francesc's embarrassment.

Bertrán de Solsona rode up to where Sanchis and Fray Francesc were talking.

"Prince Sanchis," he said, "believe me, there is little to say about the activity. It was so badly organised that I nearly drowned and I have been ridiculed as a result by people I would not normally even speak to."

Josep watched astonished as Sanchis bowed his head to Bertrán de Solsona.

"Good evening to you, Master Bertrán. I trust you are not in need of medical assistance as a result of today's little adventure."

"No, indeed, I thank your Highness but I am made of strong stuff. Stronger than these imbeciles I have to share my days with for sure."

Josep, Ramón and Guillem each looked at each other in disbelief. Josep looked more closely at Sanchis. He was expensively dressed even for a noble and was fair with green eyes. He reminded him of Bertrán.

"Return to Cavallers forthwith, Fray. We have royal business to attend to. Hand your report to Fray Arnaldo."

Josep noticed a sneer appear on the face of Bertrán de Solsona.

"Yes, of course, my lord," said Fray Francesc.

"He is a prince of the royal blood," said Bertrán. "His title is Prince Sanchis."

Sanchis held Fray Francecsc in an ice cold stare.

"Yes, Prince Sanchis," he said.

†

The party were practically falling off their horses with exhaustion when they finally got back to the Academy. They had ridden hard for two hours to arrive an hour after nightfall. It was eerie as they had seen nobody all day apart from Sanchis and his party on the roads. They were given hot milk, bread and fuet, Catalan preserved pork sausage, and packed off to bed where they fell fast asleep.

Three hours before dawn, Josep was woken by Lord Pedro and required to do some tasks. Though groggy, Josep was alert enough to realise this was no ordinary gathering from the number of horses present and the magnificence of the livery of one of them in particular. It was l'Infant Pere, the Crown Prince, and the party was heading for Antillón, the feudal town of Ferran Sanchis' mother, Blanca de Antillón.

As Josep fed and watered the prince's horse, a magnificent black Arabian stallion, a good head taller than the other horses, he noticed Crown Prince Pere was darker than Sanchis.

"Sanchis is my master here, your Highness, how can I openly disobey him?" Lord Pedro asked the prince.

"Then as you hold dear your affection for me as brother and future king, find someone who can avoid detection. Do not fail me in this!"

Moments later, the party departed. Before he went back to bed, Josep overheard two knights from the household of Compte d'Empúries.

"Sanchis wants us to get these bags of coins to the count for safe-keeping before the Christmas festivities bring business to a halt," one knight said.

"We could take them with us when we accompany Bertrán de Solsona and Mateu de Villalba back to Castelló d'Empúries," the other replied.

"If we're quick and he's smart, Sanchis might have a chance to outwit the greedy crown prince!" the first knight then said.

"You mean everyone will pay the tribute to Sanchis' representatives believing it is the king's wish?" the other replied.

"That's the point of this letter and seal, isn't it?" the first knight said, producing a sealed document from inside his jacket.

Josep checked with Lord Pedro later what they had meant and told him about meeting Sanchis' party on the road.

"While Prince Pere has been away, Sanchis seems to have been getting the towns to pay their taxes to the king through his messengers but I believe he's keeping the money for himself," Lord Pedro explained.

"Doesn't the king know?" asked Josep.

"I don't know but as he's all the way down in Murcia still, he leaves Sanchis to do much as he chooses up here. How are the roads up here at the moment, by the way, empty or full?"

"Apart from Lord Sanchis and his party, empty if you ask me," Josep replied.

"Sanchis' men are demanding money from anyone they meet on the roads, that's why."

"But can't Prince Pere stop him?"

"Not if he's out of the area, in Barcelona or in Murcia. He can't be everywhere at once, so he has to pay agents and the money that should be going to him is being taken by Sanchis."

"But Prince Pere is often here. Do they not fear him, my lord?"

"They think Sanchis is powerful and will protect them. He seems to be on better terms with his father the king at the moment and he's also on good terms with the king's second son, Jaume. I suppose they hope Crown Prince Pere's influence in these parts will continue to be minimal with Sanchis and Prince Jaume close at hand. Some of the Aragonese nobles must prefer it that way. Fewer taxes to pay and more autonomy."

Ramón walked into the stable at that moment to prepare his horse for the day's work. It was soon clear he was aware of the situation of divided loyalties that existed between the followers of Lord Ferran Sanchis and Prince Pere.

"I was invited to travel back next time with the two knights who came for Bertrán de Solsona and Mateu de Villalba but servants from Viscount Jofre Rocabertí came for me with a message from him that I was to have nothing to do with those traitors!" Ramón said quietly, looking around nervously.

"Strong words!" said Lord Pedro. Ramón looked scared for once, Josep thought.

"I don't know why Viscount Rocabertí decided to send me to a school that belongs to Sanchis."

"Fear not, jove, we are at hand should matters come to a head. Rest assured you will not be in the thick of it," Lord Pedro exchanged a glance with Josep and nodded.

"I hope not, my lord, for either of us," Josep said. Josep had never seen Ramón agitated like this. He was normally so calm and collected. At that moment, Lord Pedro produced a letter from inside his shirt.

"Deliver this to Viscount Rocabertí. You must leave and get ahead of the knights taking Bertrán de Solsona and Mateu de Villalba to Castelló d'Empúries." It was a letter bearing the seal of the Prince Pere.

"You'll earn my gratitude as well as that of the Crown Prince," Lord Pedro said.

When he had gone, Lord Pedro explained to Josep what he believed to be the contents of the letter.

"Prince Pere wants to reassure Viscount Rocabertí his instincts are right, so he wants him to distance himself from the Solsona and Villalba families and assist him in dealing with Sanchis," he said, checking the windows and doors around them.

"Sanchis introduced Crown Prince Pere to Constança of Hohenstaufen, the daughter of King Manfred of Sicily, Josep," he said.

"You mean they were on good terms once?"

"Indeed!" replied Lord Perdro. "They had been on crusade together in North Africa. Somehow Sanchis came under the influence of Count Charles of Anjou.

"But didn't Count Charles of Anjou kill Constança's father at the battle of Benevento in 1266?" Josep asked.

"Exactly, Josep. Then executed the next in line to the throne and made himself King Charles of Sicily."

"Even though Constança is the legitimate heir to the throne?" Josep asked.

"Exactly," Lord Pedro de Ayerbe said. "But it was clear Sanchis no longer wanted to have anything to do with Prince Pere or Constança when he refused to attend their wedding in 1262."

"But why does he want to cheat the legitimate heir to a throne?" Josep asked, struggling to assimilate in his mind what his master was telling him. "Prince Pere will be his king one day. And Constança should be Queen of Sicily."

"Be careful who you say that around, Josep!" his knight said. "Every man has his price. Perhaps Count Charles convinced Sanchis he had as much right to be king as Prince Pere."

"I cannot understand this," Josep shook his head. "For me it is clear the king is in a stronger position if he is the heir!"

"Perhaps Count Charles offered to help make Sanchis the king. Or he just wants our kingdom to be unstable and Sanchis was fool enough to believe his lies."

"But why?" asked Josep.

"Maybe to make the Catalan Aragonese crown weaker so that he can pursue his own ambitions more easily. King Charles also has his eye on other parts the Mediterranean. Princess Constança is still the heir to Sicily. If Prince Pere aims to reestablish her on the throne of Sicily, he will have to challenge King Charles of Sicily."

"I don't understand why he wanted to be king anyway," Josep said.

"Don't worry, Josep, it's a complicated story. King Charles, or Count Charles of Anjou, was the younger brother of the former King of France, Louis IX. He is married to Beatriz of Provence."

"Isn't she a cousin of Prince Pere's? Josep asked.

"Distant cousin, yes. Beatriz is the youngest of four beautiful sisters but was rumoured to be jealous of her elder sisters because they all married kings. Beatriz alone married a count, albeit a royal count, Charles of France. It annoyed her so much that she should be seated below her sisters at official functions that she persuaded her husband to make war on the Hohenstaufen dynasty of the Holy Roman Empire for the crown of Sicily so that she, too, could be a queen."

"So now she is Queen of Sicily, she has got what she wanted," Josep interrupted.

"Some people are never satisfied, Josep," said Lord Pedro. "Maybe being King Charles and Queen Beatriz of Sicily is not enough for them."

CHAPTER 4 ARTIGA DE LIN

A month later, intelligence came that the Count of Foix had occupied the Val d'Aran, a beautiful valley in the Pyrenees of strategic importance as it was a natural link across the mountains between the north of Catalunya and the south of France.

"There is little Crown Prince Peter can do to stop him the count," said Lord Pedro, "but he wants a secret route in the mountains researched that will allow him to enter and withdraw from the valley at will. He has entrusted us with this task."

Josep was pleased and excited. Dressed as ordinary travellers, they set out in late September, after the feast of the Mercè had been celebrated in Barcelona. From La Puebla de Castro they rode north towards Benasque along the Essera River. Life was returning to normal along these unfrequented country roads and unlike a year before when Josep had done rafting there, the roads were full of people making their way to and from work in the fields or travelling like themselves. There was also a freer atmosphere, people were chatting and laughing again on the open road.

The knight and his page made their way north. Ravenously hungry, they had been riding since after daybreak, their bread and milk a distant memory. Their path, through heavily wooded mountain slopes, was still alongside the river and the air was much cooler and damper than in La Puebla. The horses were working hard and the heat rose from them. They passed fewer people here, on the solitary road, dark with ancient beaches and chestnuts. The smell of rain and fallen leaves was in their nostrils. When Josep was about to fall off his horse with fatigue and hunger, they saw smoke rising in the distance and crossing a rickety wooden bridge they had an excellent meal at a roadside inn in Castejón de Sos.

The atmosphere was not friendly. Despite their ordinary clothes, they were clearly men of standing and when asked where they were heading, they replied Benasque and did not expand. When they resumed their ride, they knew they had to get to Benasque by nightfall. They had four hours before sunset. The plan was to follow the River Essera up to its source in the glacier of Mount Aneto, two hours on from Benasque. They were in the middle of the mountains, Aneto still by far the highest peak around. At sundown, they passed through grey stone built Benasque.

Small barraques, stone huts originally built for shepherds that travellers could use, were dotted around the Pyrenees and the plan was to spend the night in one of these at the source of the Essera and start the ascent into the Val d'Aran in the early morning before sunrise. The ascent to the pass, called La Picada, a name denoting rough, grinding conditions, was steep and tortuous, a thousand metres above them and would take them the best part of four hours. They would be visible for the first two hours of the climb till they reached sufficient height. As night was falling, they came to a barraca, unpacked their provisions and lit a fire. It was bitterly cold now that the sun had set, yet their spirits were good as they had provided well for their evening meal, knowing how hungry they would be. Though smoky in the barraca, one could breathe if seated and the warmth and glow of the fire and a full belly soon sent them to sleep. Early in the morning before dawn, Pedro de Ayerbe awoke with a start, jumped to his feet and in a flash was outside, his sword drawn, cursing someone was stealing the horses, a false alarm. The horses were awake and hungry so were snorting and whinnying. He gave them a nose bag, knowing they would need their strength for the exertion ahead of them. Josep, roused by the commotion, was already up.

"My eyes are itching," he said

"It must be the smoke from the fire," returned Lord Pedro. "It's warmer in here than it is outside, let me tell you."

"I suppose so, my lord", replied Josep, who could see the steam coming from the horses in the pale moonlight.

"How are the horses?"

"They are fine. They must eat. I want to tell you a couple of things meanwhile," Lord Pedro said, kicking over the fire while the two companions packed their meagre belongings into their saddlebags.

"We'll ride the horses as long as they can take it. If we push them too hard, we'll have to feed them more and we only have provisions for two days. We must be back in Benasque by Wednesday. We can't climb and carry provisions, so we must treat the horses with the greatest respect. If one breaks a leg, we'll have to return immediately, without accomplishing our mission."

"What exactly is our mission?" asked Josep.

"Let's start out and I'll tell you what Prince Pere has asked us to do."

They untied their horses and set off for the trail with a map from Fray Francesc, who knew all about the paths in this part of the Pyrenees. It was steep and winding but the conditions were perfect. It was clearly below freezing because there was frost on the mossy grass covering the hillocks and mountains that distinguished this marshy upland area and the Essera, a metre wide at this point, was frozen at its edges.

"The sky is the clearest I can remember seeing it, my lord," Josep said. It was absolutely pitch black and festooned with myriad stars. "How is the moon so bright?" he asked, amazed by the serene majesty of the alpine scenery around him.

"The moon is so bright as it is full moon after the Autumn equinox," said Lord Pedro. It gave a peculiarly bright light all around them, bright enough to pick out shadows on the path ahead of them. "Fray Francesc says that if the moon is full and the night is clear, the light shines off the Aneto glacier like a looking glass and can light up the way. That's why he recommended this night above all others for the ascent. Turn around for a moment and take a look at the glacier behind us," said Lord Pedro.

Josep did so and realised immediately why there were such distinct shadows on the path. The moon was beaming down on the great mountain of Aneto and the slope he could see behind him was almost glistening in the moonlight, as if water were streaming down off it. It was shining a ghostly pale blue light that lit up the valley below them as well as the path they had to follow.

"Is it actually water running down the mountainside?" asked Josep.

"I think it's too cold. The glacier is ice, I think. In the summer, it melts and causes great waterfalls halfway up at a place called Aigualluts but I think it's frozen now. As the crow flies, it's five miles from here to the pass but we're going to have to walk ten miles and that will be steep enough," said Lord Pedro.

They slowly zigzagged up the path. Josep's lips grew numb and started to freeze.

"How long will it take to get the top?" he asked through chattering teeth.

"We should be about halfway up by sunrise," Lord Pedro replied.

"Will you explain the plan to me while we are walking, Lord Pedro?" asked Josep.

"Oh, yes, of course!" he replied. "I said I would an hour ago. It must be the cold. We are to make our way to the town of Les Bordes and reconnoitre the castle there. We'll approach from the western ridge, so we'll stay as high as possible above the town, as long as possible, then try to get close and estimate the number of men the counts of Foix and Cominges have posted there. It's thickly wooded so we need have no fear of being seen. Nobody goes out there, it's no man's land."

"Why do they want it then if it's no man's land?" asked Josep.

"No, no, not the Val d'Aran, the ridge we're going to. It demarcates the land of the Count of Cominges from that of the Val d'Aran. The Val d'Aran is open to the French side of the Pyrenees, so it's easy to attack. But it's a natural route across the mountains so it's a prosperous region with good grazing land. It has plenty of water, there's more rain than on the Catalan south side of the Pyrenees and it's loyal to the Aragonese crown and always has been."

"So why is Count Roger Bernat so keen to invade it if the people are against him?" asked Josep.

"Exactly, jove. The count hates the Aragonese crown and will do anything to provoke Prince Pere. Unlike his father, Prince Pere is easy to provoke. The two of them, the Count of Foix and Prince Pere are like two old-fashioned warriors. It's in their nature to make war. Their blood calls out for it."

Josep shivered. "I hope there are none of his troops in the castle and some friendly villagers invite us in so we can eat plenty and warm ourselves," he grumbled.

Lord Pedro laughed. "There may be time for that too. Save your energy and control your horse."

By sunrise, they were halfway up to the pass. If they looked right over their shoulder, they could see the east-facing sections of the path that zigzagged up, lit up with the early morning sun streaming onto the glacier and blinding them with its blue reflected glow. They passed nobody and nothing and saw no movement, even in the valley below them. It was an eerie wilderness up here. Occasionally, an eagle could be seen circling high overhead. They had no company except for their two sturdy horses and the crunching sound of their steady footfalls, snorts and occasional whinnying.

The pass up ahead seemed closer than it was. Josep felt colder as the ridge was in the shadow of the mountain and the wind was beginning to blow harder and had an icy edge to it. He imagined that the wind would drop as soon as he got through that pass, imagined that, on the other side, it was sunny and calm and this thought spurred him on. Light wisps of high cloud decorated the V-shaped fault in the ridge that would let them through to the Val d'Aran. The wind started to blow more and more strongly as they neared the pass, the gusts developing into a steady stream of constant wind. It started to rain heavily and in moments they were soaked. They were five metres from the pass but visibility dropped in seconds. The rapid change was unnerving.

"Get off your horse and pull into the rock face as close as you can," shouted Lord Pedro. They took what shelter they could from the sudden storm and calmed their horses, which tucked their heads down away from the blasts of the wintry wind.

"Where did this come from?" shouted Josep in Lord Pedro's ear, who struggled to hear him as the wind moaned and the rain poured down.

"I have no idea! Thank goodness we have the horses to take the full force. We're going to have to sit it out," shouted Lord Pedro.

Things were getting worse. The rain had turned to hail and the horses were being stung by the icey stones. There was no shelter around, no cave or even overhanging slab of rock. They were out in the open in a mountain hailstorm and if they stood, they would be blown over by the force of the wind.

"Get the horses to lie down, then at least they'll be able to protect their legs from the hail," said Lord Pedro over the roar of the storm and both pulled down hard on the bridle of their horses and slapped the back of their flanks. The horses lay down and the two riders huddled up to the heat of their bellies as the storm raged around them. In seconds, the temperature had dropped even further below freezing. They wrapped their blankets around their heads and knees as best they could.

Then, as soon as it had started, the storm stopped. It was strange, as if someone had clicked their fingers to begin and end the storm. The two companions had gone into a trance as long as the storm had lasted and finally, realising the noise had abated, Josep was the first to shake the blanket off his head. The hailstones lay in drifts at the sheer sides of the path melting in the sudden sun. There was heat in it and the approach to the pass was perfectly visible again. Josep could see wisps of high cloud again over the pass and a bird of prey circling high in a dazzling blue sky. Josep thought the change miraculous.

"Unbelievable!" Lord Pedro shouted as if the elements could hear him. "I've never seen anything like it. Unbelievable!"

Knight and page patted the horses, checked for injuries and gave them a nose bag for ten minutes. The horses soon calmed and ate hungrily.

The wet storm-pummelled earth became stonier in front of the pass and more difficult to walk on until they reached the V-shaped pass itself. There was no earth here, only rough stone, grey and shiny, that looked like stones left behind from a quarry. They crunched through the pass and the path immediately dropped on the other side. They were crossing the high point of the ridge. It would have been easy to walk down the gravel-strewn shallow valley ahead of them. However, that was the wrong way. They had to follow the ridge around to the north-west. They could not see their way beyond two hundred metres because the path, steeper there, dipped out of sight. The scenery was magnificent. Along the ridge, they could see down over the whole of the Val d'Aran and more pertinently, the slope down to Les Bordes, where they were heading, at the head of the valley called Artiga de Lin. They could see the town in the distance, about ten miles away, trails of smoke rising from it.

"The line of trees down in the valley marks the course of the River Garonne, which flows from here to Bordeaux," said Lord Pedro. "It flows through Les Bordes, so we know where we're heading."

High up on the ridge, they admired the pine forests that surrounded them, the valley below on the right and the streams flowing from the mountainside which drained in waterfalls they could see falling over the edge on the other side of the valley. It was stunning. They stopped where Fray Francis had told Lord Pedro at a small lake with a shepherd's hut like the one they had stayed in at the foot of the mountain. It was near enough to paths down to Les Bordes to be convenient for them yet had views over the ascent path should anyone venture up towards them. It was called Cabanhes dera Montanha, an Occitan name, and had views over the town of Les Bordes and the castle.

"Tomorrow we'll retrace our steps and get as close as possible to the castle to see what activity there is. Therefore the rest of the day, we can tend to our horses, hunt for supper, if you like."

The woods around there were absolutely teeming with life, so they would have no trouble in catching a rabbit for supper, Lord Pedro said. Fray Francesc had shown Josep the technique, beautiful in its simplicity. A loop was made of twine, big enough for a rabbit's head to go through but not its body. The loop was made with a slipknot, which tightened when pulled. This loop was held open and in place by a Y- shaped stick driven into the ground. Josep and Lord Pedro made a dozen of these simple traps and placed them along rabbit runs that could easily be identified by tracing droppings between one rabbit hole and another. They set the traps a good hour away from where they were camping, using this opportunity without the noise and encumbrance of their horses to scout the zone they were in. They were therefore able to identify other paths that lead steeply down to the Castle and on the other side of the ridge into the lands of the Count of Cominges, French territory.

When they went back to their traps, an hour before sundown, many of them were untouched and some had been pushed over or had fallen but the line was taut on one of them and a good-sized brown rabbit was found in the undergrowth. Once held down, its neck was quickly broken. Making a circular incision around each paw and then another incision from paw to trunk, they peeled off the skin easily. Josep, fascinated, claimed it proudly, scraped it clean of fat and hung it out to dry. The lungs and intestines were inedible so were carefully removed and buried so as not to attract unwelcome attention wild animals. The rabbit spitted and roasted over the wood fire was ready to eat in an hour. Lord Pedro shared a small pouch of red wine with Josep and shortly after eating, Josep dozed off. Both slept till dawn next day.

They set out at first light to check the castle and its surroundings. They got so close that from a stout beech tree, they could actually see into the courtyard of the castle. There seemed to be a handful of Foix's soldiers inside, together with the regular garrison of fifty or so troops of Cao de Benós, Baron of Les, the baron in the Val d'Aran. It was at his invitation that the Count of Foix had entered the valley but there was no evidence of the Count of Cominges. The Castle keep faced north as danger was anticipated as coming from France so the south of the castle was less well guarded. In any case, there were more pennants of the distinctive tower on the blue background, the coat of arms of the Baron of Les, than the three red vertical stripes and gold background of the Count of Foix. This was good news as it meant the count's force there was small and the intelligence had been exaggerated.

"It would be easy to confuse the three red stripes of the House of Foix with the four red stripes of the Royal House of the counts of Barcelona," said Lord Pedro. "Pay attention to that, Josep. You could mistakenly stake your life on your enemy or worse attack your friend if you made that mistake in time to come."

Josep nodded. "When I first saw the coat of arms of the Count of Foix, I did think it was the royal coat of arms," he said. "How is it that it is so similar?"

"Hundreds of years ago, the Royal House of the Counts of Barcelona and the Counts of Foix had a common ancestor in Wilfred the Hirsuit, Guifré el Pilós," said Lord Pedro. "Both families have the right to use La Senyera, the Catalan flag, which is the coat of arms of Guifré de Pilós."

"He was the first Count of Urgell and Barcelona, wasn't he? Didn't he win the coat of arms in a battle?" asked Josep.

"So they say, jove. In the times of the kingdoms of Charlemagne, he made our people of the Marca Hispànica feel like a nation and encouraged them to use Catalan. The Frankish king, Charles the Bald, officially the count's king, rewarded his bravery by giving him a coat of arms after Guifré was wounded in a battle against the Moors. The king dipped Guifré's fingers in his wounds and slid his fingers over his copper shield, thus creating the Senyera, the Catalan flag, with its four stripes of red on gold, so the legend goes."

"When did that happen? Josep asked. "It sounds as old as the Romans."

"Four hundred years ago, Josep, not so long ago as the Romans, in the late eight hundreds." He paused and quickly checked around them. They had been talking for some time, which made them vulnerable. "There is little family feeling left between the counts of Barcelona and Foix in my opinion but the Senyera remains to remind us of the shared noble origins of the two houses.

"Well, it's a great story!" Josep said. Lord Pedro laughed. "I wish we could get that across to the Count of Foix. But a lot of water has gone under the bridge since then. A lot of bad has happened."

"His family were Cathars, too, once, weren't they?" Josep asked.

"That's right, jove. The count's parents were. They died, were buried in Castellbó, then declared heretics and exhumed. Their remains had to be taken closer to Foix."

"I can understand why he does not feel like family any more then," said Josep.

Their mission accomplished, they returned to their camp, tended to their horses and as they were hungry, decided to check the two remaining traps from the night before. As soon as they retraced their steps, they found one and dispatched it quickly. They kicked over the last remaining trap and were turning to leave when there was an ominous crack of wood no more than a couple of metres from them. Both Josep and Lord Pedro froze, then the nerve of the third person broke and he noisily ran from them.

"After him!" Josep heard.

He was no match for Josep's speed and agility and in seconds he had brought him down. He was a heavy man of about forty with clothes they didn't recognise and a long beard. He was also difficult to understand. They bound him immediately but he offered little resistance and switched between French and Occitan. They could understand him when he spoke Occitan but not French.

"Please do not take me down to the castle. I've done nothing wrong. I was watching you. I've never seen rabbit killed," he panted.

"Wait, wait. One moment," said Lord Pedro. "Where did you come from? How long have you been tracking us and how did you get up here without us seeing you?"

"I'm innocent, I haven't done anything wrong," the man repeated desperately.

They couldn't make him talk so bound and still gagged in case he called for help, the man was taken back to their camp.

"We mean you no harm if you have nothing to do with the castle," said Lord Pedro once they were back. "But we can't let you go until we can guarantee that you will not reveal our whereabouts to the garrison of Es Bordes."

"I never go down there. They will kill me if they know we are here."

"What do you mean "we"?" asked Lord Pedro sharply.

He whirled around, expecting at any moment to be attacked by armed assailants.

"Stupid, stupid, Amaury, first you are caught like a fat old rabbit, you cannot keep your mouth shut. Oh, how stupid am I!"

This was all he would say through his sobs. He was hysterical. They bound him to a tree, fearing less and less for their safety as neither Josep nor Lord Pedro could believe the man they had as their prisoner was on a military sortie or that his company, even if they came, would be any more dangerous than he himself had been and nobody had come so far. More than nervous, they were bemused as to who this strange man was who called himself Amaury, a name they'd never heard before. The man seemed old enough to have been Lord Pedro's father. He spoke such strange Occitan and was still weeping and thrashing his head to and fro.

"Calm down, old man!" said Lord Pedro, his voice calmer and quieter. "We are not going to harm you."

"Maybe he's hungry," volunteered Josep. "And he's annoyed with himself that he's missed his lunch," he added, laughing at the strangeness of the situation.

"He would need a good amount of food to keep that frame going!" laughed Lord Pedro, patting the man's paunch. "Are you hungry, old man, is that it?"

"We could always share a rabbit with him, couldn't we?" asked Josep.

The rabbit had been spitted and roasting for a good half an hour by and both knight and page's mouths were watering. There was a hungry look in the old man's eyes but neither Lord Pedro nor Josep could make him speak any further.

They decided to eat but felt uncomfortable as they did. He would not take his eyes off them once. What is more, he seemed to follow every movement from knife to mouth as if tantalising himself with a visual feast that he couldn't share in reality. He was repeatedly offered parts of the rabbit, better and better parts, as his captors satisfied their own appetite but it became clear that he wouldn't accept. Finally, all the rabbit was devoured and with renewed vigour, the two companions contemplated what they were going to do with Amaury.

"He's not from the castle, nor is he some wild man from the woods. His clothes are rough but clean and strong and mended in parts. I vote that we take him to the pass. Then, when we enter Ribagorça and are safe from the men of Cao de Benós and Foix, we can release him and he can do as he wishes," said Lord Pedro.

"But what if he follows us down and reveals to whomever he meets who we are?" countered Josep.

"That's an important consideration, Josep, good thinking but of course he'd have to get past us first and we'll see what happens if he tries. Something tells me he won't."

Once they got to the pass, they released Amaury. He looked confused for a moment, then, realising he was free, lumbered off at great speed in case knight and page should change their mind. He disappeared along the trail they had taken when they had arrived but Josep noticed he soon cut left onto a track they hadn't noticed before.

"He's gone further west towards the ridge, my Lord," said Josep. "There can't be a party there that could harm us, could there?"

"Good observation, young Josep," replied his knight. "I don't know is the answer to your question."

They moved quickly over the loose stone leading to the entrance to the pass and both shuddered at the idea of being pursued in a freak storm. Certain capture if not serious injury and death would certainly ensue for both, they well knew. However, the day couldn't have been finer and as there was nobody on their tail, within an hour they started laughing and enjoyed their journey back down the mountain, making it to Benasque by late afternoon.

"I wonder if we'll ever find out who Amaury was," Josep mused during an excellent and welcome hot meal at the inn in Benasque." Little did he imagine how important he was to be to him. "Perhaps we'll bump into him again when we next go to the Val d'Aran. He owes us a favour."

CHAPTER 5 CHRISTMAS CHILL

As Lord Pedro de Ayerbe had been invited to spend Christmas with Josep, they arrived at Can Baró de la Cabrera on Christmas Eve. After the traditional meal, carn d'olla and sopa de galets, a light casserole and pasta shell soup, and nuelles, Catalan honey-flavoured wafer spirals, for dessert, Josep dozed off while Catarina and Clara sat chatting by the fire. He slept so soundly he was awake by six. He put his head out of the window as soon as he leapt out of bed. The temperature had dropped in the night and frost was all around, dusting the vineyards white, leaving white crowns on the upper branches of the pines on the hillside opposite. At first he didn't recognise Bru as he looked more like a wild animal than a human being. There was a blankness in his eyes that reminded Josep of the look of wild dogs before they attacked. He had obviously not been in human society for some time and Clara had been the first to witness his condition on his return. He was almost black against the pale dawn frosty light yet it was a strange, patchy black as if grimy layers had been irregularly overlaid, baked by the sun, blasted by the wind and etched in by the chilly nights as summer had yielded to autumn and autumn in turn to winter since Josep had last seen him. He wore nothing against the cold but his gonella, or outer garment, which was torn around his neck and gathered at the waist by his cinturó, the belt, from which his coltell hung. His espardenyes were of the same colour as his face and over his back he had his sageta, his arrow sheath, which contained his bread and a couple of short spears.

"No, Bru," Clara was saying to him by way of returning his greeting. "I cannot let you enter my house like this!" she recoiled from his appearance.

"Go away until you can accustom yourself again to civilized life!" She closed the door in his face. It was clear to Josep, shocked though he was to see him like this, that he had been doing what almogavers do: where for centuries before they had used their shepherd skills to hunt wolves in order to protect the flock, these days they used the same skills to track and trap victims in the mountains, kill them, plunder their possessions and then move on to the next victim. He was back later that day bearing gifts. He arrived and left what he had brought on the front doorstep. Clara watched him through the window.

"I'm sorry, I should have known I should bring you something. Merry Christmas!" he said but Clara steadfastly refused to let him in. Then he was gone.

In a handwoven bag decorated with geometric patterns, he left handwoven silk scarves, fabulously fashioned golden earrings with parts so small they must have been beaten with a thimble-sized hammer, intricately inlaid with emeralds, rubies and sapphires. He also left a beautifully-crafted scimitar, complete with scabbard of beaten silver so highly polished you could see your reflection in it, so sharp it dented your finger if you so little as touched the blade. Clara was horrified.

"Where did he get these things this time? Which innocent's blood lies cooling to furnish his gift? How dare he celebrate Christ's birth with presents dripping in Muslim blood?"

Before anyone could stop her, she had set off to track down Bru's latest victim. Catarina, Josep and Lord Pedro caught up with her at la Cova Negra. As they drew near, a trail of blood appeared, leading into the cave. A woman with her knees drawn up to her chest lay there still breathing lightly.

"Take her back to our house, if you please, Jacques, and do for her what you can. There is a trail of blood leading to where the attack was carried out. There may be more victims there," Clara said.

The woman's simple brown cotton dress was drenched with blood and she groaned as Jacques picked her up. She was small, about Catarina's age and seemed to weigh little more than a child. The way she clutched at her belly indicated where she was wounded. Her hands and feet were dyed with henna, Catarina noticed. Lord Pedro wasted no time in leaving.

The trail of blood leading away from the cave was easy to track up into the hills of the Garraf, the high moorland neighbouring Sant Pere de Ribes. Josep and Catarina could barely keep up with Clara, who seemed to be verging on hysterical. She said nothing but choked cries of horror and sorrow escaped from her time and time again.

"Let it not be a child!" Josep whispered to himself.

The blood was harder to follow as rocks lay in the path, pitted and irregular and all but abandoned.

"Perhaps it was a secret path the Muslims knew about leading to where they lived," Josep thought to himself. He dreaded his mother's reaction. Here, deeper stains in the sandy soil showed where the woman must have stopped for a moment, consistent with the heavy bleeding of initial blood loss. They found themselves in front of another cave.

Catarina and Josep followed Clara inside. At first, in the gloom, Clara could not see the supine form lying there and tripped over the inert body. All three of them then saw the outline of the victim they had been seeking. Josep slumped down as he saw it was a man dressed in the long outer garment typical of Muslims. He was older, perhaps in his sixties. His thin hair and long beard were white and he was frail. As Clara wiped her eyes, she could make out what she dreaded. The body was brutally mutilated. The throat of the man had been slashed from one side to the other and the head was all but parted from the neck. The body seemed to have been flung powerfully to the right of the assailant, who must have attacked from behind, as the body lay with its shoulders against the wall of the cave, the limbs sprawled across the entrance that Clara had stumbled over.

"Whose blood have we followed to get here?" asked Clara.

"The woman's of course," answered Catarina.

"So she walked down to the riverbed after she was attacked?" Clara asked, trying to make all the pieces fit.

"Maybe she was looking for help," answered Catarina.

"But why would she take shelter in a cave that she knew was being used by an almogaver?" asked Clara. "La Cova Negra is the place Bru took you to that night when you found the dying Muslim man, isn't it, Josep?" she asked.

"Yes, Bru brought me to it the night you came looking for me," Josep said.

"But that doesn't mean he always uses it, does it?" asked Catarina. "Maybe the couple knew about the cave first and were regularly using it to take shelter. Their attacker also knew about it and had been watching them for some time and had followed them from the cave to their home cave in the hills. Then, when the couple were attacked, the woman went to find help but only made it as far as the Cova Negra," she said.

"So both Bru and the couple knew about the Cova Negra and Bru was able to follow the couple back to their home cave after he'd seen them here. We've always thought it was Bru's cave and he used it to store his bloody pickings," said Clara.

"But that doesn't make sense, he has no interest in storing dying bodies, he leaves them behind as he left this man behind. In which case Bru might not have been responsible for the death of the first man we found in the summer! We assumed he was guilty but the evidence was purely circumstantial. He was in the wrong place at the wrong time!"

"He didn't deny it!" said Clara a little too vehemently.

"Well, to be honest, nobody ever stopped to ask him either," said Catarina. "Maybe he had nothing to do with any of these deaths. Perhaps we have jumped to conclusions and done Bru a great injustice."

"I don't think Bru would have taken me to see a dying man that night no matter how bad we think he is," said Josep, obviously eager to believe the man who had effectively been an uncle to him all his life was not responsible for committing such barbarities.

"There's no real evidence he had anything to do with either of these attacks," said Catarina.

"But wait, what is this in the corner?" Clara said. They had all seen the gifts Bru had left on Clara's doorstep and as their eyes further adjusted to the light, they saw a small wooden loom with cloth still stretched over it, cotton threads neatly tied under it, the frame of which was smashed causing the woven fabric to fold over on itself thereby obscuring the pattern. Picking it up, she examined it in the light at the front of the cave.

She went quiet. The pattern on the loom was the same as that on the cloth Bru had presented as a present to her.

"If he's not the murderer, he was close behind him!" Clara hissed as if her worst fears had been confirmed.

"We've jumped to conclusions the other way: even if the man found in the cave in the summer was not his victim, these people might well be. It's impossible to know for sure. The hills are full of these marauding warriors preying on Muslims living outside the law, beyond protection. They pick them off one by one for the sake of their paltry possessions," she said clenching her fists.

They cast an eye around the cave. Everything you would expect to find in a home was there: bedding for two, cooking equipment, a small ring of stones serving as fireplace near the entrance. A few decorations on the walls, which the attacker had missed, made the place less austere.

"Let's return home," said Clara. "We need to bury this man as we did the last one but the woman worries me of a sudden!"

A chill that Christmas Day lodged in Josep's heart, a splinter of ice etched itself into Clara's expression and never left. The next day Lord Pedro and Josep returned to what they had started to call the "Home Cave" to bury the body of the man. Meanwhile, the Muslim woman clung onto life without uttering a word. Lord Pedro said her wounds were flesh wounds and therefore had bled a lot at first but needn't be fatal. After three days, she accepted her first warm milk and bread and her hands felt warm for the first time since she had been at Can Baró although the room where she was, an outhouse, had had a fire lit since the first day of her arrival. Her expression was distant and frozen like someone locked into the past in a place that was inaccessible to anyone else. Her stolen belongings were restored to her, together with whatever could be salvaged from the Home Cave. Yet she continued to lie on her back and stare up at the ceiling not even acknowledging the occupants of the house. Lord Pedro left for Ayerbe that day.

On New Year's Eve, she seemed to notice more what was going on around her. Clara sat down at one point to feed her warm milk with Catarina and Josep in attendance. Habiba sat and looked Clara straight in the eye and patting her chest with both her hands, said clearly, "Habiba."

Clara replied with the same gesture.

Then Habiba began speaking. She spoke in Mozarabe, as she could not speak Catalan or Spanish but had communicated, she said, with a small group of people outside her immediate circle not in her native Arabic but in this Arabised form of Spanish that had developed during the six centuries of the Moorish occupation. Clara understood Mozarabe well enough to translate for Catarina and Josep listening carefully to what Habiba was saying. After a while, they started to understand snatches of what sounded at times like archaic Spanish with a great deal of incomprehensible Arabic vocabulary and a style of speech that was immediately exotic, full of religious references and repetitions. It was a tragic monologue Josep would never forget.

"We are of this land Clara, this land that our ancestors cultivated by the grace of Allah for six hundred years and that Allah in his mercy showed us how to bring out its riches, from this land we brought out its riches, green and good things by the grace of Allah.

These stone walls and terraces, these we built again though they were ruins when we arrived, we rebuilt them with the skill and wisdom that Allah in his mercy gave us, built them, built this land that Allah gave us in his mercy, we built with our own hands this land of plenty that Allah gave us.

With our own tools that Allah in his mercy showed us how to use, we built and farmed this land this land that Allah in his providence gave us, we farmed it and nurtured this land our land, we tended it like a mother tends a child, we nourished it and it nourished us. This was done according to Allah's will. We were one with the land as Allah saw fit, we nurtured it and it nurtured us. We built the walls of the fields, we shaped the hills with our walls and with our walls we stopped the soil running away with the rain water thanks to the grace and wisdom of Allah. And we planted rice in the fields where we used the water from the rain that fell by the grace of Allah, we used the water to nurture our rice. And we lived well with the food that the land gave us. And it was in accordance with the will of Allah.

And the vine that you see today everywhere planted, we found this planted and tended it with Allah's grace and wisdom, we tended the vine next to the orange tree and the lemon tree and the olive tree and this land had all manner of fruits that Allah in his wisdom showed us how to plant and tend. And we lived well with it and it was in accordance with the will of Allah.

The vine that gives sweet fruit, you use the same fruit to make your melancholic wine that sends men mad. The same fruit in the same fields in the same land that Allah gave us you use to make your melancholic wine that sends men mad.

This land that for generations nourished us, our blood stains it. You in your victory, you spill our blood that stains the soil that gives you your red wine and you drink the melancholic wine that sends men mad and I ask: is this in accordance with the will of Allah?

Your God, I hear you eat the flesh and drink the blood of your God. And I cannot understand why you do this and I shake to imagine what your people are capable of. May Allah have mercy upon us."

"Can we not protect her at least and make sure sure she is safe and well?" Catarina asked Clara later. "Then at least Habiba will know our Christian beliefs of forgiveness, charity and gentleness. I feel we must help her but I also feel loyalty to our own people and the values we are at least supposed to live by."

Clara rose visibly fighting back tears.

"I knew this was happening and I did nothing to stop it," she said. Then she went outside and daubed a crude picture of an almogaver on a square of wood with a red cross through it as a warning to Bru or any other vagrant hill warrior that under no circumstances were they in any way welcome at Can Baró. She nailed this sign to the post next to the track to Can Baró.

Another evening, Habiba sat weeping in her room. Her fire was lit as usual and it was comfortable as Josep sat there again with Clara and Catarina. Catarina noticed she was still attractive, dark despite her present pallor. She was petite and shapely, with tiny hands. Her henna-dyed, copper hair, streaked with grey, was drawn back from her face, her features fine but gaunt, her lips full, her eyes dark and penetrating.

"In the old days, when this land was our land my family lived in the old stone house that is fallen down up the hill next to Can Baró. Six generations of my family lived there before they had to leave, they had their children there by the grace of Allah and lived, farmed and died there. They are buried on the hill. Our family name is Atuel, this means "tall" in Arabic and we built another stone house and had a little land next to the Jafra river in the hills just outside Ripis. You call it Ribes. We are seven generations living a poor life in the hills. I lived there with my father and husband. My little boy and girl died before they were ten, they were never strong, we had little food."

"I am living on your family's land by a stroke of good fortune, Habiba. You are welcome to stay here as long as you wish," Clara said.

"Every generation the community was smaller but my generation is the last to have children, now dead. My man did not come back one day last summer."

"Habiba," Clara said, "in the cave where we found you, we found a man in the summer. He was badly injured. We carried him here and tried to heal his wounds but that night, he died praying. He is buried up the hill here, near where you say your family home was. He left this set of prayer beads but we buried him with his ring on his finger. We imagined a wife and children waiting for him to come home." She handed the beads to Habiba.

When she saw the beads, Habiba let out a deep moan. Everyone's hair stood on end. Habiba cried then and hid her face in her hands. She spoke for some minutes in Arabic. Then she turned to Clara.

"Why did you help my man?" she asked in Mozarabe.

"It is normal for us to help people if we find them and they are injured," replied Clara, glad at last to be able to apologise to some extent for her culture and redress the balance.

"Thank you for helping my husband. He was a good man. You are a good person. My mother was sick and died so I cooked and did these things that she did when she was alive for my father and husband. I knew one or two Christian families when we lived in the hills. They did not help us but they did not harm us. We exchanged things that we needed but nothing more. We were not friends." She kept her head low, refusing to look Clara in the eye.

"Habiba, do you know who killed your husband?"

"How can I know that?"

"Because the night we found your husband, another man was there. A Catalan soldier, we call them almogavers."

"It is an Arabic word, it means destroyer. There are some in the hills here."

Clara leant forward and looked into Habiba's eyes.

"Habiba, was it a soldier who destroyed your home and killed your father?"

"We had the fire and were cooking sitting next to it to keep warm. The man appeared quickly and attacked us. He wounded me with his knife and then hit me in the face. My spirit left me for some minutes. When my spirit returned, I saw all the things destroyed in the cave and I saw my father. I wanted to help him so I ran to find help but I could find nobody."

"Are there other people like you living in the hills?"

"We feared to go to the aljama in Barcelona where we would be protected by the king. How could we travel safely to the city? Only one or two small communities like our one remain but they are secret and hidden," she said a little suspiciously so Clara dropped the subject.

"I was so tired and there was a lot blood. I couldn't find anyone so I lay down to rest in the cave. I thought it was safe. Then you found me."

"Did you recognise the man who attacked you? Was he an almogaver?"

"He was wild and mad with wine. I could smell it on his breath. But he was big and like an animal. His eyes were cold and black. His hair was long and unwashed. His clothes were dirty and his skin was white but covered in black."

"Did you recognise him?"

"They all look the same to me," she replied.

"We think it might be an almogaver that we know. Tell me, did your husband know where the Cova Negra where we found you was?

"We have always used that cave. For shelter in storms sometimes."

"Do you think the almogaver took your husband and left him there?"

"No, the almogavers never leave things there. We do not leave things there. It is an open cave, anyone can use it but it is not safe to leave things there. He knew where it was. You say that you found my husband there so maybe he needed to find shelter there when he was injured, like me. The almogaver do not leave people alive to return to them later. They kill, steal and destroy."

Clara turned to Catarina.

"It sounds as if it was an almogaver who killed her father and it might have been Bru," Catarina said. Habiba sat rocking quietly, clutching her husband's beads.

"Bru is not welcome here. None of them is. I want nothing to do with any of them again," Clara whispered, her eyes red. Catarina did not argue with her.

Later that evening, Josep overheard Clara talking to his mother.

"I'm tired of war and killing, Catarina. I have this house through chance by being born into the Mir family. Yet my two brothers died in war and the original Mir acquired the house and land by dispossessing the family of the woman who is presently recovering from an attack, whose ancestral house is not twenty metres from this house in ruins. Where is the Christian message in all this?" she asked.

"Where is the message of peace in the fact that Muslim soldiers took the land from Christians six hundred years ago?" replied Catarina. "We are no better or worse than our Muslim counterparts."

"But at the moment, our Christian God is pounding the Muslim God into the red soil of this land!" said Clara.

Josep struggled to reconcile this weariness of war, this horror of violence, this empathy and pity for other people's suffering with the education he was receiving. Though not overtly religious, the women in his life embodied beliefs in values like love, hope, charity, mercy, neighbourliness. Yet his education at the hands of holy men and knights was focused on competition, domination and cleverness on the one hand; and religious ideals, on the other, that he found curious but unconvincing that had to be swallowed for regurgitation. Death for Josep was real, all too familiar to him already and was a much more cogent teacher. His education was clothed in idealism but was focused on survival, his own and that of the narrow sector of society represented by the education of the stamp and pedigree he was receiving. He struggled in his thirteen-year-old mind to square this circle but couldn't. In the interests of survival, he put the conundrum to the back of his mind.

He thought about Bru, the old raw thumping heart of this country. He imagined he was older than the House of the Counts of Barcelona and the Crown of Catalunya Aragón, older than Guifré el Pilós, Sunyer, Bella, Charlemagne and all the Franks, the Visigoths, more ancient than the Romans, the Celts, the Iberians. Faced with the Moors, whether in open battle for the king or in guerrilla warfare for his own private livelihood, he was of a breed of warriors perfectly adapted to a mountain environment from shepherd origins. Bru's bones were formed from the earth his leathery feet were planted on, his ancestors for countless generations had been born, bred, buried in the Vale of Montgròs, the mountain of Sant Pere de Ribes, as long as anyone could remember. Bru was one with the crumbly limey soil of the vineyards, the dusty pines that gave no shade in summer, the dry riverbed that cut like an old scar into the ripis or riverbank that gave the town its Latin name aeons later. His kind had been employed traditionally as shepherds because of their knowledge of nature and the land but he was more than that. He was one with the moist ravine, the one that nobody ever went into because it was dark, damp and creepy, where many secrets had lain buried since time immemorial. He was one with the black caves that snaked under the labyrinthine limestone passages that lattice the mountains of the Garraf. How many wonders of nature or human remains had he seen by torchlight in the depths of those natural vaults? They were places daylight never visited, seen by one or two others in every generation who had dared or were driven to explore what remained hidden or deliberately unobserved by "normal folk". He could appear and disappear at will. He knew every track, crevice, spring and bend in the river in this, his land. He was born of the land, a natural product of it. Josep had not seen the last of him.

CHAPTER 6 THE DROWNING

Two years passed in which Josep, away at Cavallers, saw nothing of Bru. Meanwhile, the antagonism between Ferran Sanchis and Prince Pere became more and more heated when Josep returned to Cavallers in the spring of 1276. Although he applied himself to his studies, which were overseen by Fray Francesc, Fray Arnaldo el Zurdo, though not much in evidence around the school, was still present. He was said to be helping Ferran Sanchis more in his tasks.

Josep was being called to attend Lord Pedro de Ayerbe in the middle of the night on a weekly basis and three times, once in February, once in April and once in May, in the presence of Prince Pere himself. The heir to the throne immediately recognised Josep. Guillem de Queralt's father, Pere de Queralt, who always attended the Crown Prince, explained that Josep had been a good friend to Guillem.

"So, he'll be a natural enemy of Fray Arnaldo el Zurdo!" Prince Pere said and everyone laughed knowing about the friar's cruel reputation and also how closely connected Fray Arnaldo el Zurdo was to Ferran Sanchis.

"My father the king has done everything in his power to bring about a reconciliation between the nobles of Aragón and Catalunya and himself but Sanchis continues to frustrate every attempt," said the Crown Prince, finishing a silver goblet of wine and passing it to Josep.

"But why will the nobles not side with the king and Prince Pere now that it is clear that the king has broken off all relations with Sanchis?" Lord Pedro de Ayerbe asked.

"They are playing a waiting game, " replied Prince Pere. "Whoever controls the castles in the end is the paymaster. The king has debts with all the nobles that remain unpaid as a result of the trouble Sanchis has stirred up. If I can eliminate Sanchis, I can take back all the possessions of mine he presently controls and start calling in our debts. Then the nobles will do homage again to the king."

"What do you mean by eliminate, your Highness? Do you mean to send him into exile? His faction might find the resources to bring him back and his mother, Blanca de Antillón, is still popular with the king."

As he said this, Lord Pedro de Ayerbe could not look the Crown Prince in the eye. Ferran Sanchis was one illegitimate son of King Jaume, while he, Lord Pedro de Ayerbe, was another.

"I do not choose to contemplate the past relationships of my father," replied the prince. "The illegitimate offspring of the king should know where they stand. On the other side of the royal bed. You, Lord Pedro de Ayerbe, are not only my half-brother but also my namesake. Would that all siblings were as loyal. And this young man who has attended you unfailingly, quietly, correctly and obediently, doing our bidding day and night," he strode over to Josep. Everyone was murmuring and there was laughter in the Crown Prince's voice.

"Your Highness," Josep said.

There were louder noises of assent and several knights approached him and clapped him on the back. The Crown Prince turned to his horse, mounted it in one motion and said to Lord Pedro de Ayerbe, "Make sure this young man has a horse saddled next time I come. I'll need both your help if I finally find Sanchis and you'll need a page."

A few days later, while the boys were tending to the horses, a party of ten soldiers arrived bearing penants with five gold stars on a blue background, the shield of Antillón. They accompanied a beautiful noble woman. She was magnificently attired in silk and ermine furs against the chill of the May morning. It was Ferran Sanchis' mother, Blanca de Antillón. She had a brief interview with the director of the school and then promptly left with several heavy saddle bags that clinked with the sound of silver coins. She also took Sanchis' three best horses, together with saddles and harnesses.

The moment she had left, Josep's knight found him.

"Josep, the moment has come!" he whispered urgently. "Saddle your horse and ride as fast as you can to Huesca where you will find the king. Tell him Sanchis' mother has removed the last of his possessions from the academy so he must be running out of money and expecting to be besieged. He moves nightly under cover of darkness between the various castles he controls but his mother coming here in broad daylight has betrayed him unwittingly and I am convinced this means he will be in Antillón this evening."

"You mean that I should go alone my Lord? The road is long and I have never travelled it alone!" Josep said.

"But they will not question a boy of thirteen, Josep, whereas If I were to accompany you, I would be stopped immediately as the roads are crowded with Sanchis' men. The message has to get through!"

His heart in his mouth, Josep saddled his horse and wrapping a cloak around him, leapt upon his horse and was ready for off.

"What shall I say if I am stopped?" asked Josep.

"Tell them you're on your way to the market in Huesca to sell your horse," Lord Pedro de Ayerbe murmured loud enough for Josep to hear as he held the bridle of Josep's horse in his hands. He let go, gave the horse a slap on the rump and Josep skilfully turned his palfrey and galloped out of the grounds of the academy along the dusty, pine-clad road that led to Barbastro.

It didn't take long till he saw the rear of the party of Sanchis' mother. He put his head down, spurred on his horse and galloped past them as fast as he could. For several minutes, he dared not look back, his heart pounding in his chest but clearly nobody suspected him, out for a canter on his horse. In any case, if they were heading to Antillón, their paths would diverge after a few miles.

The Crown Prince had spent the night in Monte Aragón, a few miles east of Huesca and was on the road early as Josep saw. He was meeting his father's steward, Jaume de Xèrica, Lord Pedro de Ayerbe's brother, in Huesca. More and more work was being delegated to the king's inner circle as the burden of the Muslim revolt in Valencia and Murcia and the nobles' revolts in the north of his dominions weighed down the ageing monarch, who was not well. Crown Prince Pere was two miles outside Huesca enjoying the view of the plane open all the way to Saragossa in the south and to the Pyrenees to the north and the cool breezes of a late May morning.

There was a sudden commotion around the Prince and young Josep Goodman burst through the ranks of knights around him.

De Queralt was the first to recognise him and he grasped the bridle of Josep's horse, which was startled at being stopped. The horse reared up and Josep had to struggle to stay in the saddle.

He gave his message breathlessly still panting form the exertion of the hour-long gallop but there was a thrill of understanding that charged the features of all those gathered round him as he finished.

"When did they leave?" asked the Crown Prince.

"I passed them on the road after leaving La Puebla, your Highness!" replied Josep.

"Post an ambush here in case they flee this way later," said the Crown Prince. Send a message to Jaume de Xèrica to meet me at Antillón by the most direct route. Give me a guide!"

"I know these roads, your Highness," said Josep. "We have been using them for our own riding practice for the past year. There is a little used path running directly from here to Antillón across the garriga," Josep said, pointing out towards the featureless moorland countryside.

Prince Pere cast him a momentary glance, barely able to believe his ears that this young page had brought him the vital intelligence he had been long awaiting.

Most of the prince's party arrived at Antillón in less than an hour. They had been seen arriving from a distance of course, so the portcullis gate had been lowered preventing their entry into the town. But this also barred two knights of Blanca de Antillón's party who had been bringing up the rear and were delayed catching one of Sanchis' three horses, which had broken loose. It did not take Crown Prince Pere long to extract the information he needed from them. Sanchis was indeed inside the town's castle and Josep was immediately summoned.

"Master Josep, I wonder if you can imagine the importance of what you've done! I shall not forget!" said the Crown Prince.

He wasted no time in having siege engines brought in from Huesca and before long, huge catapults, called mangonels, were hurling great boulders against the castle walls, which seemed impregnable to Josep. Lord Pedro de Ayerbe's brother Jaume de Xèrica also arrived with twenty knights, fresh horses and fifty head of cattle as well as a carriage laden with money. The odds against Antillón were enormous. The two captured knights also revealed that little provision had yet been stored up inside the town as those inside had planned to finalise their preparations that morning. Josep's information had been a total coup. The word in the Crown Prince's camp was that those inside Antillón had thought a siege was a possibility but had never considered it inevitable. The next step they had anticipated was the arrival of help from from Compte d'Empúries and his followers. It would certainly not reach the town now.

Antillón fell quickly under the barrage of heavy stones flung at all angles against the walls. Soon weaknesses were revealed and specially trained soldiers called sappers went in under cover of the siege engines to hack away at the smashed and crumbling stones at the foot of the the town walls. A breach was opened and a squadron of knights twenty strong each with two footsoldiers for support poured into the hole in the town. The unfortunate and blameless townspeople suffered the violence and destruction to their property that civilians always bear in this kind of military manoeuvre but there were strict instructions from the Crown Prince himself, repeated time and time again by the senior knights, that nobody was to be killed or raped and no booty was to be taken and as far as the Crown Prince was aware, this order was respected. The townspeople, who quickly assembled in front of the church once the gates to the town had been opened, begged the Crown Prince abjectly for mercy.

"I would have your loyalty but you cannot have two masters. I would have you as my people as this is my town. The rest depends on you!"

The mayor summoned up the courage to express the gratitude and loyalty of all the townspeople and the matter came to a close. The people were allowed to return to their houses, once the soldiers had checked that they were not harbouring the fugitive half-brother of the Crown Prince in case he had slipped out of the castle unawares. The Crown Prince called Jaume de Xèrica to talk to him as it was he who had brought the prince the sealed document from King Jaume granting permission to use any means necessary to subdue Sanchis. It was an agonising dilemma King Jaume had had to decide on: with which son was he going to side? Both his flesh and blood, one legitimate, loyal but unpopular, the other disloyal to him but with the loyalty of much of the Aragonese and northern Catalan nobility.

"There is no way he can escape," began the Crown Prince. "Sooner or later we will have him!"

"Then you will have to be judge and executioner, my brother," said Lord Pedro de Ayerbe, "for if you allow Sanchis to slip through your fingers, his supporters will rally to rescue him and the conflict will escalate, more lives will be lost and further damage caused. You will have to be swift and decisive."

"You have our father's permission to do whatever may be necessary," said Jaume de Xèrica.

It was Tuesday evening, the twenty-ninth of May, 1275. The town had fallen almost immediately so no provisions lay secretly waiting to be passed through to the castle. It was a matter of starving them out. Camp set up outside the town was convivial if not festive. Fifty knights were present, thirty owing allegiance directly to the prince twenty to Jaume de Xèrica. Two huge oxen were roasting, enormous on the spit, outside the shattered main gate to the town. Passage in and out was strictly controlled in case anyone should take flight. The surrounding area was billeted with sentries working day and night in threes to guard all routes out. The townspeople unable to leave had to pay an exorbitant price for food from the camp followers who had attached themselves to the camp of the besieging force. They provided fresh bread and meat to whomever could afford to pay. The wind blew the smoke of the roasting beef over the gate of the town drifting tantalisingly to the highest castle tower. Many a face was imagined seen peeping out from the ramparts or through the arrowslits, drawn by the delicious smells coming from the besieging camp. As evening drew on, there were drunken cries from some of the tents, accompanied by the bawdy laughter of prostitutes themselves seduced away from Huesca, Barbastro and Monzón to Antillón by rumours of easy money.

The scene was repeated the following evening. During the day the castle had been subjected to increased bombardment as more trebuchets and mangonels hurled out their destruction. Antillón was nearly smashed to pieces and the barbican alone remained intact. Over the lip of this circular tower any offensive material that could be found was also hurled. This included the parts of the slaughtered cow that could not be used and had lain festering in the sun prone to disease: heads, feet, intestines, lungs were bundled up mixed with animal dung in case it crossed anyone's mind to eat the vile offal. Sooner or later, it was known that disease would break out. Several enemy soldiers had also been killed protecting the castle towers and had fallen camp side. Their bodies were mutilated almost beyond recognition and sent back over the walls in the trebuchets. It was clear that beset as it was by every form of warfare imaginable, hunger, brutal violence, psychological torture and the threat of disease, the castle could hold out no longer. Morale must have been at rock bottom.

As evening's first pink shadows played on the walls of the castle, Sanchis, bearing the shield with five gold stars, bolted on horseback from a rear gate obscured by undergrowth, galloping at full pelt for the Monzón road.

The shout went up and in the confusion, stalls were knocked over, tents torn up and mayhem soon reigned. Pere de Queralt was the first to give chase and the whole camp was in hot pursuit, including the Crown Prince, Lord Pedro de Ayerbe and Josep. Of course Sanchis' horse was a fine one and would not be easy to catch.

Yet Josep sensed something strange. Sanchis seemed to be thrown about on the back of the horse as if he lacked firm hold of the reigns to command the horse to gallop as if life itself depended on it. The prince's knights were gaining on him when disaster struck. The horse, a thoroughbred and highly strung, had enough of its rider and reared all of a sudden sending the rider sprawling into the undergrowth, motionless in his exquisite garments, the shield lying by his side.

No sooner were they on him than they saw he had shrunk and his hair had turned grey and been tonsured. They had been tricked. Josep drew in closer and saw the unmistakable features of Fray Arnaldo el Zurdo. He shouted out his name in the sudden commotion of rearing horses and clash of metal on metal as the knights beat their shields with their swords when they realized Fray Arnaldo el Zurdo had switched places with Sanchis.

"Sanchis!" roared Prince Pere, wheeling around and scanning the horizon wildly. As Josep then looked, he saw some of the camp followers jumping and waving and even at this distance heard the faint din they were raising by striking any metal object they could to draw attention frantically to the direction Sanchis' horse was heading.

The Crown Prince had the right idea and was already desperately riding after the real fugitive. The only option for Sanchis was the river. Sanchis had used a decoy to make his getaway and was planning to cross the River Cinca on horseback.

"He intends to cross the river at Pomar de Cinca and ride like fury to Ceret, the first place that will give him shelter," cried Lord Pedro de Ayerbe to Josep as they tried to catch up with the Prince. At that moment, the Crown Prince uttered a strangled cry of rage. Sanchis's escape was not just a possibility but a real threat. Both men were riding for their lives because it was clear that if Sanchis escaped, the Crown

Prince would look an incompetent fool and his reputation and therefore authority would be in tatters. If Sanchis was caught he would die.

There were no bridges at this point of the river, the closest one being at Monzón, twenty miles to the north.

"Perhaps Sanchis intends to make his horse swim across the river and carry him over," Josep thought.

Josep and Lord Pedro were just behind the Prince. Could they catch Sanchis before he got to the river? How far across the river could Sanchis get before the Prince caught up with him? The chase was on. Prince Pere's horse was fast but so was Sanchis'. The Prince perhaps hoped when Sanchis got to the river, the horse would refuse to enter the water. Or he could try to follow him across. Or he could shoot him with an arrow but Josep doubted the Prince had such a weapon on his person. He was, however, famous for his knife throwing. How well could he throw a knife across a river thirty metres wide in the dying light of the day? Josep had his doubts.

They arrived at the river and crashed through the alders, ashes and reeds that lined the shore. They threw themselves out of the saddle leaving the steaming horses and saw the Crown Prince already up to his knees in the river water about five metres from the bank. He looked steadily out over the placid water. Sanchis was about thirty metres from them and half way across the river on his horse. Prince Pere's silence was eerie. This was the closest he and his half-brother had been to each other in half a year. There was nothing to say. Sanchis' survival depended on his horse and the river currents. His horse's head dipped momentarily under the water and the poor animal started neighing pitifully. They could hear Sanchis shouting and cursing the animal. It seemed to be trapped, it was thrashing its head around wildly but had stopped going forward.

"I do believe it's got its hooves caught in the reeds on the other side but the water is still too deep for the horse to stand. It's panicking and as it stamps about, it's enmeshing itself even more deeply into the reeds," said Lord Pedro de Ayerbe. The Crown Prince growled in reply.

Sanchis' horse continued to thrash about and whinny but was going nowhere. Then Sanchis started beating the horse around the head before finally throwing off his steel breastplate. Freeing himself from the animal, he made a desperate bid for the opposite bank. He was about the same distance from the bank as he had come but the currents took him being lighter than the horse and as the horse continued to struggle he did what he could to stay afloat but luck was not with him. The current was clearly bringing him back to the near side and Prince Pere wasted no time in splashing his way downstream to intercept him when he hit the bank. He disappeared from view on account of the height of the reeds as the river swept him along. Prince Pere started swearing loudly as he feared the man would slip out of sight somehow. Meanwhile, Sanchis' horse neighed once more and finally went under the water never to reappear.

"Master Josep, fetch a detachment immediately," shouted Prince Pere. Station men every fifty yards along the river for two miles. Make sure Sanchis doesn't disappear up a tree or into the long grass or corn when he finally makes dry land. My brother," he then said turning to Lord Pedro de Ayerbe, "fetch your two most trusted lieutenants. I need men capable of carrying out any order."

"Yes, your Highness," both replied.

The sun had gone down, the moon was out and the light shone coldly down over the riverbank converting the familiar shapes of trees and reeds into ghostly sentinels of the night. The men had been stationed along the river bank for two hours as Prince Pere had commanded and Lord Pedro de Ayerbe and his two trusted henchmen, one of them Guillem's father, Pere de Queralt, the most senior knight there, awaited the prince's orders on horseback next to him. Prince Pere sat there high on his horse and a gust of wind caught his hair and blew it out like a lion's mane. All was silent on his express instructions. Every creak, whistle or snap might be the fugitive making his getaway.

Then there was a sudden commotion. There was a cry for help from one of the soldiers posted along the river bank.

"I've seen him. He's there heading back into the cornfield. He must have got lost and wandered back to the riverbank."

"Fool, he should have waited till morning when he could see something!" shouted de Queralt triumphantly. "Now we have him."

The soldiers fanned out and surrounded the area they expected him to be and within minutes, he was in their midst and Prince Pere on horseback was next to him.

"I have you, do not cause any more trouble, it will be the worse for you!" he said, laying a hand firmly on his head. "Summon the other traitor, Sanchis' monk accomplice."

"You are charged with high treason. How do you plead?" he began without preliminaries.

"Guilty!" all the knights and soldiers gathered around the trial shouted.

"Silence if you please. Let me hear it from the lips of the accused. How do you plead?"

"Long live the king!" shouted Sanchis provocative, defiant and fearless.

"Pass on my regards to our forefathers in the afterlife!" muttered the Crown Prince, his hand still on his head, staring coldly into his eyes.

Fray Arnaldo el Zurdo dropped to his knees and begged for mercy. He knew all too well the penalty for high treason was death. He was weeping, beseeching Josep also with his eyes to intercede on his behalf.

"Your Highness, the boy is too young to see such things," said one of de Queralt's men.

"Nonsense!" replied the Prince. "If it hadn't been for this young man, we would never even have known Sanchis was in Antillón. It was the beginning of the end for Sanchis. The choice is yours, jove. Stay or leave, as you wish but harden your heart to your true enemies!"

Josep looked at his former tutor, completely beaten. He felt a sudden pang of pity for him. Fray Arnaldo el Zurdo sensed the turmoil in the young boy's heart, shrewdly even then reading his expression. He prostrated himself at Josep's feet, wetting his espardenyes with his tears and dribble. Josep was both appalled and dumbstruck. How could he go against the will of the prince and all these knights? His heart shrank back in horror. If it was a quick, painless death that was better but death was death and he suspected, there was no such thing as a quick, painless death in war. It was always brutal and vicious and sordid and unskillful and terrifying.

"Harden your heart, young man!" the Prince said. "Remember what he did to your friend!"

Where did the Prince drag that memory up from?" Josep thought. He was paralysed. He could no longer think straight. Going against the prince's wishes, pleading for this man was a terrifying option. He couldn't do it. He looked at the man. What mercy had he shown any of the weaker boys all that term he had taught them chivalry? Where was the chivalry in that? Where had human kindness been when he swiped the boys across the face, what kind of miscreant prepared his victims with a gentle caress to the back of the legs, where was the mercy in the blinding speed with which he struck those who could not defend themselves? He moved back a step, shook his foot as if to free it from the hands of his supplicant. He looked at Guillem's father. He was granite-like in his resolve. Lord Pedro de Ayerbe wore the same grim expression. Face after face was the same. The conflict in Josep's mind came back to him: Life or death. Mercy and kindness or survival and privilege? If he showed mercy he might as well resign any ambition to be in the prince's service. He felt ill. He knew what had to happen but he couldn't bear to witness it. Here was death so near again waiting for these two men. He could do nothing to change it. Pere de Queralt would not let Fray Arnaldo el Zurdo escape as Crown Prince Pere would not relax his grip on Sanchis. Josep stiffened his back and half turned away from Fray Arnaldo el Zurdo, who continued to sob.

The Prince put his hand on Fray Arnaldo el Zurdo's shoulder and heaved him up to his feet. "Meet your death like a man for God's sake." That was all he said and there was a murmur of approval from the assembled knights.

Still near enough to know what was going on though far enough away not to actually witness it, Josep heard everything as the prisoners were bound and taken to the river. He heard the lieutenants, one of whom was Pere de Queralt, instruct the soldiers to lay the men face down on the river bank. "Pin down their legs," he said, "as they will struggle like pigs being slaughtered."

Josep vomited. He could still hear the muffled cries of Fray Arnaldo el Zurdo and the grunts of effort as the soldiers positioned themselves on top of the men's legs. Josep then heard Pere de Queralt utter an exclamation to indicate he was about to begin.

"Go ahead, Queralt. May God have mercy on their souls!" said the Prince.

"Grasp their shoulders," the prince continued. "Hold them down men as they are pulled in, then pin down their legs," he said.

Josep could hear as the men were pulled face first into the water. The whimpering from Fray Arnaldo el Zurdo ceased.

"Men, hold down their legs. Hold them, hold them, hold them!" shouted de Queralt.

Josep heard frantic twisting and splashing and several stamps, he presumed, to the backs and legs of the prisoners to subdue them further.

"A moment longer to be sure!" Pere de Queralt said.

Josep heard the sound of a body being lifted out of the water, water streaming and dripping, consultations, then the sound, one then another, of a heavy body sploshing into the water. Josep was sick again. From that moment in his life, the thought of drowning unconsciously haunted him, causing him to feel nauseous, provoking a deep sense of unease and almost guilt in him.

†

The ordinary people considered the death of Ferran Sanchis to be so tragic that for months after his funeral, in La Puebla de Castro and Antillón and the other surrounding villages like Pomar de Cinca and Graus, as far as Monzón, they sang the song composed for Sanchis' death by the troubadour Cerverí de Girona.

Far from me be all joy and song

For he has parted from Aragón

A man whose charm was greater than

The strength that possesses the dragon.

So hear the cry, alas! So loud and strong

Heard from the River Cinca to Monzón

Behold the people bear his bones

Whose death a crime their plaint bemoans.

A tragic end

For all his charm

But envy the calm

Of the drowning man!

CHAPTER 7 THE COUNT AND THE KING

Once Josep was back at Cavallers, news came in a letter to Josep from his mother that Jacques de Molay had finally been sent to the Crusades.

"I want you to sit down and read this," said Fray Domènech, the principal of the academy. Josep had never been summoned to the principal's office so feared it had something to do with Sanchis' death, which had happened some weeks before. Josep reached out to take the letter.

"My dear Josep

By now you will have heard from the Principal the news that Jacques de Molay has been sent to the island of Cyprus to serve the Templars in the Crusades. I know that you will be saddened not to have been able to see him before he went as your life has been so turbulent and I am sure you would want to talk to him about everything that has happened. He has asked me to reassure you that he will be in contact with you as soon as he reaches his destination.

I am so sorry to send such unwelcome news to you by letter but know Fray Domènech will be kind in preparing you for it. I hope you can understand why I cannot travel in person to see you.

Your loving Mother."

The news was a blow to Josep. Jacques was effectively on the other side of the world now. Without Jacques, his mother would not travel to see him as she could not travel alone. He knew he could only rarely get back to Sant Pere de Ribes now as he could not travel alone himself. He felt abandoned, by his mother, by Jacques and by the principal who had handled him so coldly.

"My mother said you would prepare me for the bad news."

"The two letters, one for me, one for you, arrived at the same time. There seemed little point." The principal's tone was neutral. Josep therefore left the letter on the table and went out of the principal's office, gently closing the heavy oak door in silence, not wanting to disturb the principal any more, feeling again frozen out.

The shadow of Sanchis' death loomed over the situation, as if Josep were a monstrous child by association rather than an innocent dragged into the brutal world of kings and nobles. Luckily, he ran into Fray Francesc.

"What you witnessed at Pomar was not for someone of your years. But sometimes life marks us out for certain experiences and you have won the trust and thanks of Crown Prince Peter. However, you should be careful. You've made enemies."

Josep didn't know what to say. A numbness had descended upon him since that fateful afternoon. When Pere de Queralt had withdrawn Guillem from the college, taking away one of Josep's best friends, he had felt nothing. The only thing that made any impression on him was this news from Jacques and that had hurt him deeply.

"All the other boys want to talk to me about Sanchis and all I want to do is forget about it," he confided, hoping Fray Francesc could help him. "And they dislike me even more than before!" he added. "I don't feel like I have any friends, my mother is four days' ride away and my benefactor is the other side of the world."

"You and Muntaner are still friends, are you not?" Fray Francesc pointed out. Josep nodded. Yet his loneliness at that moment made everything seem pointless and left him feeling sluggish.

He kept having dreams that he was fighting for air underwater. The sound of blood pumping through his head changed to the high-pitched ringing in his ears of absolute emergency. He would wake up with a rasping gasp of air so loud and chilling it would wake several other boys in the dormitory, who would then complain that he had woken them up again.

"What would you do if you kept having nightmares, you idiots?" he shouted in fury and exasperation one night.

"Go to the nurse, maybe she'll tuck you in like your mother!" spat Bertrán de Solsona, which silenced Josep.

As Sanchis had suffered a traitor's death, all his property was forfeited to Prince Pere. Within a week, the town of La Puebla de Castro had been compelled to swear fidelity to him. The prince's lawyers, Giovanni da Procida and Vidal de Canyelles, stayed at the Academy while the papers were being drawn up.

There was an impatience about the whole affair that some accredited to the natural irascibility of lawyers while others read into it the prince's disinclination to spend more time than necessary in these parts of the realm. After all, the old king was ailing and many believed him to have but few months to live.

Giovanni da Procida read the following proclamation in all the town squares from Monday to Friday that week.

"All properties of Sanchis and his supporters, of Blanca de Antillón and of the Urrea family to whom she is related by marriage, are confiscated. Sanchis' close followers, as well as the Aragonese knight Jordan de Pena, Sanchis' half brother, are banished for life."

"Where do you think they have gone?" Josep asked Ramón while rubbing down Lord Pedro's horse when they returned to Cavallers that Friday evening.

"Rumour has it they have joined forces across the border with the Count of Foix, one of Prince Pere's great friends," Ramón replied laughing.

"Who is this Giovanni da Procida, anyway?" Josep asked absently, clearly exhausted after the exertions of a week on the road. He was spattered with mud and stank of sweat and horse droppings.

"I gather he's one of the most able lawyers of his generation," said Ramón in his easy, precocious, confident manner. Somehow, he still looked as fresh as he had on Monday.

"He's at least seventy but he is so belligerent that he'll exploit any weakness he can find for the king. Dalmau Rocabertí says if property is not specifically protected by the Fuero de Aragón, the statutes of the kingdom, it is appropriated for the king by him and his legal experts."

"Well, I suppose it might amount to a castle here and a village there," Josep said, paying more attention to his task than to what he was actually saying. He desperately wanted to change and get something to eat.

"I'm not so sure," replied Muntaner, rubbing down Rocabertí's horse. "You know about the county of Urgell, the ancient fief of Guifré el Pelós, don't you?" he asked.

"Yes, it's a disputed inheritance," Josep said the words with difficulty, "or something like that, I think."

"It's been disputed for at least a generation," Ramón said, looking at Josep to make sure he was listening. "But the thing is, the Crown Prince is renting it out to the present claimant Àlvar d'Urgell for a small fortune and wants his share in the final settlement."

"And Procida can get that for him?" Josep asked.

"Apparently, that's how good he is," Muntaner nodded. "And whose protégé is Àlvar d'Urgell?" he continued. Josep shook his head.

"You were born into these matters, Ramón. How should I know?"

"I'll tell you, Josep. He has always been protected by the Count of Foix. So by keeping the Viscount of Cardona his ally, Crown Prince Pere is hoping to soften up the count. And remember too, Foix's mother, Brunisende de Cardona, is Viscount Cardona's aunt."

Just at that moment, they were interrupted.

"Prince Pere's cruelty and high-handed dealings in the north of Aragón have lost him many noble friends, in Aragón, Catalunya and Valencia," Bertrán de Solsona said as he came into the stables with Mateu de Villalba.

"Ramón Folc of Cardona is so angry with the prince, not only because of the murder of Sanchis but also the way the prince has occupied various lands and estates. He has no respect for the barons of his realm and he must count on our enmity, my father says," he said.

Once they had finished with the horses, Josep and Ramón headed for the kitchens. Josep was laughing about Solsona's pomposity. "He's just repeating what he's heard. He thinks it makes him look like an expert in the matter and part of things."

"You're right, of course, my friend," Ramón agreed. However, Josep knew immediately he was going to be corrected again. "But what Solsona says shows that even the nobles who were previously well disposed to the royal family are turning against the prince. Dalmau Rocabertí says the Compte d' Empúries opposed the creation of the new town of Figueres, a new town created by the prince, I might add, and has recently attacked the lands of the Baron of Ceret, Guillem de Castellnou, while Guillem accompanied the king in France. The prince has never warmed to him."

"What friends do these traitors have?" Josep said outraged.

"Well be careful there, my dear friend!" Ramón again corrected him gently. "Dalmau de Rocabertí's father, Jofre, actually entertained Ramón Folc of Cardona last week. Why? Because of his influence with all the leading families in the north of Catalunya. He's known as the Prohom Vinculador."

"The Link Baron," Josep said to himself in English.

"He's the king's link to all the Barons of northern Catalunya, " Muntaner said. They're thinking if Ferran Sanchis is any indication, their rights to their property will be fought out either in the courts or, if there is the merest whiff of treason, on the battlefield. It could be a choice between bankruptcy or death."

Josep blinked tiredly. Ramón put an arm around his shoulder.

"It's a bit complicated, isn't it, Pep? And it may not come to that! Let's hope not, hey? Let's go and get something to eat and freshen up a bit. You could do with a bath!" He cuffed Josep around the head. Josep put his head down and roared and drove him backwards towards the kitchens.

No more than a month after the fratricide at Pomar, the prince returned to Valencia to aid his father once more against Muslim uprisings north of the Xuquer River. Many nobles from the north failed to heed the call of the king.

Josep's mother corresponded occasionally with scant news of Jacques: he was established in the city called Famagusta and was busy fortifying an island off the coast of Acre called Ruad that they had renamed Tortosa, like the Catalan city. He sent greetings, which only sharpened Josep's disappointment that he could see neither him nor his mother.

News also came at the end of the summer that old King Jaume had died.

"I must attend my father's funeral, Josep," Lord Pedro said. "While I am in Valencia with Crown Prince Pere, I shall visit my mother in her convent."

"I am your page, my lord and my place is at your side," Josep said. "Which convent is it? Does she have friends there?" he said imagining that she might have a similar relationship with the other women in the convent as his mother had with Clara and Habiba.

"I do not know jove. She founded the convent Monestir de la Saïdia, so she's not in a position to have friends. She is the authority in the convent. I do not know who she can confide in but many will not go near the convent, thinking that she has leprosy. This was the reason my father gave for abandoning her." He was talking not to Josep but to himself. Josep went and stood next to his knight, who put his hand on Josep's shoulder and patted it absent-mindedly.

Later, Josep heard Lord Pedro talking to Fray Francesc.

"I'd had no contact with the king for nearly ten years since he confirmed me as Lord of Ayerbe and my brother as Lord of Xèrica," Lord Pedro said. "Crown Prince Pere passed on his greetings but it was always perfunctory: "Our father sends his greetings and is pleased with you," was the typical message. I think Prince Pere was jealous that my mother had become the king's lover again after Queen Iolanda's death. At least my mother is still alive!"

"That's right, Lord Pedro and remember prince Pere has always treated you fairly and honestly and with affection as far as he is capable of that. He is such a highly-strung and secretive fellow, Constança alone knows the secrets and joys of his heart," said Fray Francesc.

They made their preparations and left quickly for it was Lord Pedro's intention to accompany his father's body from Valencia to the Monastery of Poblet where he would be buried, a journey that would take them six days on horseback. They passed through Vilafranca the second evening, so rode over to Sant Pere de Ribes, where they were received rapturously by the three women in Clara's house, who seemed well and in tune with running a small holding and living together. Josep of course was delighted to be able to see his mother after all he had gone through recently and his disappointment about Jacques. However, something inside him stopped him getting too close to her, as if separation would therefore be easier. There was a sad but resigned expression on Catarinas' face when they parted the next morning.

They passed on through the laden vineyards of the Penedès countryside and after two more days travelled through the orange groves of Castellón, the heady scent of oranges in their nostrils. It was the harvest and the entire coastal plain between Tortosa and Castellón was ablaze with orange against the green of the trees and the red of the earth. It took a further two days keen riding to get to Valencia, where they could finally rest properly in an inn on the square behind the Cathedral. The following morning, Lord Pedro visited his mother.

"She feels it's a release for her," he said later to Josep. "She's finally free of him. I hope that she can pray for his soul and die in peace," he said about his visit. "She is and has been in perfect health for her entire life," was his last comment.

After the formal state funeral in the Cathedral of Valencia, Lord Pedro and Josep joined the smaller funeral cortège and travelled slowly to the Royal Monastery of Poblet where the king was to be buried. They travelled together with the family of the newly appointed Commander of Loarre castle, Richard of Benavent, distantly related to the noble Aragonese family of Pinós, in command or twenty-five knights and a hundred men in the castle should they be needed either in Val d'Aran or on the Navarese border. He was with his beautiful wife Sancha and their twin daughters Alba and Bella, two years younger than Josep. It was a moment Josep was to remember for the rest of his life. Alba and Bella looked alike but Bella was more withdrawn and shy, while Alba was bright and constantly suppressing laughter. They soon realised they had Loarre in common and Josep's mind and heart raced in a way that left him almost breathless at the idea that they could see each other again.

The burial was solemn. Grief was etched into the faces of Crown Prince Pere and his brother Prince Jaume, the Princesses Elisabet and Iolanda, and all the members of the Royal family present. However, the setting for the ceremony was magnificent and Josep and Alba actually received permission the morning after to go for a ride around the vineyards of Vimbodí and Esplugues de Francolí with Lord Pedro as chaperone.

"I hope to see you at the coronation in Saragossa," said Josep.

"I will be there if I can!" Alba replied when they parted at Barbastro, where Ricard Benavent de Pinós and his entourage continued on to Loarre.

The coronation at the Cathedral of Saragossa was magnificent and the entire court was present, including the as-yet-uncrowned King of Majorca, Jaume, Pere's younger brother, who had yet to swear loyalty to his new monarch, King Pere II of Catalunya Aragón. Their mother, Queen Iolanda, had insisted before her death on the division of the kingdom between the two eldest sons and her lawyers were punctilious in the application of the letter of the law.

The creation of the new Kingdom of Majorca represented a potential threat to Catalunya Aragón. However, the new king's lawyers, Giovanni da Procida among them, insisted and specified that this was a relationship of vasellage. In other words, King Jaume de Majorca would have to do homage to the new King Pere for his kingdom, hence limiting his power.

Josep had never seen such magnificence. The fifty thousand ounces of gold that were Constança's dowry were put to use increasing the prestige of the royal house of the counts of Barcelona. Queen Constança's crown was modern, for the land of which she would be queen, and distinctly imperial with its ruby encrusted golden tresses that would frame her features. At the age of twenty-eight, she was considered at the height of her beauty, as wife to the new king and mother of two boys of twelve and ten, serene and mature beyond her years. She was of fair complexion but had long, dark hair, a long Italian nose and blue-green eyes that could turn from warm and teasing to cold and imperious in a flash, the inheritance of her red-haired German forefathers, the Hohenstaufen dynasty of Holy Roman Emperors.

Josep thought she was the most beautiful woman he had seen in his life.

†

After some weeks, romance was in the air. The Count of Foix had an important proposal to make. As his rights and privileges, together with those of many other nobles had not been confirmed since Prince Pere had become king, he decided to take matters into his own hands and embarked on a diplomatic initiative that took everyone by surprise. He was a skilled matchmaker, as demonstrated by his success in arranging the marriage of his sister Esclaramonda to the newly created King Jaume of Majorca. He himself had received the county of Bearn as his wife's dowry when he married Margaret of Bearn, from a branch of the Moncada family, which was well connected with the House of the Counts of Barcelona. He proposed the marriage of his daughter, also called Constança, to King Pere's second son, Jaume. It was a dynastic move that would extend his influence in Catalunya and was seen as a means of guaranteeing and furthering his power.

King Pere's inner thoughts were impossible to guess but he momentarily knitted his brow and narrowed his eyes when the Count of Foix made his proposal in the Royal Palace of Aljafería, in Saragossa. For a few telling moments, Josep could see the king hadn't been able to look the Count of Foix in the eye. However, implicitly trusting his wife, Josep saw him look at her. He read an imperceptible sign from her and his face relaxed and he became sociable and chearful. Later that day, as Josep ran a late-night errand for Lord Pedro, he heard the Queen speaking.

"Humour him my love, keep him happy and on your side. There's no point in alienating potential allies unnecessarily. You are king, you decide and nobody need know your mind if you do not wish it!"

When Josep reported to Lord Pedro what he had heard Constança confide to the king in their private chambers, he again explained the Queen's background to Josep, this time in more detail.

As the daughter of the heir to the Hohenstaufen Imperial dynasty, she was well used to the subtleties of court intrigue. She had grown up amid the deadly struggle between her family on one hand and the Capets, the French monarchy and the Papacy on the other. Subtlety and diplomacy were etched into every line of her lovely face.

Highly accomplished in the refined arts of her time, she was an excellent musician and often soothed her husband's spirit by playing to him on the lute. She spoke German, Napolitano, Sicilian, Catalan, Castillian, French and Arabic and was said to be knowledgeable about Aristotelian philosophy through the reading of Averroes.

Her hatred of Charles of Anjou, now King Charles of Sicily, derived from when he killed her father King Manfred of Sicily and Naples then left him unburied for the dogs to eat, captured her mother and starved her to death in prison, then beheaded her 16-year-old half brother, the heir to the throne, Conradín.

Instead of culture, he had French chauvinism, Lord Pedro said. Far from Frederic and Manfred's cultivation of art, culture and learning at the courts of Sicily and Naples, he was cold and austere and referred contemptuously to any belief not officially sanctioned by the Vatican as heresy. Queen Constança's hatred for Charles of Anjou was matched by King Pere's. If King Pere excused the present French monarchy anything it was because of his sister Isabel of Aragón, who had been Queen of France and mother of Philippe, the heir to the throne. She had been happily married but was dead two years. Josep never forgot the lesson Lord Pedro gave him that night. It explained so well the background to what was happening in the Western Mediterranean at the time and was a key for understanding what was to happen over the next decade, if not a whole generation.

King Pere's instructions to Lord Pedro de Ayerbe had not changed. He and therefore Josep, too, were to continue their observation of movements on the border with Val d'Aran. The Academy was to stay open but Josep was spending two days a week away, so he had desperate problems catching up with his studies when he returned. Fray Domènech was to remain principal of the academy and Fray Francesc was appointed Cura Pastoralis, the Head of Studies and Theology at the centre.

Later that year, 1277, King Pere won the most important victory of the whole Valencia uprising when he defeated rebels in the mountain fortress of Montesa, after which all resistance ceased. He was a proud and triumphant new king and he and his wife enjoyed enormous prestige and popularity. Their entourage numbered a hundred or more, including ladies-in-waiting for the Queen, mainly Catalan, while the king's courtiers were mainly Aragonese, among them lawyers, councillors, couriers, tailors and cooks, as well as translators, who were normally Muslims from Granada. The king always travelled with a small squadron of five knights and twenty almogavers, his trusted household guard. They visited the king's dominions bringing glamour and spectacle and therefore much trade to every county town they passed through, which of course made them immensely popular with the common folk.

Lord Pedro also kept Josep up-to-date on the various developments and intrigues taking place in Barcelona, which he got to hear about through the Procuradors and Veguers, with whom he was friendly. One of the more exotic and curious episodes involved the Count of Foix and was especially interesting as it went right to the heart of the problems which any new king would have with enforcing his will within his realm. Yet it also had a lot to do with King Pere inheriting the problems of his father. Where previously discontentment had crystalised around Ferran Sanchis, similar discontentment galvanised around Roger Bernat IV, the Count of Foix though this time involving Catalan nobles.

At this moment, the count decided to try his marriage proposal once again. The privileges of the counts and nobles of Catalunya had still not been confirmed because the new king needed to levy further taxes out of his realms for his missions abroad. He therefore needed to leave his nobles as legally exposed as possible in order to make this easier. Nobody knew what his plans might be. Lord Pedro said to Josep, they might be the consolidation of his North African initiative and trade with the present and well-disposed King of Tunis. The nobles, however, felt if they were to contribute to the king's projects, they should be privy to his plans. King Pere deliberately did not hold court in Barcelona, therefore, to avoid having to confirm the privileges of the nobles, unquestionable though some of those privileges were. What irked the king was the unfair privileges some of the nobles had had written, in the times of his father when a boy, into the usatges and furs, the agreements about money and manpower by which the monarch and the nobility were bound. Moreover, the new king preferred to demand what he needed anyway and fight for it, if necessary, not in court but in the field. His demands were made through his chief financial functionary Ferris de Liçana, Procurador of Catalunya, who appointed and controlled the Veguers, who in turn levied taxes and troops from each town. The Veguers were therefore always well supplied with their own troops, often almogavers, to enforce the king's wishes. It was a case of might was right.

The king wanted the Count of Foix as his ally but was determined to keep him on the back foot. For example, it was rumoured that the young king was behind new litigation actually against the Count of Foix himself, in which the count was accused of having attacked and damaged property belonging to the Bishop of Urgell. The accusation was preposterous. For the past one hundred years, the Bishops of Urgell had relentlessly pursued and exterminated Cathar heretics. Some had even been members of the Foix family. It had been the Bishop of Urgell who had insisted that the Count of Foix disinter his family's remains, including those of his father and mother, who had been executed as heretics, because they were buried in hallowed ground. The new king's spurious and especially insulting case therefore showed the extent of the aggression and single-mindedness of the new king and was intended to cow all nobles, whether Catalan or Aragonese, into submission. Hence the Count of Foix's offer of marriage and reconciliation.

Guillem de Molina, King Pere's closest friend, was with the king in Barcelona when the count made his proposal in private. Guillem himself repeated the scene to Lord Pedro de Ayerbe.

"I remember thinking, "He's as sly as a fox," Molina said, "What a pity he isn't as sleek as a fox!"

"God bless His Majesty and peace be upon his father." Molina imitated the count well. "I trust the king is rested from his extensive travels through his realms and has recovered from the leg wound he sustained in Montesa."

He told Lord Pedro de Ayerbe and Josep how he and the king had laughed later about the Count of Foix's corpulence. He added that the king himself had laughed when he heard the count wheezing on his knees while kissing the king's hand. His expression had quickly hardened into one of contempt when he saw how much weight the count had gained since they had last seen each other.

"I am well, thank you for the enquiry, and the wound is completely recovered," the king replied. Guillem de Molina said the king then shot him a glance.

"Where did he get that information from?"

Guillem de Molina's eyes swept the room.

"The count has spies everywhere!"

"I trust the count's lands are sufficient to satisfy his appetites." He then raised the count to his feet and looked him square in the face.

"Or is it to increase your standing that you approach me, my dear Count?" the conversation continued.

"Your Majesty is most observant and is, I hope, pleased at the use that we make of our lands to secure the king's frontiers. There is more wild boar in my lands than I can find use for and as I police my borders, often in remote snowy reaches, there is good sport to be had in the hunting of the boar and plenty of meat to keep my squadrons contented," the count replied.

"I am pleased to see that you are not suffering too much hardship on your king's behalf, my lord," the king quipped.

"Nothing gives me more pleasure than to serve your Majesty and it is with this thought in mind that I would remind his Majesty of the advantages that I can offer him in securing his borders more permanently, were he disposed to condescend to contemplate a union between our two families."

Guillem de Molina said King Pere had winced at the excessive obsequiousness of the request, quick as he was to sense mockery in overwrought phraseology. He was an astute commander and his sense of personal safety was highly developed: he was able to divine loyalty and disloyalty among his men, so essential for an effective leader and subscribed to the saying: Keep your friends close and your enemies closer. There was nothing worse than a close ally who then turned against you; a trusted family member who betrayed you; an enemy in the camp. He was utterly ruthless in these cases, as his summary execution of Ferran Sanchis had shown.

"I am delighted to receive your request once again, my dear Count and am willing to accept the terms established by our respective advocates. I believe there are certain fiefs in and around Barcelona that may well be of interest to you," the king said gracefully.

"Your Majesty is most gracious and I shall await news from his advocates as to when negotiations can begin," the count replied.

"Whose marriage does the Count of Foix want to arrange?" asked Josep a little mystified when he heard all this.

"The count wants King Pere's second son Jaume to marry his daughter, Constança" replied Lord Pedro patiently.

"Have you ever met the count's daughter Constança?" Josep asked

"I haven't and I don't think many people have. It's not right to make a young girl like that go through such an ordeal!" said Lord Pedro.

"What do you mean? Where is she?"

"She's been living away from her family and friends in a castle called Castellbó near La Seu d'Urgell for two years waiting for her father to organise her wedding, with only a couple of ladies-in-waiting for company, apart from the guards. She's a captive in her own castle, a rich commodity to be bartered for."

"Castellbó," said Josep thoughtfully. "I think we passed it on our way to La Seu d'Urgell but it's a long way from Foix, the other side of the Pyrenees for a start.

Josep then asked after a pause, barely audibly: "How old is she?"

"She's ten" came the reply.

"Poor thing!" said Josep.

"What kind of father would hatch such a plan?" asked Lord Pedro, almost to himself.

"...and what kind of mother?" added Josep.

Lord Pedro shot him a look of surprise, tinged with pity. He was blushing and his eyes had widened but were down-turned.

"You're old beyond your years, Josep. Maybe I shouldn't talk about such adult issues with you."

"I am fifteen, my lord," said Josep.

"Yes, you are old enough, it is true." Lord Pedro said, putting an avuncular hand on his shoulder. It was a small gesture but Josep in years to come remembered this detail. Lord Pedro had been with him during his childhood and as he grew into a man, he was still with him.

CHAPTER 8 TO FOIX

Lord Pedro was dispatched to Foix within a week bearing a message from the king, who had left Barcelona and resumed his endless travels this time to Lleida and Agramunt. It was early December and the usual path up to the pass at la Porta Picada was snowed under. For once Lord Pedro and his young page went over to Tremp and then to La Seu d'Urgell following the Segre River as it cut its valleys into the timeless landscape of the Catalan Pyrenees. As they passed Castellbó, Josep remembered the Count of Foix's proposal and thought of the lonely girl captive in her father's castle. But what could they do? Josep promised himself if there was anything he could do to pay back the Count of Foix he would do it, so deeply did he despise him already.

They crossed the winding but well travelled passes of Andorra's snowy summits and blue sky accompanied them across the French border and all the way to Foix. As they were on public business, not reconnaissance, they travelled comfortably in their regular clothes, which kept them warmer than they would have otherwise been for despite the sun there was a fierce wind and it was bitterly cold.

Though dominated by its castle upon a bluff of rock at the top of the town, Foix felt like a Catalan town. Here, of course, they spoke Occitan and French not Catalan and Aragonese but if you ignored the position of the sun, you could believe you were looking north to the Pyrenees from La Seu d'Urgell when you gazed south at the mountains from Foix.

Once they had climbed the steep cobbled road up to the castle with its high tower and had been ushered in, they heard the soft wheezy voice of the count.

"Well, well, well," he began. "Who do we have here if not one of the king's other brothers bearing his young page with him. How sweet!" he simpered to Eustache de Beaumarchais, the Governor of Navarra, who was on business in Foix at the time. Josep noticed Beaumarchais stiffen. He coughed and looked away. Josep wondered if he found this kind of behaviour to be inappropriate. Yet Josep was soon to learn the count was also accompanied by a certain Guillaume de Nogaret, one of the most able advisers to the French Crown Prince Philippe.

Tough old French soldiers like Eustace de Beaumarchais may have been embarrassed but Guillaume de Nogaret seemed much more amused by the count's affectations. The two whispered and laughed about the weary messengers as they divested themselves of their onerous clothing and prepared to be formally announced.

The knight and his page handed over their message, which was taken by the count and opened ostentatiously so that Guillaume de Nogaret could also see its contents.

The Count of Foix desired keenly that the future King Philippe of France should know what dynastic links were being forged in his court between the House of Foix and the crown of Catalunya Aragón.

"Tell your Master that I shall send my lawyers to Castellbó within the week if the king's lawyers wish to meet them there. They will be well looked after," said the count.

This was their mission accomplished but they were hospitably entertained that evening. During dinner, Josep had the uncomfortable feeling he was being minutely examined by Guillaume de Nogaret. After dinner, Guillaume approached Lord Pedro and started a conversation with him in Latin.

"So you are here on a little business, are you? And where do you head back to?"

"We head back to La Puebla de Castro tomorrow, your excellency," Lord Pedro managed to reply in his broken Latin.

"Your young page. Where does he come from? He is fair. I detect perhaps northern blood, am I not right? Nonne septemtrionalis est, ipse?" he drawled, "Is he not northern?"

"Indeed, your excellency, his mother is English, connected to the Grailly family of Bordeaux and his patron is Jacques de Molay," replied Lord Pedro. Two surprises in a single sentence were too much for Guillaume de Nogaret and he choked a little on his wine.

"Am I to take it that you have no father boy?" he said to Josep in French, luckily, Josep thought as he read but did not speak Latin.

"Yes, sir, your Excellency," and Josep stammered back in French.

"And your patron is a rising star in the order of the Templars, based at present in Famagusta, if I'm not mistaken, is that not so?" he asked.

"That is so, your excellency," Lord Pedro replied for Josep.

"Good, good. I have always been such an admirer of the Knights Templar, so rugged, so brave, so... powerful!" said Nogaret.

"I should greatly like to meet him. I hear he is due back in France soon."

It was incredible. Nogaret had known them no more than a few hours and yet knew intimate details about them and more about the movements of people like Jacques de Molay than Lord Pedro and Josep knew themselves. There was something unsettling about his manner, his face, so mobile, his eyes constantly widening and narrowing, green and brown, concentric rings in the pupils that seemed to draw you in and drink the truth out of you. His way of speaking was silky, constantly almost catching up with itself as if his mouth were asking questions which when answered his mind immediately formed into chunks that he hungrily devoured. His neck was in a perpetual peristaltic surge formulating questions, weaving his small head this way and that, his eyes fixed on his interlocutor, made to feel like something for the eating, or at least, sniffing. He seemed to be permanently surrounded by hooded youngsters, who gave Josep the impression they were looking at himself and Lord Pedro but then looking away before they were noticed. It was an unsettling feeling and it made Josep feel on-edge and defensive.

Yet once free from Nogaret and the posturing count, they returned safely to La Puebla de Castro, welcoming the icey blasts that seemed to scour their cloying hosts from them.

Things at Cavallers were no better, however. Bertrán de Solsona seemed to have decided to make Josep's life as uncomfortable as possible. Josep had received a letter from Alba saying that they were snowed in and didn't expect to be able to go anywhere for the duration of the winter. Bertrán de Solsona kept having visits from young men in hoods, similar to the ones Josep had seen in Foix but they would stay the evening then be gone the next day. He and his sidekick Mateu de Villalba were always whispering in the corner, turning away and laughing every time they saw Josep.

He accompanied Ramón Muntaner but he had his own commitments with his knight, Dalmau de Rocabertí. Between his own missions with Lord Pedro and his schoolwork, he didn't have much time for himself but when he did, he generally found himself wandering aimlessly around the corridors of Cavallers or in the courtyard or helping in the stables with the horses but he could not keep his mind off Alba Benavent de Pinós and wondered if she ever thought of him. It was three months since they had last seen each other and though messages came, they were few and brief.

Josep at fifteen years of age was meanwhile undergoing adolescence. His voice was cracking, he was covered in spots around his chin and jaw line and he was growing taller at an alarming rate. Hair was sprouting on his face, arms and legs and his frame was filling out with taut muscles in response to the constant demands he made of his body in weapons training and horsemanship. Yet he couldn't keep his mind off Alba. He was so tightly wound up that the smallest incident could set him off.

Bertrán de Solsona would never forget the day he meddled with him and consciously or not touched that raw nerve.

"I have heard," he started in his pompous drawl, "that there is a young lady who holds your affection." He sniggered to Mateu de Villalba.

"You should learn to keep your nose out of business that doesn't concern you," Josep snapped back, regretting his words and turning his back on him.

"You mean to say that this note I'm reading is for you?" asked Bertrán de Solsona, eyeing Josep as he held the paper note between thumb and forefinger of his right hand. Josep whirled round to face him, breaking into a cold sweat. His ears ringing as if he had been beaten over the back of the head, he snatched at the piece of paper Bertrán de Solsona was holding with such speed and force that he sent Bertrán de Solsona flying backwards. He stopped himself from falling back and, regaining his balance, sped away from him out into the courtyard. The enclosure was a quagmire of mud and horse manure and every lunge that Josep made for Bertrán nearly had him sprawled on the floor. Bertrán was wiry and fast and as the provoker of the incident, prepared for the chase. Yet Josep was a frightening prospect. His head down, his eyes burned from under his brow. There was nowhere else to run except out of the gate down the muddy, sloping cornfield that led to the woods separating the college from the river. Josep dived for Bertrán's legs and managed to catch a foot but miraculously Bertrán remained upright. Josep dragged himself out of the mud freezing on his face. The intense cold warmed, then his whole face became a mass of pins and needles, as the cold reacted with the heat of his exertion, desperation and embarrassment. That note was one of the only things he had from Alba. How did Bertrán de Solsona know? Where had he found it? Had he or one of his shifty friends intercepted another note from a messenger from Loarre? He had to get it, silence Bertrán de Solsona and keep the secret.

Bertrán de Solsona had expected to get a rise out of Josep but not this cold fury and for the first time he looked nervous. He had been dismissive of Josep's missions with Lord Pedro de Ayerbe as Josep never talked much about them, which left Bertrán de Solsona jealous and frustrated. Yet it was clear to everyone Josep had obviously put his body through duress and was therefore fit for he was fast and tireless in his pursuit. Bertrán de Solsona tossed the paper as high into the air as he could so the wind blew it and fled into the woods, not daring to check behind him till he was well and truly hidden in the fallen branches and undergrowth. He paused, panting and sweating, gasping for air. Josep chased after the note full speed and caught it in a headlong dive that catapulted him several metres along a muddy furrow. Despite the wet, he lay on his back, looked up, his mouth tasting of blood and metal, and feverishly opened up the piece of paper. He couldn't believe his eyes. It was blank. Blank one side, blank the other. He examined it closely for faded lettering but clearly there was nothing on it, nor had there ever been. He groaned, let his head fall back and closed his eyes as he fought for breath and an explanation. He felt relieved at first, mighty relieved. His secret was still safe. Obviously a rumour had started that there was a girl but from where the rumour had come in the first place was a mystery. Neither Ramón nor Lord Pedro would say a word, of course, so it was simply a rumour.

"Oh my God! I've confirmed the rumour! What a fool!" he thought: first verbally, by telling Bertrán de Solsona to keep his nose out, then visibly by chasing him. And for what? A note that didn't even exist.

Then another feeling hit him. He was wet, cold and… there was a hollow feeling in the pit of his stomach. There was no message. No word from Alba, he could have wept with disappointment. Then the fury kicked in. He would tear Bertrán de Solsona to pieces when he could get his hands on him.

He didn't have to wait long. That evening, when all the boys met for supper, Josep sent younger boys and stools flying as he made a beeline for Bertrán de Solsona, he couldn't believe it was so easy. He was standing there asking for it. Josep drew back his right arm and delivered a blow to Bertrán's left cheek that sent the boy flying onto the table, bringing the wood-paneled dining room to a halt and silence in seconds. Josep didn't know what happened next because he woke up the following morning in the infirmary.

"How are you feeling Josep?" Lord Pedro was asking him. Josep managed to open his eyes and a shooting pain like a dagger between his eyeballs made him gasp with agony.

"Don't open your eyes, Josep, you took a blow to the back of the head and a real beating before they could drag you off Bertrán de Solsona."

"Oh my head. It feels like it's going to split open!" groaned Josep screwing his eyes up against the pain.

"You landed the most almighty blow on Bertrán's jaw", said another voice. "You smashed it… and two teeth!" It was Ramón Muntaner, Josep immediately recognised the voice of his good friend at the academy.

"Don't talk too loud," he said. "He's in the bed on the other side of the room," he added, whispering in Josep's ear.

Josep lurched onto his side as if he was going to jump out of bed, to be laid low by another shooting pain in his left-hand side from the shoulder to the ribs.

"Don't move, jove!" said Lord Pedro. "You're in a bit of a bad way. Worse, I'd say, than Bertrán de Solsona."

"Not once I've finished with him," was all Josep could say and then fell back onto the bed with a cry, his head crashing against the wall. He cried out in pain.

"Well, you'll have to get past Fray Francesc!" Ramón said. "He's attending to him having seen to you first," he whispered.

Josep laughed but this brought on a convulsion of coughing. He struggled for some moments to control his coughing.

"There's more bad blood between you and Bertrán de Solsona than I knew." Lord Pedro said.

"You try living with his constant snide remarks," said Josep "You should hear what he says about you and your mother…" Another spasm of coughing cut Josep off.

"Well, he's not without his supporters, Josep," replied Lord Pedro levelly refusing to rise to the bait. "By the way, would you like to know how many kids jumped on you? All the two lower years, so about twelve kids in all. Apart from the stool that was smashed on the back of your head, you are being held responsible for the damage, totalling about two months' wages for a working man. The dining room was half destroyed and most of it on your shoulders, back and legs.

"It feels like it!" Josep groaned. "It was a personal argument, I didn't attack him with my henchmen!"

"But Bertrán de Solsona was waiting for you with his," Josep heard Lord Pedro sigh and Ramón cough to suppress a laugh.

"He took a real battering, if I may give my opinion," said Lord Pedro. Then Josep fell asleep again.

Lord Pedro had business to attend to in west Aragón and it took about a week for Josep to recover. It was by that time mid-December. Bertrán de Solsona was still in the infirmary but Josep could feel the atmosphere of antipathy towards him as keenly as the freezing blasts of the wintry winds blowing off the peaks. Ramón would always be his good friend and of course there were Lord Pedro and Fray Francesc that he could count on but the principal, Fray Domènech, was his usual terse, cold self with Josep.

Josep pondered why this had always been so. Perhaps he thought him too low-born to be at the academy. This thought depressed him. Maybe he was an upstart who had no right to be there. His patron was foreign. He did not have a father, his mother was foreign as well and stuck four days' ride away. He felt rootless, restless and irritable. On an impulse, he saddled his horse one morning in December, with minimal food and set out towards the Val d'Aran. He didn't know exactly where he was going or why, he headed where he and Lord Pedro usually went.

He made good progress and was at the foot of the pass at Porta Picada by nightfall. He camped in the barraca he had stayed in with Lord Pedro the first time they had ascended to the pass. It seemed like a long time ago yet it was little more than two years before. He felt he had left childhood behind and was somewhere between boy and young man and this gave him courage to look after himself.

He rose early the next morning and headed up the winding path to the pass and made it into the upper hills of the Val d'Aran by nightfall. There, he stopped at another refugi and as the light was fading, ate the last of his provisions and gave a nose bag to the horse. If he didn't find more food, he would have to start eating the horse's oats as well, he thought to himself. He lay down to sleep and when he awoke the following morning, came out of the shelter to find that there had been snow during the night. His horse was well provisioned and contented but he had no food. He had not counted on having to hunt in the snow and though he laid traps, six hours later they had brought him nothing. He was cold and hungry but determined not to return until he absolutely had to.

The following day, when he finally found a small rabbit in one of the traps, he killed it, cooked it and ate it ravenously but by the next morning he was dizzy with hunger again and his nerves were a-jangle. Several times he thought he heard the soft pad of footsteps in the snow around him or in the undergrowth as he scoured the forest floor for anything to eat. It was bitterly cold. The wind was blowing in from the north, freezing the snow and making all the paths icy. Worse still, it was impossible to see the ice on the paths and he slipped several times, once narrowly missing a steep edge that plunged down into a crevice, the bottom of which he couldn't see. Luckily, he was holding on to the horse's reigns, otherwise he dreaded to think what might have happened. It was when he had decided to turn back that disaster struck his horse itself, which had not only saved him but also provided him with warmth and on whose back he could make better progress if he decided to turn back. It showed him that the horse was as accident-prone on the ice as any other creature. The poor animal slipped and hobbled itself. It was not a bad injury but it did make the horse unridable. So Josep abandoned his plans and headed back to the less exposed paths in the forest. It was dark by then and he was light-headed with tiredness, hunger and worse, he was dispirited. He turned left onto what he thought was a path leading to the shelter but after two hours, to his horror, found himself in an area of forest he did not recognise at all. He had learned enough to know that in these cases it was best to stop, conserve warmth and wait till first light. He pulled the horse down onto the undergrowth, gave it a nose bag, ate a handful of the oats and quickly lost his appetite, then pulled his cloak over him and positioned himself as well as he could up against the horse's warm belly and went straight to sleep.

The following morning when he opened his eyes, he couldn't believe what he could see ahead of him. It was a clearing in the forest overhung by the crowns of trees so that light entered dimly. There were fires going but there seemed to be no smoke around the enclosure. He was sure he would have seen smoke if he had been anywhere near this settlement before so he couldn't understand it.

As he struggled to his feet and rubbed his eyes, who should approach him but the wild man of the woods they had met the year before. He was friendly and offered Josep food and tended to his horse. Josep couldn't believe his luck. He was taken to the centre of the clearing and introduced to the wood dwellers. They lived in low wooden huts with thatched roofs. Fires were lit in the centre of the hut and the smoke filled the huts but this seemed to dissipate and left little trace outside and the overarching tree crowns seemed to diffuse the rest

All the men looked the same. They all wore the same rough green heavy cotton clothes, had long beards and hair and spoke the curious Occitan which Josep could partially understand. Josep thought they must be Jews because of their appearance but the leader of the village, when told this, looked offended but didn't explain who they were immediately. The leader was much more interested in Josep and how he had found them.

"I was lost and wandering around for several hours and I didn't see or hear you, though I was a hundred yards away. Don't you make any noise at night?" Josep asked.

A flicker of amusement crossed the heavy-browed features of his interrogator but he responded with another question.

"Why should we release you?" Josep's mouth went dry, his heart started pounding and he jumped to his feet, ready to fight.

"You are by your own admission lost, young man," continued the leader. "Without our aid, you would have died. It would be as irresponsible for us to let you go unguided as it would be imprudent for us to allow you to go and reveal our whereabouts," he said in Occitan.

"I swear I won't tell anyone about you, just let me go! Point me in the right direction and I swear your secret will be safe with me!" Josep replied in Catalan.

"You take oaths easily, jove. Does that mean you take them lightly or is your word your bond? How can we know that you can be trusted?" the old man continued.

"Sir, I give you my word of honour that I can be trusted."

"How can you be of service to us?" was the old man's next question?

"Ask, sir, and I will endeavour to fulfil your request."

At this, the old man, who had been looking intently deep into Josep's eyes the entire interview seemed satisfied and Josep was released into the custody of Amaury, the woodman.

"What are they going to do with me?" asked Josep.

"I can respond not to the questions. First, I receive the consent of the Perfect, then I shall respond," Amaury said in his French-accented Occitan.

"I might as well have a look around in that case." Josep thought. Amaury accompanied him but it seemed that he was allowed a free run of the place.

Josep found it amazing. Every effort had been made to maintain as much of the natural look of the woods as possible. Some of the huts were built around trees, the lower branches of which served as the basis of the thatched roof that had then been woven into them. The resulting abode looked like something a giant insect or bird might have made. Though it was smoky inside, this was only the case if you stood upright. If you crouched down, it was possible to breathe more easily.

"I suppose you use these huts mainly for sleeping, don't you?" Josep said to Amaury and Amaury repeated what he'd said before.

"Yes, yes that's right, sorry. I should have remembered that is a secret, too," Josep quipped. Amaury said nothing and looked blankly back at him.

The meeting house was the largest of the huts and was constructed within a square formed by four great beech trees. It was dark inside and when Josep was told to go in, he had to blink to see the old man, whom they seemed to call the Perfect.

"Sit down," the old man said.

"I am the Perfect of this community," the old man said, speaking rusty Catalan, his back to Josep and looking into the fire. "It is, as far as I know, the only Cathar community in the mountains. We have lived like this for more than thirty years. Amaury is my protégé, he will be the Perfect when I surpass this life."

"You mean when you die, Prefect" said Josep struggling to hear the old man as he had his back to him and had a strong Occitan accent.

"Perfect, my boy, the Cathar title is the Perfect. Not Prefect, I am not a Roman official. We oppose everything Roman. In our faith, when we die we unite with the Father. Our spirits unite. That is our deepest wish. We fear not death but await the moment our Father calls us. This world is evil. We are persecuted. We will be tortured and killed if they catch us. Christians hate us because their leaders tell them that we are evil. Their leaders want our possessions. They want our land and they persecute us because they can. They have the power and they want more, so they took our lands in the past. They killed us to take our lands. It is not more complicated than this. Maybe the Pope in Rome wishes to convert us to their Catholic faith but his agents are hungry for land, possessions and power. You see how we live. We are simple people. We eat not flesh. Amaury, the day he met you for the first time, he saw you but then he saw a rabbit in a trap. It is necessary that we free the rabbit if we see this. You captured him when he tried to free the rabbit, then you tried to give him the rabbit's flesh to eat but he cannot eat flesh. It is not permitted. We live to contemplate God and we can eat only vegetables. Our bread is made from wild grass, it grows behind this hall and everywhere, and we drink only water. We have one or two metal tools to help to work the land. We desire our freedom to exist. We feed the body for this and we exist to contemplate God and await our union with him."

Josep was stunned and deeply impressed by the clarity and simplicity of the old man's expression and his explanation of life and remembered dimly what Fray Arnaldo had told them in class about the Cathars: that they were heretics and devil worshippers. That they stole and ate babies and the pyre was too good for them. Burning a heretic saved his or her soul by purifying it through the flames of hell on earth. The heretic purified could enter heaven. Fray Arnaldo was for executing the Cathars in other equally atrocious ways but sending them to eternal hell as well. He had delighted in horrifying the boys with stories of the crusade against the Albigensians the people of Albi, many of whom were Cathars.

"The lucky ones were burned," he always ended with a cold smile.

"We will unite with our Father, all of us, soon." The old man had started speaking again. "But we want to live in our way with our traditions, with our beliefs. We do not seek pain but we will die in pain for our beliefs but we do not want that anyone finds us. We are human, we have fear. We love our family," he said.

"Perfect, how can I help you"? asked Josep. These people seemed good, simple, generous people, who had helped him and he wanted to help them in return. He clearly understood how secret their community had to remain.

"We left our loved ones and family. We ask ourselves still if they are alive and if not, how they died. Can you take a message to our town?"

"Of course!" said Josep, without even thinking about it.

"It is a town near Carcassonne, east of Foix," said the Perfect. "It is a long journey. The name of the village is Rennes. Please take this note to the Blancfort family. They are the lords of this town. The note is for Madeleine Fabre, whose family has worked for them for several generations."

"I will endeavour to my utmost to do this," said Josep in reply, almost embarrassing himself in his earnestness, "but I must return to my academy first."

It was true, depressing but true. Josep had been gone for five days and he thought they must be despairing of him.

"Most likely, they have sent my knight up here to try to find me and he may have returned to the academy empty-handed," said Josep.

"Please take great care not to reveal our camp. We have lived here for many years and our journey to escape was dangerous, travelling always at night, old people, young people and children, too. We do not want anything more from our life but we do not want to have to move once more. A year is necessary to have a crop after planting. This would be a hungry year of waiting.

Amaury acted as Josep's guide. His horse, its near left shank tightly bound in the same coarse green cloth as the Cathars all wore could be ridden again. Josep was immediately glad of the guide as the forest on the mountain ridge was dense and there were no paths, only undergrowth. They rode in silence at first but after half an hour or so Josep had to speak.

"How do you know the way Amaury?" Josep wondered if this time Amaury would reply. It would be the first time.

"This tree is called Caterpillar Tree because it is the favourite home of those creatures. Many trees here have names, Josep, this is our home. I was your age when I left Rennes thirty years ago and we have been in this camp for twenty-five years, so we know all the landmarks like you know your friends."

"I don't seem to have many of them," Josep thought to himself. He didn't know what to expect when he got back to Cavallers.

It was clear that someone had been up the pass in the last few days because there were fresh horse droppings on the path. Josep and Amaury compared them with older droppings which they assumed were from Josep's horse and concluded they were no more than two days old. Amaury left Josep at the entrance to the pass.

"How will I find you again, Amaury?" asked Josep.

"You can go to your usual refugi and I will find you," Amaury replied. "Pax tecum, Amaury," Josep said in Latin.

"Pax tecumque, Josep," Amaury replied and they parted.

"I fought over a note that didn't exist and confirmed the rumour by defending a secret. I now have a real note and a secret and a community stands or falls on my never revealing either. How am I going to conceal this from Lord Pedro? The best way of keeping a secret is by telling nobody but will he allow me to say that I can't tell him where I have been and that I am sworn to secrecy? I'll say nothing, no matter what!" Josep thought to himself as he travelled back to Cavallers. The chill in the air was conducive to clear thinking.

However, the indifference and repressed hostility he experienced when he returned marked Josep for the rest of his life. He remembered to his dying day the coldness of the principal who seemed to regret his safe return and complained about the worry and disruption he had caused.

"You understand I am too busy a man to play mother to the boys," he said.

It stung Josep. He might as well have slapped him across the face. It woke him up to what people felt, would always feel about him, recognising neither his personal qualities, of which he was becoming aware, nor his development from boy to man. He looked down and away and held his tongue.

Ramón Muntaner had left the morning he himself had gone so knew nothing of the affair. Fray Francesc had accompanied Lord Pedro to the foot of the Porta Picada looking for Josep and seemed reproachful of Josep.

"You've given your enemies a weapon to use against you, Josep," he said. "People were sympathetic with you following the incident with Bertrán de Solsona but your recent absence and the extra work it has caused the academy have been interpreted as great selfishness on your part. Needless to say, Lord Pedro is worried about you. The principal Fray Domènech has also been in contact with Berenguer de Belvís, Knight Commander of Monzón, who has been providing for your upkeep on behalf of Jacques de Molay while he is in the Holy Land. I think you need to pay him a visit."

Yet, there was a twinkle in Fray Francesc's eye that Josep didn't fail to notice and Josep smiled.

"I am sorry if I have inconvenienced you, Fray Francesc. I shall visit Berenguer de Belvís as soon as I can. Thank you for being so understanding, Master. I am grateful and relieved. This is what I need! It will put my mind at ease."

"Better for all our sakes!" replied Fray Francesc.

Josep left word for Lord Pedro that he was heading for Monzón and would be back in a week. He calculated that if he travelled hard he could make it to Monzón, over to La Seu d'Urgell, across to Foix and on to Rennes in three days' riding and so long as he was back within that time, nobody should worry about him. He figured that if he kept a low profile, nobody would even notice him.

A nostalgic pang made him turn back one last time. Had he not done so, he would not have seen the small group of three huddled together. He could have sworn it was Fray Domènech and Bertrán de Solsona but he couldn't recognise the third person, a hooded character, who stood apart from the other two, motionless, faceless, nameless to Josep. He turned to the road ahead of him and banished any feelings of fondness for the place. Had Josep looked back once again, he would have seen the hooded figure mount his horse and set out in the same direction as Josep.

Josep did not know how to interpret Berenguer de Belvís when he arrived in Monzón.

"You are wayward, young man," said Belvís de Berenguer, "and would do well to consider the effects of your actions."

"I have come to apologise, my lord," Josep said to Belvís de Berenguer.

"I don't want apologies or excuses!" replied the wolf-like warrior monk. "What I want is your commitment to behave within reasonable limits. In other words, grow up! I have had no option but to communicate with your patron Jacques de Molay about recent events and await his instructions. How old are you?

"Fifteen, my lord, I'll turn sixteen in March."

"Good, good! You're old enough to look after yourself, then. I hear from Fray Francesc that you are a linguist, good at your classes and an excellent horseman but that you are also willful and headstrong." There was a slight inflection to this resumé that invited comment.

"My Lord, perhaps the constrictions placed upon me are too tight," Josep said.

"Are you a boy or a man? Jaques de Molay and your mother decided to send you to Cavallers because you were too much for your mother to handle. Here you are three years later repeating the same mistake!"

"I do feel I can look after myself these days, my lord, and I do not feel at home there any longer."

Belvís turned from the window he had been pretending to look out of and looked Josep straight in the eye.

"I am aware of the invaluable intelligence collected by Lord Pedro de Ayerbe from Val d'Aran. I take it from your recent escapade you have assisted him in these matters?" Lord Belvís raised an eyebrow in question.

"Yes, my Lord!" Josep was actually taken aback that Lord Belvís should know about this and make the connection.

"We are the first line of defence in this land, no matter where the attack may come along the border, in answer to your unspoken question. I also know of your involvement in the execution of Ferrán Sanchis, so be careful. I will tell you something that may make the hair on the back of your neck stand on end. You have already made some serious enemies."

"I have?" Josep said.

"I understand that Lord Pedro de Ayerbe was recently introduced to Guillaume de Nogaret in Foix. You might like to know that following your meeting there, Count Roger Bernat of Foix asked a few questions and found that you were the one who informed the king about where Ferrán Sanchis was. This information, as you know, led to his death."

"How does anyone know that?"

"The count of Foix and Sanchis were close allies. Foix hates the new king because of his fratricide, as he puts it, and therefore by association, you, young man."

"But I was following instructions."

"It matters not, young man. You may also wish to defend yourself by saying that it was two years ago now and you were barely more than a child but hatred is no respecter of age and revenge matures with time. Keep a low profile, Josep, because Guillaume de Nogaret will take any opportunity to promote himself and that could be by eliminating you. Once his eye has rested upon you, you are easy pickings for such a man."

Josep remembered the impression of being interrogated by him and started to sweat.

"You may think that this is your own concern but bear in mind you could be used against Jacques de Molay, an important member of our community. One further consideration, Foix's closest ally is Ramón Folc, the Viscount of Cardona."

"He is Bertrán de Solsona's patron, my Lord and I am his sworn enemy!" Josep said. His throat felt constricted.

"The net tightens, young man," replied Lord Belvís. "You are already on the wrong side of three powerful players. Make your moves with great caution, young knight."

"My Lord, I feel it best not to return to Cavallers. They know where I am there."

"The principal is a slippery character. There is a rumour he is secretly in league with Blanca de Antillón, Sanchis' mother but nothing can be proved. King Pere drew the line at eliminating Sanchis and refused to go after anyone else connected with him in case he made himself even more unpopular. I suppose you know of Sanchis' connections with Charles of Anjou, King Charles of Sicily?"

Josep nodded. "Yes, my lord, Lord Pedro de Ayerbe has explained this to me."

"I believe Sanchis was acting as King Charles' agent in Catalunya Aragón. It would not surprise me if Fray Domènech were in league with the Count of Foix. Perhaps the Count of Foix has taken on Sanchis' role. But he is under observation."

"Who is observing him, my lord?" asked Josep.

"Lord Pedro, of course!"

Josep was stunned. "I shall return to Lord Pedro's residence in Ayerbe, my Lord. I feel my time at Cavallers has come to an end," he managed to say.

"I think that is the sensible thing to do. If you wish, I shall arrange for your belongings to be moved to Ayerbe and I shall write to Jacques and request instructions on where to send your allowance."

"Thank you, my Lord," said Josep.

"One final observatrion, jove. The Count of Foix is the brother-in-law of the new king, Jaume of Mayorca, King Pere's brother, as you know. It would not surprise me if King Jaume has been turned against King Pere by King Charles of Sicily. If so, the connection goes all the way to the French Crown and the Pope."

Josep nodded. "You mean, there is a plot for France and the papacy to take over the whole Mediterranean?"

"I could not have put it better myself, young man," the commander said.

No further questions were asked. Josep wondered why the commander had explained these matters to him. But he had the impression that Belvis's attitude to him had shifted in the last hour. It seemed that he had won his respect as a young knight-in-the-making. However, perhaps more importantly, Josep's perception of himself had changed. As he walked out of the Cyclopean castle gate of Monzón, he stepped briskly along the winding cobblestoned passage.

It was still well before midday. He stocked up on provisions, bought himself a warmer rug and set off without a moment to waste. He wore his ordinary clothes to make himself as inconspicuous as possible, though to find a young lad of fifteen riding on his own on these pre-Pyrenean backroads made him conspicuous enough. However, he looked older than he was.

He stayed the first night in Ballaguer and marvelled at its bridge over the mighty River Noguera Pallaresa. The town was well defended, he noted, almost impregnable. He kept a low profile. He did feel he was in enemy territory and felt a flash of anger at the disloyalty these individuals showed to the king.

From Balaguer, he followed the Segre River to La Seu d'Urgell. Here, he decided not to cross Andorra and reach Rennes via Foix, firstly because it was snowing heavily at nights and the roads were impassable but, secondly, because he'd dreamt that night of those penetrating eyes of Guillaume de Nogaret and felt it was an unnecessary risk to come too close to Foix. Therefore, he headed east to the source of the Segre River and continued along the higher spurs above the Tet River.

He stayed the third night in Prades and noticed Occitan was being spoken as much as Catalan. Then he reached Rennes the following day and realised there was no way he was going to be back in Ayerbe within the week. He was exhausted when he finally arrived at the Blancfort residence.

The view from the village was spectacular, overlooking a river valley surrounded by high hills with craggy, snowbound summits. As evening faded into night, fires appeared on the hilltops, evidence of castles, fortresses and small forts, which were invisible to the eye during the day, perched on the hilltops.

"My young friend!" Madeleine Fabre, dark, slim and gentle, addressed him, "I don't know if you realise what joyous news you have delivered, joyous news of the survival of our brethren!" Her eyes were shining and she was looking at the young man in front of her with awe, even disbelief.

"We have mourned our lost families for over a generation. Please do us the honour of being our guest tonight and feel free to stay as long as you need to." Josep, a little thrown by this heroic reception, smiled and nodded. He could still see the fires leaping up in the distant hills behind her as she spoke and he couldn't help his attention being distracted by them.

"Thank you," he said finally, coming to his senses. "I'm sorry but I find those fires unusual and dramatic."

"Dramatic is one word for it," Madeleine said. She frowned turning to face the direction Josep was looking.

"The fires that you see used to be lit by our Cathar brethren. They are kindled by troops loyal to the Northern Barons, the inheritors of de Montfort, who carved out of living flesh their blood-soaked fiefdoms." She paused. "But this is not the moment for sombre reflections. It is a moment of joy. Take your rest and partake of our simple fare. A letter to return to our brethren is being drafted as we speak. Please know the gratitude of several generations of our community. The Perfect you have met is Serge, whom I last saw when I was sixteen and he was eighteen, thirty years ago. At that time, our noble Lord St Giles and Lord Trencavel betrayed their faith and their people putting the material world that they know to be evil before their eternal union with Almighty God. Our brethren were rounded up and burned throughout Languedoc."

"I have heard of these wars from my teachers," Josep replied.

"You will understand we could not bear to see our children die in agony so many of us fled before we were taken and tortured. There are secret passages under the town."

"Where I live we have the same even though it is not so mountainous," Josep said.

"The mountains are our resource," she said. "Serge and all the other children fled when the town was put to the torch."

"Madam, what is the Perfect?"

"That is the highest level of priest in our faith. Serge was a very young man when he escaped. I stayed to look after my mother. She died ten years ago. Oh, I rejoice that they have survived!"

She lapsed into silence. Josep shared a simple meal of vegetable broth with plenty of bread and wine with Madeleine and her cousins. He then slipped easily into a deep dreamless sleep.

His return journey was uneventful and he made all haste. He had been gone more than a week but felt it urgent to deliver his message as quickly as possible. He stayed two nights later in the barraca in Val d'Aran as Amaury had instructed.

He was joyfully awoken by Amaury himself the following morning. When they heard the news Josep brought, the entire community treated him like a conquering hero hanging on his every word requesting repetitions of Madeleine's words, asking about her appearance. Her gentle manner and clear complexion had not changed, they concluded. They quizzed him about details of his travels, whether he had seen this person or that and if landmarks once familiar to them were still there. There was more laughter and high spirits than the community had known for years. Josep was congratulated and thanked by everyone.

He left early the following morning and was accompanied as usual by Amaury who this time went all the way down to the bottom of the track from the Pass. He was greatly excited, his long hair and beard blowing wildly in the wind. Josep said his goodbyes and made his way as quickly as he could to Barbastro completely avoiding Cavallers.

The next day he arrived in Ayerbe. It was three days before Christmas.

"Josep, I barely recognise you. How can one month make such a difference?" Lord Pedro greeted him as soon as he saw him and he listened with genuine amusement as Josep described his interview with Lord Belvís, the Knight Commander of Monzón.

"What the commander told you is of the most secret nature, Josep. Reveal this to no one and guard it with your life," said Lord Pedro.

"I am sworn to secrecy about this and my other activities, my Lord, and would rather not speak more about them but have travelled extensively in France recently."

"Discretion is one of my virtues, Josep!" the older man said laughing. "I hope they looked after you well! Am I permitted to renew my claim upon your service? Now you have had your adventure, that is?" His hearty tone relaxed Josep. "I hear there is someone you would like to see in Loarre, too, so please get it out of your system and let's get back to normal. Your belongings are in the room at the end of the hall and I'm instructed to furnish you with a monthly allowance,"

"My word, good news travels fast." Josep said. Lord Belvís must have heard from Jacques already!"

"Clear lines of communication, jove, that's the secret! Swift horses and hardworking couriers, hundreds of them for each message. It costs a small fortune to keep the channels open and fluid."

That Christmas in Ayerbe was unforgettable. He was graciously received in Loarre Castle by Ricard Benavent de Pinós and his family. Of course, his meeting with Alba was formal but they were allowed to wander alone in the courtyard. Later, on the castle parapet, they gazed out over practically the whole of lower Aragón to the Moncayo hills west of Saragossa. Josep declared his love for Alba, kissed her hands and finally her cheek and felt happier than he had ever felt. He was funny and attentive and even made Alba's mother laugh so that her father entered the room and asked what they were laughing about. He then looked on Josep in a different light and later they discussed the castle and his responsibilities as the commander of the castle garrison.

"If we are invaded from Navarra or the French counties of Bigora or Comminges, they have to get past us first. We guard the plane and hold the key to upper Aragón," said Benavent.

Josep went out to the terrace to clear his head. He felt his luck and his life were so good. He was laughing to himself, sometimes speaking to himself, muttering snatches of scenarios that he was enacting in his head.

"If my Lord would care to have me with his entourage, I should be delighted to accompany him," he was saying to himself, half in shadow. The moon was full. Clouds scudded across an otherwise clear sky, so that light followed dark in the moonlight. He was about to go back in having rehearsed the words he was going to use should Ricard Benevent de Pinós invite him to join the squadron he was organising to march to Barcelona.

He walked towards the wooden door and grasped the handle. Dark turned to light as moonlight flooded down momentarily and he saw someone out of the corner of his eye. He was so taken off his guard that the breath caught inside his chest and his mind refused the information. Nobody could be standing there so still. He walked through the door and paused. No movement. He froze. Was his mind playing tricks on him? A chill went up and down his spine and the hair on the back of his neck stood on end. His heart was pounding. If he didn't turn, he might be attacked from behind. He span around, tried to shout, managed a hoarse croak, leapt back out, drawing his short sword in one movement and saw what he hadn't wanted to see: half in shadow with the shifting pattern from the moonlight was Bru. He was there as solid and real as the granite doorway he stood next to, flush with the wall. He stared into and beyond Josep.

"Josep, fear not. I mean you no harm!" he muttered in a low tone that was at once both hushed and yet perfectly audible.

"Bru! I nearly attacked you." Josep said. Then he realized, after all, it was Christmas and Bru always made an appearance at Christmas.

"I see you think you understand why I am here, young master, and it is true we have a long-standing Christmas tradition. Yet, young master, I must inform you of a matter of the utmost urgency. Your friend has been murdered and your life is in danger."

"Bru, you are a madman!" Josep thought to himself. "Once again, I do not know how you have found me. How did you get over the castle wall? How did you get past the guards?"

"A grappling hook and rope, sir!" said Bru. "Besides, it's Christmas. The guards are a little tipsy."

He imagined that wedge of a man dangling off a rope some one hundred and fifty metres beneath the parapet.

"Josep, your young woodman friend," Bru said. "The hooded man drowned him in Aigualluts because he would not reveal your whereabouts or anything about his people." Bru paused. Josep staggered forward. Bru held him tightly.

"In truth, we have much explaining to do. I know how much these people mean to you. We also have our matters to discuss but I'll save that for later. We must away to the Val d'Aran post haste."

Josep slack-jawed fought to take in what he was hearing.

"You mean someone has drowned Amaury?"

"If that is what his name was, yes, young master."

"Who do you say is responsible?" Josep continued.

"Have you not noticed that you have been followed since your visit to Rennes?"

"How long have you been trailing me?" shouted Josep embarrassed he had been so unaware that he had been trailed not by one but by two people.

"Since you left Cavallers," Bru replied. "The last time I saw you up close, you looked battered and bruised, actually."

Josep remembered his fight with Bertrán de Solsona. It seemed a long time ago.

"My God!" was all he could think to say as the truth sank in.

"The hooded man was good. He tracked you expertly after you left the woodman's village…"

"You were there, too?" Josep interrupted him in disbelief.

"Yes, master, at a safe distance, you know, far enough to pass unnoticed by you and the hooded man. When you returned from Rennes, the hooded man ambushed the woodman, Amaury you say his name was."

The use of the past tense in relation to Amaury sent another jolt through Josep. He was starting to accept the dreadful reality. Another horrible death by drowning, another friend he would never see or speak to again. He remembered times during his journey when he'd felt uncomfortable but couldn't think why. Shadows out of the corner of his eye, a stray footfall, an uncanny silence among the birds. All these things he remembered in an instant. And all the time, Bru had been tracking the hooded man tracking him.

"Where did he go after he killed him?"

"Master Josep, he disappeared into the passes around Mount Aneto. I don't know where he went. All I know is that he tortured Amaury for several hours in the stream by the waterfall of Aigualluts. One moment, your friend struggled for the next breath, the next he was limp. The waters took him and he disappeared. The hooded man was as mystified as I was when later I looked for him and there was no trace. He sank head first underwater and disappeared. The hooded man checked the area carefully, then left heading around the glacier. All I can tell you is he spoke Occitan and French."

"And Amaury said nothing?" Josep asked in horror.

"Now there is the thing. He didn't utter a sound, not a word or even a cry, only gasps for breath."

"Poor, brave Amaury!" said Josep. "We'll have to let the Cathars know." He suddenly looked alarmed. "We'll have to get to the Cathar camp and back in two days otherwise he will miss the expedition to Barcelona."

"How will you get out of the castle tomorrow?" asked Josep.

"The same way I got in," said Bru."Don't worry, meet me as early as you can on the Osca Road," he finished.

Josep nodded. Then Bru attached his hook and was gone. Josep entered by another entrance to give Bru time to get away.

There were so many questions to answer but Josep could only say he would be back in two days. Alba looked terribly upset and disappointed. He apologised and swore he'd be back as soon as he could. Nobody could understand how this urgency could have happened.

CHAPTER 9 MOUNTAIN AND CITY

Josep met Bru as planned the following morning. Josep had been let out on his horse at first light by the soldiers on the gate, who seemed sleepy and unperturbed as he produced the token from Ricard Pinós de Benavent. Bru was, as usual, without a horse. The almogavers were infantry, foot soldiers after all.

It had snowed and the town and castle of Loarre looked as if it were part of the rock on which it was built. The snow made everything gaunt and played tricks on the eye of depth and distance. The towering Pyrenees in the distance looked like hills just behind them. There was no sound as if they were riding on a blanket. It was also bitterly cold and the only way to keep from freezing was to ride hard. Josep was grateful for his good horse, he thought, able to carry two riders, as even Bru on his own two feet could not have kept up with a horse, Josep thought. Then, by mid-morning, the horse began to tire. Bru dismounted from the trotting horse and, to Josep's amazement, began to run alongside the horse and Josep was therefore able to keep up a steady pace albeit not as swift as before.

However, it was fast enough and by watering and feeding the horse and eating rapidly themselves, they made excellent time. When they rode together, Bru explained what he understood to have happened to Amaury.

"We'll need to talk to the Perfect to understand exactly what happened and why," said Josep. "They may have found his body by now."

By afternoon they were at Barbastro, by evening at Benasque. They had covered a hundred miles in twelve hours and Bru had run half of that, alternately riding with Josep for two hours, then running alongside for two hours, then riding for two hours and so on, through the day. Josep was astounded. It was three times what a soldier could march at full speed.

"We'll have to rest here for the night. I know a small cabin at the foot of the ascent to la Porta Picada," said Josep.

"I know the cabin, too," replied Bru. "If you must rest, so be it. But I am for making it to the village before we rest for the night. Otherwise, we might not make it back to Loarre in time."

"But Bru, I'm exhausted and so is the horse," argued Josep.

"Master Josep, the horse is good for another four hours with one rider. I can continue. You must decide."

"But we might be ambushed by the woodsmen if we arrive at night!" countered Josep, digging deep for energy he knew he was going to have to find.

"That's likely, master, but they will recognise you quickly enough."

They passed the barraca where Josep had imagined getting a good night's sleep, two hours after sunset. They were going to ascend the pass in darkness with snow underfoot. Not wanting to injure the horse accidentally, Josep dismounted on Bru's advice and walked the ten miles up the pass. At the pass, Josep thought he had never been so physically exhausted in his life. Yet they paused only to feed and water the horses before they set off in search of the Cathar camp.

Within an hour, they were surrounded on all sides and then taken, bound and marched to the camp. It didn't take long for their identity to be verified.

They were brought before the Perfect, the sinewy leader of their community, who was with several other elders, one of them clearly older than the others. The Perfect greeted Josep, who introduced Bru as his uncle. The Perfect explained when they had noticed Amaury was gone and how they had set out to find him.

"We found him next to an old spring. He lay there for two more days," said the Perfect. "We couldn't decide what to do. We didn't even know if it was an accident. We even thought it might be a trap and his body had been left there to lure us out," he said.

"I am afraid we can assure you Amaury was murdered," Josep said.

"This is terrible news to us," the Perfect said. "The day after we found him, some soldiers from the Baron de Les came. We were close enough to hear them. They think he drowned. But no one can understand how he came to be at that spring. It is strictly off-limits as it is frequented by the soldiers at the top of Artiga de Lin, soldiers of the Count of Foix and the Baron of Les."

"How did you find his body?" asked Josep, "if this spring is off-limits, as you say?"

"We can observe the narrow, beautiful valley of Artiga de Lin but never descend into it. We could see a body from the top of the ridge here. I myself came with an experienced tracker and we had to use all our skill to pass unnoticed. We are still as mystified as we were as to how Amaury died there. If indeed he died there. Perhaps his body was left there at night. But who would go to the trouble?"

"He did not die there," Josep said. "He died at the waterfall at the foot of Aneto called Aigualluts. My uncle Bru saw him being interrogated." Bru stepped forward as if to introduce himself and the Perfect acknowledged his presence with a polite inclination of the head.

"Interrogated?" asked the Perfect.

"Yes, Perfect, but Bru can vouch that he said nothing. He did not say a word either about you or the village. My uncle saw it all."

"I understand not why the assailant waited for Amaury at the waterfall of Aneto. It is the other side of the pass. Why did he not track him to the village?"

"Bru and I have talked about this. The only explanation seems to be that the murderer needed to know where Amaury had come from and who you were. He needed information to explain what he saw. Maybe he had spied on the village already and you are still in danger. There is no way of knowing."

"The hooded man didn't ascend the pass, Master," Bru said to Josep, deferentially speaking to the Perfect through him.

"The hooded man?" asked the Perfect.

"We know the murderer by that name, Perfect," said Josep, "as he wore a hood. That is all we can say about his appearance. His clothes were nondescript peasant clothing without colour or distinguishing features."

"I tracked him and saw he was camped for the period in woods not far from Aigualluts which have a good view onto the pass," said Bru. "I believe he was awaiting your descent, Master Josep. But you came accompanied by Amaury. He chose to interrogate Amaury to find out what he could about both of you but Amaury refused to talk. The hooded man became angry and frustrated so he drowned him but I believe he did not intend to, not at that moment anyway."

"Why do you say that?" asked the Perfect.

"You don't kill a man you're interrogating till you have the information you need. It's a skilfull procedure. You must first make sure…"

The Perfect looked shocked.

"Thank you, Bru," said Josep cutting him off. "You say his body just disappeared from under his assailant's hands at Mount Aneto?" he asked Bru, refocusing the discussion onto Amaury and the hooded man not Bru's experience as a torturer.

"That is so, Master," said Bru.

"So how did his body reappear here?" asked Josep.

"On my honour, I know not!" said Bru. There was silence for a moment.

"There is an old tale," began the oldest of the men with the Perfect, "that these hills are full of holes and passages which take water to and from the different springs in the mountains."

"This is the tracker I mentioned," said the Perfect. "He is the one who lead me to the spring where we had seen the body from the ridge," he said.

"We know things lost in certain water points reappear in strange places," continued the tracker. "We think it is due to the flow of the water in these passages. His body could have disappeared as it could have been sucked down a channel under the spring at Aigualluts at Mount Aneto. Then it reappeared sometime later at the spring where he was found in Artiga de Lin. We knew about these channels when we lived in the villages of Rosellón. This is how many of us escaped from those towns, by following these passages when they were unflooded."

Josep remembered Madeleine Fabre had mentioned such tunnels when he had been in Rennes. Images stirred in his imagination, or was it his memory? He knew these tunnels flooded. Presumably, people drowned if they did while there were people inside them.

"Did you know he had drowned from his face?" Josep asked the tracker.

"Yes," he replied. "His face showed the signs of death by drowning. His face was bloated and his eyes were bulging, like…."

"Like those of a drowned man who has spent some time underwater?" Josep finished his sentence for him.

"Exactly, jove, how did you know?" the old man said.

"I have witnessed execution by drowning and have dreamt these images repeatedly ever since," said Josep.

"Maybe your mother could explain, Josep. She has a bad history around water," Bru said.

Josep didn't know why Bru said that or why it made him nervous so he tried to ignore it. He looked away but said nothing.

"In any case they thought he was a Jew," he said.

"Why?" asked Josep, glad for the change of subject.

"Because of his strange clothes," continued the old tracker, "and his wild hair and beard. The people around here have started calling the spring where he was found "Uelhs deth Joèu," in Occità, or "Ulls del Jueu" in Catalan, which means "Eyes of the Jew." The old tracker lapsed into silence.

"But why a Jew?" asked Josep.

"They have little to do with Jews," said the Perfect. "He looked strange, so they thought he was a Jew. That is the way of people."

"But he looks like a typical member of your community," Josep said.

"Young man," the Perfect replied. "No one has seen a Cathar for a generation or more. People can forget quickly."

Josep was stunned into silence. This was the Cathars' reality. Their kind had been extinguished, annihilated. They were the last of their kind, except for secret remnants like Madeleine Fabre in towns like Rennes. No one even remembered how they had looked these days.

"He had a good end and served us faithfully," said the Perfect. Through his silence, which cost him an agonizing death, he nobly saved his community," he said. "We will retrieve the body tonight. We thank you for your information, which has solved this sorrowful mystery. We will bury Amaury in the camp in accordance with our customs. Stay and partake of our simple food but do not delay if time presses upon you. God speed you."

After eating, Josep and Bru slept deeply. They were leaving at sunrise, as the party returned from Artiga de Lin, bearing Amaury's body. Josep paid his respects and Bru confirmed it was the woodsman he had seen and there was quiet lament from all around. Josep and Bru could not delay to witness the funeral.

"I caused his death, Bru. If I hadn't been followed, none of this would have happened. I feel I have betrayed them."

"Young Master, without your heroic deed, this community would still be lost. Their brethren in Rennes know they are here now. For both communities, a link has been restored. What was lost has been found again. Both communities have a lot to thank you for."

"But if I'd been more careful…!"

"Master, you cannot learn everything all at once and I shall endeavour to teach you all I know of tracking and being tracked."

"But I still feel I have another man's blood on my hands," Josep said, his voice cracking. "Both drowned. I am disgusted with myself."

"Young master, we live in dangerous times. I know not what else to say," Bru said. He witnessed in the lonely depths of the night Josep's anguished sleep as he once again fought for air underwater in his dreams, images that would mark him forever, that would fade but would never wholly disappear.

†

As Josep expected, Lord Pedro was annoyed with him when he returned to Ayerbe via Loarre. However, when he heard what had befallen Amaury, he expressed his deep regret at his death.

"He saved your life when you ran off that time," was his comment.

"We permanently need to be checking in case we are being followed." He was clearly both amazed and deeply impressed by Bru, who accompanied Josep and about whom Josep had spoken obliquely as the almogaver half uncle who appeared from time to time and caused problems. As Lord Pedro himself was too young to have taken part in the Valencia and Murcia campaigns of his own father, King Jaume, his contact with almogavers had been as guides in the foothills of the Navarese Pyrenees and they were almogatens, or almogaver commanders, who were, unlike the ordinary soldiers, always on horseback.

When he heard how far Josep and Bru had managed to get in a single day, one hundred miles, he was astonished.

"Is that typical?" he asked.

"I know not, my Lord," replied Bru. "We had to get there as fast as possible but I was glad to get off that horse each time, I can tell you!"

"You travelled at twice the normal speed. You'd never have made the distance in so short a time otherwise," exclaimed Lord Pedro.

"Be that as it may, my Lord, my place is on the ground on these two legs, not on horseback. I dread to think what would have happened if we'd been attacked. I was so unsteady, I couldn't even have unsheathed my coltell." Bru mimicked being thrown around on horseback, his left arm round Josep's waist the other trying to draw his coltell, also on his left side.

"I might have stabbed Josep in the back," he said. "No, no, put me on the ground. I can fell a horse sooner than ride one!"

Once back in Loarre to join the mission to Barcelona, Ricard Pinós was greatly taken with Bru and delighted to hear he could accompany them to Barcelona.

"I shall take up the rear," Bru said, "and show you how to track those who would track you."

They set out the next morning and planned to get to Barcelona four days later. King Pere had summoned all his troops to gather there as there were new reports of disturbances from the Veguer of the city, Gombau de Benavent, a cousin of Ricard Pinós de Benavent.

Despite the snow, they made good time and arrived in Lleida by nightfall the following day. Josep couldn't find Bru when they came to be billeted in one of the hostels of the city. There wasn't time to set up and take down a camp. They ate and slept with Ricard's immediate entourage.

"Where did you get to yesterday evening?" Josep asked Bru the following day as the troops left the city and crossed the River Segre en route to Anglesola.

"Remember I am tracking those who might be tracking us so I didn't arrive until two hours later. Also, I had to make sure I wasn't being tracked myself. I didn't see anyone behind me but you can never be absolutely sure."

"Believe me, I feel all the safer knowing you are there," said Josep.

"I'd better fall back now," said Bru as they entered open country.

It was so wide and flat around El Pla d'Urgell that it was difficult to see how anyone could stay hidden and launch a surprise attack on the rear but Bru was also there to catch spies, Josep thought as he rode on towards Barcelona. He was glad to have Bru there because he was obviously so experienced. He was an asset to any force. He pondered the various incidents surrounding his relationship with Bru and found himself back at the cave in the Garraf with the Morisc bleeding on the floor in front of him and Jacques de Molay warning Bru not to kill him. Yet the man had died despite everyone's efforts to save his life. Bru was a killer, a cold hearted hunter who took no prisoners, took what he wanted, when it suited him. Hadn't he made a present of the few possessions that remained to Habiba after slaughtering her father and leaving her for dead? The decorated blade, the cloth on the broken loom. He couldn't make any sense of it and he worried about it all day unable to reconcile the actions of this man with the man Bru was at this moment. He was a dangerous killer not even allowed on the grounds of Clara's house any more. Yet he had tracked Josep from Cavallers to Val d'Aran and Rennes and back to Loarre and had been responsible for informing him of the death of Amaury and the danger this meant to him. Two conflicts collided at that moment in Josep's mind. He felt proud to have Bru there but the question nagged at the back of his mind: why had he not tried to save Amaury? The implications of this question were horrifying: Bru had watched Amaury being killed, tortured to death and had done nothing to stop it. At this point, his thoughts became muddled. He imagined himself there intervening and being overcome by Amaury's assailant. Then he imagined him overcoming the assailant and in turn trying to drown him but not being able to do it. That was, after all, his nightmare death and he couldn't inflict that on anyone, no matter who it was. Against these thoughts, he imagined other scenarios involving Bru. Bru was skilful enough to disable the assailant without killing him and releasing Amaury. So why had he not done that? Then he could have taken the hooded man prisoner and found out who he was thereby further helping Josep by clearly identifying his enemies. He wanted to talk to Bru about that.

Later that day, as they were on the last stretch to Barcelona and heading for the Creu Coberta, Bru rejoined the main group. There were so many people on the road, it was pointless for Bru to try to identify possible threats and madness for anyone to launch an attack on them, surrounded as they were by so many people.

"That's my job done, Josep!" he said, with a broad smile looking to Josep for recognition. Josep, however, looked away and Bru's face fell.

"What is it, young Master?"

"Bru, why did you not save Amaury? Did you sit there and watch as he was tortured to death? Why didn't you intervene? You needn't have killed the hooded man but then at least I'd know who he was and who my enemies are and Amaury would have gone free and still be alive."

"If I'd have gone for him, I'd have killed him, Master Josep, that is my way! I didn't know he was going to kill Amaury. Besides, it was not my fight."

Josep looked disgusted at him.

"Master, it's not my way. I don't know anything about taking prisoners. I've never done it and his death was so sudden. I was watching him one moment and the next he went limp."

There was a call from up front as the squadron was ordered to halt.

"Word has come that a hostile force is burning fields and ransacking property due north of here around the village of Gràcia," said one of Pinós de Benavent's captains. "They have made an attempt on the Porta de l'Àngel but it has been repulsed. It is the Viscount of Cardona, Ramón Folc and his knights about ten in all and fifty infantry poorly armed. They are taking a great risk. They are outnumbered and can easily be defeated. The nightly disturbances in the city have stopped, Gombau de Benavent has arrested an agent provocateur who happens to be a spy working for the Count of Foix. Apparently, his mission was to spread rumours of poor yields in the countryside to push up the prices of flour, in which he has succeeded. People started protesting and there was some trouble for a few nights but it's all under control. We are awaiting instructions about how to proceed."

They set up camp next to the little hill they call Creu Coberta. This was the place of execution of ordinary criminals. The gallows had an old desiccated body swinging from them. The crow on top of the gallows completed the picture. It was the first time Josep had seen a man hanging from the gallows and he couldn't help looking.

"Why do they call this place Creu Coberta he asked an old passer-by. "Are the gallows in the shape of a cross but it used to be covered?"

"No, young master," said the old man, "it's because of the little chapel over there on that little hill. There's a cross inside it and as it is sheltered from the weather, it's called the covered cross. Last rites for the condemned man are performed there before they hang him. That's why."

Josep shivered. It was ironic that the place was named after the cross and not the gallows. Life seemed strange and bleak to Josep and the place with its ironic name deepened that impression. He could not take his eyes off the hanging man swinging in the breeze. He went to bed and dreamt of Bru hanging on the end of the rope.

CHAPTER 10 IMPOSSIBLE ALLIANCES

The following morning, when the small detachment visited Gombau de Benavent at the Casa del Veguer, Bru immediately recognised the Count of Foix's agent as the hooded man who'd been tracking Josep and had murdered Amaury. He always spoke so forthrightly. He nearly informed all present of this fact, in which case he would have given away the secret of the Cathars in the Val d'Aran. Josep silenced him quickly and made sure it was to him that Bru revealed this information.

"He claims to be working for the Count of Foix," said the Veguer. "We shall have him tried and the king can decide what to do with him. In any case, the disturbances have died down."

"I shall deal with him once I have dealt with Ramón Folc, the Viscount of Cardona," said a booming voice as the king entered, a good head taller than anyone else in the room, sending servants scurrying off in all directions. Everyone fell to their knees in the king's presence.

"But first to Gracia to deal with the troublesome count!" the king then said. They made all haste to follow the king, who exchanged glances of greeting with those gathered in the hall of the Casa del Veguer, the residence of the most senior official in the city, the king's representative. He nodded briefly at Josep, as if he'd expected to see him there. Josep had not seen the king for two years and yet he had recognised him immediately. When they arrived, the king dismounted and strode up to where the first tents of Ramón Folc's force were pitched. He met with no resistance.

"Viscount Cardona, I wish to speak to you," he said. Out came Ramón Folc, accompanied by his page, Bertrán de Solsona. Josep couldn't believe his eyes.

"Young Master," Bru said to Josep, "is this the young lad you fought with?"

"Yes, Bru, the very one."

"He was the young man who was with the hooded man when he left Cavallers on your trail."

Everything fitted into place. The hooded man was a spy for the Count of Foix whom Bertrán de Solsona had also somehow met at Cavallers.

"There was a third man, tonsured, dry and stern and older than all the other teachers at the school that I also saw," said Bru.

"That must have been the principal," said Josep. So all the rumours are true, he thought. Cavallers was still a base for all the nobles in revolt in the area, backed by the Count of Foix and the Viscount of Cardona.

"I must let his Majesty know this at once," Josep said half to himself half to Bru. But before he could move, his knight Lord Pedro was at his elbow. He had heard what Josep had said.

"It is as the king expected!" he whispered in his ear.

"He has had you and me at Cavallers for all these years, keeping an eye on developments there and also in the Val d'Aran, knowing all along that Fray Domènech was in league with the rebels. We have done a good job keeping him informed of the developments. The principal's antipathy to you and that of Bertrán de Solsona are no longer a mystery to you, I take it."

"I have my own antipathy to Bertán de Solsona," Josep said. "As far as I know, it has always been reciprocated. I hate him and would gladly kill him myself. He was complicit in the death of Amaury."

Josep couldn't understand why the king was so calm with Ramón Folc.

"They're playing cat and mouse again," Josep said to himself, "but as the king finally outwitted Sanchis, so he will Foix. He has more agents and soldiers and commands more loyalty than Ramón Folc or the Count of Foix. There is more to this than meets the eye."

There was a sudden commotion and at an unseen signal all Foix's knights mounted and fled in the direction of the River Llobregat, hoping to put distance and water between themselves and their pursuers. They were followed by the infantry, who fled on foot as fast as they could. The king was still deep in discussion with Viscount Ramón Folc, the king dark, the viscount fair but both equally tall. King Pere was doing the talking and held his head higher than did Folc, who, for all his swagger, looked nervous. The king summoned the Crown Prince Alfons and gave him brief instructions. The king then left the scene, returning briefly to the veguer to discuss the issue of the agent provocateur.

"If he's found guilty, we'll hang him at Creu Coberta like a common criminal. If he's not my subject, I will send him to Prince Alfons to imprison him and we will deliberate what profit to make of him."

King Pere at that point left the side of Josep's small detachment and went back inside the palace.

As soon as the Viscount of Cardona's battalion had fled the city and the Viscount himself was in the custody of Crown Prince Alfons, the veguer, Gombau de

Benevent, and the soldiers at his disposal prepared to pursue the fleeing soldiers. The veguer's men numbered at least one thousand five hundred, three times the number of Folc's force as the king had issued summonses to many of his knights to meet him with their companies in Barcelona. Among those illustrious names were Dalmau Rocabertí and his page Ramón Muntaner, who immediately rode up to Josep and quizzed him about what he had seen. Josep was flattered by the attention and pleased to see practically the only person he could still call his friend from his days in Cavallers. Guillem Moliner, one of the king's most trusted knights, rode with the king, together with Ramón de Molina, the Veguer of Ribagorça and Pallars, whom Josep recognised as he had been several times to Cavallers to pay Lord Pedro his expenses. He was joking that he was getting too old for the job but his companion, the Italian Josep recognized as Giovanni da Procida, made him look youthful. He was at least eighty years of age, a venerable, shrivelled up prune of a man with a long nose, for intrigue, they said, and sparkling blue eyes.

"Imagine how that makes me feel," was his response to Ramón de Molina's complaint.

"Nevertheless, I shall have to recruit some new blood," said King Pere. "This young man is a fine candidate to succeed his master in that role," he laughed by way of introducing Josep and Lord Pedro to Giovanni da Procida.

"I have a feeling we have already met, have we not?" said Giovanni da Procida without missing a beat and transfixing both Josep and Lord Pedro with his penetrating gaze.

"That is so, Sir Giovanni," said Lord Pedro with Josep nodding in agreement. "We met at Cavallers two years ago after the Sanchis incident, if I am not mistaken."

"Indeed, indeed, I remember you both well," replied da Procida. "Well, let us hope that we can aid his majesty in quelling these northern rebellions once and for all. He needs a free hand to develop his realm and make up for lost ground, wouldn't you say?" the old man transfixed them both again with his steely ice-cold gaze.

Lord Pedro felt as though he were being interrogated himself, he later confessed to Josep.

"Naturally, naturally!" was all he could reply. Josep had the impression Lord Pedro and Guillem de Molina, who also heard the exchange, were not entirely sure what he meant.

As they made their pursuit of Folc's force along the Llobregat, more knights, private soldiers and even almogavers, drawn from the hills by rumours that the northern rebellion was to be quelled once and for all, joined King Pere's force as it marched behind and drove away Folc's much smaller force.

That afternoon, Josep heard a rumour that the pursuit of Folc was incidental. What was happening was the king was using Folc's attack on Barcelona as a test case, a rallying call to gauge the loyalty he commanded. Given the force he had amassed, support for him was clearly significant.

Night fell and Viscount Folc's force crossed the River Llobregat at Corbera in complete darkness. They had no idea what was going on. They had been instructed by him to march to Barcelona. He had then attacked the gate for a day and then submitted to the king and left his army to fend for itself. One soldier was left behind the following day. Josep heard him say several had drowned in the crossing but he'd lost his horse and his nerve. The king, who happened to be there, sent him home after making him swear loyalty to him in the future. The man couldn't believe his luck and disappeared as quickly as he could. King Pere's force crossed the river in daylight and pushed on towards Lleida.

The force was swelling as they rode across Catalunya and more knights, having received the call to arms from the king, arrived with their companies. The king's spies, scouts and messengers were also hard at work. The king's army occupied the countryside as far as the eye could see and his scouts were constantly going to and fro, reporting to the army's various commanders what was happening, where certain elements were and who had arrived.

Outside Balaguer, two men were arrested. Around the king's company, for a moment Josep couldn't make out what was happening. Then it became clear that a young messenger had been captured and was being led to the king by an almogaver on foot. Josep immediately recognised the almogaver as Bru. The young messenger had given himself away by displaying the arms of the Count of Pallars, a two-headed black eagle on a yellow background. Under interrogation, it transpired that the messenger was bearing a message for a number of knights who had issued letters of deseixement to the king, the formal breaking of the oath of loyalty to him. Among these knights were Arnau, Count of Pallars, Ermengol, the Count of Urgell and Arnau d'Espanya, the Count of Pallar's nephew.

The message was addressed to the Count of Foix in Balaguer. King Pere had the information he needed. A shout went up: "To Balaguer!"

Foix had concentrated all his nobles and forces and was in open defiance of the king in Balaguer. He was staging a revolt there. Ramón Folc had used his attack on Barcelona as a decoy to distract attention from Foix's build up of forces in Balaguer. Hence, his easy surrender and indifferent retreat from Barcelona.

Once in Balaguer, the other captive was taken to the king and identified as Esquiu de Miralpeix, a knight from Tolzà, a village between Foix and Toulouse. He had come to aid his cousin the Count of Foix. So the king pressed him for all the information he could give him about the Count of Foix's resources north of the Pyrenees, which were extensive and in many cases contentious, as he claimed to own properties the king had considered his own.

"I seem to remember the Count of Foix was imprisoned by my cousin, the King of France, for sedition and rebellion in the early 1270s. He should keep his hands off other people's property. He's too hot-headed to be a successful rebel. He hasn't got the forces to back up his plans. Better Count of the mountains than the Prince of nothing."

This raised a laugh, even from Esquiu de Miralpeix. The count was overambitious and apt to make powerful enemies.

"He has always been a thorn in our side over the succession of Urgell. He has imprisoned his own daughter in the hope I would marry her to my son, Jaume, has married his sister to my treacherous brother and seeks to defy an army of five hundred knights and a hundred thousand men with a force ten, twenty or even a hundred times smaller. How many men does he have under arms?" King Pere asked.

"About fifty knights, Majesty, and two thousand men," Esquiu de Miralpeix replied.

"They will starve in a matter of days unless they have laid up provisions with great care. Can you not persuade them to lay down their arms?"

"I thank his Majesty for his mercy and will do my utmost!" the Languedeoc knight replied.

Several days later, it was clear the deputation had failed and Foix was as defiant as ever.

"His ambition and pride have blinded him," the king said and the order was given immediately to set up the trebuchets and start knocking down the walls. At the same time, all roads around Balaguer were guarded to stop anyone coming in and out of the city and the fields and vines were systematically torched. After two weeks valiantly rebuilding their walls at night and watching their possessions around the town being destroyed, the townspeople prevailed on their rebellious aristocrats to surrender. The gates were opened and the townspeople ran across the bridge weeping, imploring the king for mercy. Last to come out were the nobles including Foix, head down. Josep and Bru couldn't believe what they were seeing, such defiance laid so low. King Pere's son Alfons was again entrusted with the custody of the nobles and they were transferred to La Paeria, the royal castle and prison.

Lord Pedro de Ayerbe appointed Ricard Pinós de Benavent commander of the garrison at La Paeria, in Lleida, where the nobles were held until 1281, when they were released after swearing allegiance to King Pere. Ramón Folc of Cardona and

Arnau Roger of Pallars became exemplary loyal servants of the king from then on. In July 1281, the Count of Foix was required to swear allegiance to the king in his prison cell but refused and was therefore secretly transferred to the Castle of Siurana and cut off from any contact with the town of Foix.

Ricard Pinós de Benavent visited Lleida frequently, often accompanied by his wife and twin daughters, Alba and Bella, and Josep's relationship with Alba blossomed. Josep rode frequently to Lleida to meet her with her family, where they stayed in La Paeria. Josep always had a bed available in the Castle of Gardeny, the ancient castle nearby built on Roman and Moorish remains with many details of Templar military design added at a later date, which fascinated Josep.

Josep felt he was part of a prestigious corps of almogavers guarding important nobles in the area. He was well liked by the almogavers and was respected by them for his affability and physical toughness. He was the page of Lord Pedro de Ayerbe but was happy to be subordinate to Ricard Pinós de Benavent.

Josep would organise days of rest with Bru so that he could be together with Alba in Lleida and on those days, they would wander around the streets of the city, especially the beautiful Carrer de Cavallers, which always brought to mind his days at the academy with the same name. They would wander in the cloisters of the Monasteri del Roser or walk up the hill to the cathedral, La Seu, climb up the tower and admire the view over the orchards of the city, the river running down from Balaguer and the castle on the opposite hill.

Josep told Alba about his dreams, serving the king in Catalunya but also in foreign lands and his desire to go overseas. This idea clutched at his stomach, he didn't know if it was out of fear or excitement, every time. This always led them to a discussion on the state of the nation.

"The king has a lot of discontented and jealous nobles sitting on their lands waiting to be granted the same privileges they had under his father," said Alba.

"But King Pere has seen that they were demanding too much for too little in return," Josep answered. "I think he's postponing a settlement with the nobles until they agree to contribute to his plans, whatever they may be."

"What do you mean?" Alba replied. Do they now have to provide endless troops and money to get what they already have?"

"Exactly! But what they have is exaggerated. King Jaume offered them too much when he finally came to power," Josep argued, referring to the fact that King Jaume became king at five years of age but had no power of his own till he was twenty or so. "He did what he had to do at the time to ensure some support from the nobles who wouldn't have supported him at all otherwise."

"Land is what the aristocrats want. But what land is the king going to offer his unhappy aristocrats in return for their support?" asked Alba.

"Well, that's the question. We've gone as far south as we can into old Almohad lands, maybe the king is looking overseas to find occupations and rewards for them."

"Where do you mean? I cannot see his nobles settling happily in the kingdom of Tunis," she said.

"Do you never dream about us in the future?" Josep cut in quickly taking the initiative.

"Of course I do. We were talking. I did not know I had to be so careful around you," Alba replied.

"God, if I could, I would marry you tomorrow!" Josep said.

"To whom?" Alba quipped in her own self-defence, not wanting to enter a conversation about matrimony or hurt Josep's feelings. But it was unavoidable. They started arguing as usual.

CHAPTER 11 LOVE AND HATE

Lleida, December, 1281.

Months passed. Josep continued with his knight in Lleida. He was now known as his squire but his duties effectively remained unchanged. He heard rumours that the Count of Anjou and the King of France were aiming to take control of possessions of the Catalans in North Africa, that the Sultan of Morocco had a secret pact with the Sultan of Granada to push all the Christians out of North Africa and that King Sancho Bravo, the Castillian usurper, had his eye on these North African fiefs and was in league with all the other parties to achieve his aims. As with all rumours, there was probably a grain of truth in all of them. He made his way up Carrer de Cavallers, trying to banish old memories of being there with Alba. After all, he was due to meet her father that morning to receive his orders. He found the commander in an expansive mood when he asked him about North Africa.

"The Almohads invaded Iberia, conquered the Almoravids throughout Spain and expelled them. The Almohads themselves are all but extinct on this side of the Straits of Gibraltar except for vestiges in Granada and Estepona. We are invading them so the idea they want to expel us is not surprising," Ricard Benavent de Pinós said.

Josep understood what he meant except for the word vestiges. "You mean, the Muslims in Granada are related to the Almohads?" he asked.

"They are Nazarids but they are related distantly to them through the Almohad Sultans of Morocco and Tunis. Old King Jaume drove out the Almohads south of Valencia and Murcia. Yet their cousins still rule in North Africa from Morocco to Tunis." He made a high sweeping wave as if to suggest they were all around but on the horizon.

"There is trouble closer to home in Castilla, Lord Pedro tells me, sir," Josep said.

"We will have to be careful with Sancho el Bravo, the present King of Castilla. He is capable of anything!" the commander said.

"He usurped the throne from the infant twin sons of Fernando de la Cerda, the Infante of Castilla, didn't he?" asked Josep, saddling the commander's horse and pleased to be able to contribute in some way.

"Indeed, Josep, despite their royal French blood. King Pere is their uncle and has them in Xérica, down in Murcia, for their protection," the commander said.

"Do they have French royal blood?" Josep asked.

"The twins' grandmother, Blanche, was the daughter of King Louis The Pious of France and so they are of royal blood three times over, Catalunya Aragón, Castilla and France."

"My lord, do you think France has something to do with the barons leading the northern rebellions?"

"Ferran Sanchis met influential French leaders in the crusades, as you know," Benavent de Pinós said. "Yet I know not if there is French support for the Aragonese and Catalan Barons. Apart from the Count of Foix, who seems to have connections to the Crown Prince Philippe. It is as well he is behind bars."

Josep had plenty to occupy him checking security in Castell Siurana, where the count was held. One morning in September, he noticed at different points while making his rounds at least half a dozen overturned carts at the roadside. The harvest of corn once proudly stacked in tight bushels high on the cart was again and again hopelessly overturned and the farmers trying to recover their livelihood.

"Jump down from your horse, young sir, and help me with this wheel," one farmer shouted to him. Josep did not mention he was the sixth farmer he'd seen in this predicament so far that morning.

"What seems to have been the problem?" he asked the farmer.

"No seems about it, jove, the wheel went and broke without warning and off the road we comes. It's going to take me all night to re-tie all these bushels. And it looks like rain! That'll ruin the whole lot!"

While they were talking, the two cows that had been pulling the farmer's cart started munching on the corn and Josep's own horse was quick to do the same. The farmer looked cross and Josep steered his horse away. He dismounted and helped the farmer right the cart and get it back on the road and saw that the solid back wheel had split from the centre out and come out of its metal rim in two pieces.

"I don't know how it could have happened," said the farmer, "because the cartright put it on for me but a week ago. If I didn't know better, I'd say someone's been tampering with it and weakened it."

When Josep returned to Castell Siurana, he mentioned these incidents to Lord Pedro.

"I can't believe you stopped and lent a hand," the nobleman said. "You shouldn't sully your hands in peasant's work!"

This bothered Josep. He had helped the farmer and was being criticised for it. He turned to look Lord Pedro straight in the eye.

"Anyway, I trust our prisoners are in good health?" Lord Pedro continued before Josep could say anything.

"Too good for my liking," Josep replied.

"That may well be so," Lord Pedro said, ignoring Josep's remark. "But it does not reflect well on King Pere if our prisoners are in anything other than the best of health."

Josep now felt his work was under scrutiny.

"Is there a problem, my lord?" he asked.

Lord Pedro eyed Josep coldly for a moment. "Josep, you are becoming a young man," he said. "But I demand respect at all times. Therefore, I do not appreciate witty answers to my questions. Remember, your role is important and part of it is to serve me," he raised an eyebrow as he said this.

Josep understood he was expected to agree. "Yes, my Lord. I did not mean to be disrespectful," he said, putting his head down.

"Very well," replied Lord Pedro. "King Pere will be here tomorrow," he said, "so make all necessary preparations for Foix to accompany us across the border. We are to visit the king's brother, King Jaume of Mayorca, in Perpignan," he nodded in farewell and turned his horse out of the gate.

Josep took a deep breath and told himself to control himself. The fact was, as Josep knew very well, his position was one of great responsibility. Lord Pedro had told him where they would be going the following day. Surely that meant he still trusted him completely. Josep felt reassured when he realized this. But he realized he was changing and his attitudes to those around him were also changing. His now saw that his words and actions were sometimes inappropriate. He had to be careful, he thought to himself. He did not stop work that day from that moment till everything had been arranged.

The following morning, the king's entourage arrived at the first hour. Josep had arranged everything to happen with minimum fuss. The count was brought out with his hands bound behind his back. He'd lost some weight over his eighteen months in captivity.

"I remember you even if you don't remember me, you little miscreant," he said addressing Josep directly, "and I swear that I shall have my revenge on you and your family, on your master, Lord Pedro, on your people, on your country, on your king. I spit on your filthy country, I regret the time I ever set foot in your miserable little kingdom. I regret ever having befriended Ramón Folc, my sworn enemy having taken sides with your king again. You will be wiped out. We shall overrun your puny nation. We will flow out like a river bursting its banks over the Pyrenees. When you least expect us we will be there and we will engulf you like a flood and you will be utterly wiped off the face of the Earth!" Spittle was forming at the corners of his mouth. He looked demented.

Josep took a deep breath and told himself to control himself. This raving tirade would have been enough to provoke many a young man but Josep said nothing and did not allow even a flicker of emotion to cross his face.

Bru helped Josep install the count in a windowless carriage. "Best none see him and he sees none, isn't it, young master?" Bru said.

"Yes, Bru, quite right," Josep replied.

Later that day, once they were on their way, Josep rode up next to Lord Pedro.

"What does the king expect in return for Count Roger Bernat, my lord?" he asked him without lowering his voice. "Doesn't anyone know the king's plans?"

"For God's sake, Josep, please keep your voice down!" Lord Pedro answered. "Of course nobody knows the king's intentions and if anyone did and were asked they would be wise to deny it," he said. "Come on, Josep, play the game!"

It was another rebuke and Josep simply fell back behind Lord Pedro and told himself he was going to have to rethink his entire attitude to his knight. He clearly did not expect Josep to ask the questions he had always asked him. Maybe there was something boyish about his questions or his manner. Then he realised he was no longer calling him, "jove." He suddenly understood Lord Pedro was treating him like a man and he had to behave accordingly.

The open landscape of the northern Empordà, was ablaze with the leaves of the beech trees and vines turning red in the December sun. Josep was wondering about a connection between Sanchis, the count and the king's brother, King Jaume of Majorca. He then remembered Blanca de Antillón, Ferran Sanchis' mother, and thinking she was the most beautiful woman he had seen in his life. Yet he thought Queen Constança seemed even more beautiful. Josep realised he had been staring fixedly at the Queen for some time and she now fixed him with her own gaze.

They stopped at the Castle of Recasens, the Rocaberti's ancient family seat. Perched on the highest point overlooking the pass of Portus and Panissars, it was the gateway to Languedoc and the kingdom of Majorca.

That evening, the mood was relaxed and informal. All the business of the day had been done, dinner was on the table, roast duck from the River Ter, with its subtle fishy taste, seabass and gilthead bream from Llançà, the nearest port, wild boar from the hills of the Pyrenees that surrounded them, pigs trotters and prawns, a classic Catalan dish, small noodles called fideos flavoured with squid ink, Valencian rice dishes with rabbit and vegetables straight from the Moorish cookbooks, mountain salt-cured ham in translucent slices, white wines from the Penedès and robust red wines from the king's favourite vineyards in Tarragona.

The king, looking more relaxed than Josep had ever seen him, was conversing with Viscount Jofré Rocabertí, lord of the castle, an old man but spry and witty, Dalmau, his son, Ramón Muntaner's sponsor, Guillem Moliner, the king's closest friend and Aaron Abinafia and Giovanni da Procida, the king's legal experts. The conversation had turned to politics.

"But the King of France Philippe III of the House of Capet is the most powerful monarch in Europe and has the support of Rome together with the Count of Anjou in denying the Hohenstaufen the crown of Sicily," Guillem Moliner was saying. "It would be foolish to provoke such powerful figures at the moment."

"This is the right moment," said Giovanni da Procida. "The Papacy is always occupied by supporters of the Capetian monarchs and members of families inimical to the Hohenstaufen Holy Roman Emperors. Despite the fact that King Pere is married into the Hohenstaufen, his relationship with King Philippe is cordial. He was, after all, married to King Pere's sister, Princess Isabel."

"I do not think there is much family feeling left on his side since she died," the king said.

The Queen made a special effort to engage Josep in conversation as they had dinner.

"May I help you to some food?" Josep hadn't been deliberately listening but inevitably he could hear what was being discussed. As she was effectively the topic of conversation, perhaps Queen Constança felt uncomfortable that Josep could hear what was being said. He was embarrassed.

"Your Majesty is most kind and gracious," Josep said, realising the Queen was effectively proposing to serve him. "But let me serve your Majesty first!"

"You'll go to sleep if you wait any longer," she flashed a look of liquid emerald at him which was enough to stop him in his tracks.

"Take the plate and come and sit by me. It seems that we have certain things in common. Did you not know your father?"

"No, your Majesty. My mother never talks about him but I have heard from another person he was an Andaluz knight, working in the English court in Bordeaux and that he was a good man but that is all I know, hence my name, Josep Goodman."

"Who told you these things?" asked the Queen, motioning for Josep to continue eating while tentatively prodding some fish on her plate.

"My godfather, your Majesty, Jacques de Molay." He thought at that moment she had an accent similar to Jacques's when she spoke Catalan.

"There are few men of such talent, bravery and integrity. You should feel privileged. You ought to tell him so. This is what we would do if we had our fathers with us, wouldn't we?"

"Indeed I would, your Majesty."

"I noticed you looking at me today. What were you thinking?"

"I was thinking you are probably the most beautiful woman I have ever seen," he replied.

She raised her head a little, opened her eyes wide and laughed.

"Probably, Josep? You sweet boy. I shall save the kiss I was going to give you till you are sure!"

"No, no, I meant no disrespect, your Majesty." The Queen, seeing his mounting anxiety, smiled at him, cocking her head to one side.

"Diplomacy will not be your forté Josep," she laughed.

When the entourage finally arrived at the Palace of the King of Majorca, Josep hung back to observe how the two brothers would react to each other. King Pere was as solid as a rock, affable but perfectly in control. King Jaume started blathering about not knowing exactly when to expect them, thinking they would call at Collioure, even though that was his summer residence. He seemed not to know their scouts were good and had checked and ascertained where to find him. It was almost as if he were trying to evade them, Josep thought, but he'd run out of places to run to or hadn't seen the plan through. Even though King Jaume had sworn vassalage to his brother, King Pere wanted a personal assurance from him that he was loyal to him not to the French crown. Without that guarantee, Catalunya Aragón was open to French attack.

That evening at dinner, Josep overheard King Jaume stuttering and stammering scenarios and excuses all mixed up about Montpelier.

"King Philippe occupies many of the strongholds but says he will relinquish them when the right time comes," King Jaume said.

"I will be delighted for both of us when that day arrives," King Pere said suavely, though that was the end of the conversation. So Count Roger Bernat of Foix was being used as a pawn in exchange for certain properties in the Montpellier area, Josep concluded to himself. Out of the corner of his eye Josep saw the Queen smile at him.

Philippe III of France was magnificent in his royal palace in Toulouse. King Pere's sister Isabel had been Philippe's queen but she had been dead for ten years now. The two kings called each other brother but no mention was made of her. The atmosphere was cordial but chilly. However, the other guest present at that time was King Charles of Sicily's eldest son, Charles of Salerno. When he entered the room, King Pere would not look at him and when the prince tried to engage him in conversation, the king looked the other way, or grunted a monosyllabic response and then began an animated conversation about something completely different with King Philippe. With the Prince of Salerno was Prince Philippe, the heir to the French throne. Though he was King Pere's nephew and Prince Alfons, King Pere's eldest son, was present, he preferred the company of his paternal cousin, Prince Charles of Salerno.

"Anyone would think King Pere was the king of a great and powerful country," the Prince of Salerno said at one point in earshot of Josep.

"He has ambitions far beyond his station," Prince Philippe replied.

Josep's eyes met those of a man he had not noticed among the courtiers in the background as his hood must have been up but his face was momentarily clearly visible. The serpent-like eyes of Guillaume Nogaret let escape a look so patently malevolent that the hairs stood up on the back of Josep's neck and a chill ran down his spine. He hadn't seen him since the visit Lord Pedro de Ayerbe and Josep had paid Count Roger Bernat at his castle in Foix. Certain faces are imprinted on the mind from an early age, faces deeply associated with a strong emotion. Etched into the subconscious mind, they serve as a summary of a lesson in life. In this case, "This man hates you. Fear him." This man was his lethal enemy.

As for diplomacy, no progress was made between King Pere and King Philippe in negotiations about the contested possessions in Montpellier so the Count of Foix was to return across the border in Josep's custody.

"My dear brother," King Pere was heard to sympathise with King Philippe. "I do hope you can manage to subdue and reward your troublesome clergy in Montpellier so that we can once again find a good home for Count Roger Bernat. Siurana is secure but bleak, especially in winter. He would far prefer Foix!"

"Were the Bishop of Urgell more flexible with properties on your side of the Pyrenees belonging as we feel to a vassal of the kingdom of France, we might encounter more movement on the other side of the mountains, my dear brother. But we know well what an avaricious lot the Bishops are."

They both laughed unconvincingly.

The entourage passed back into Catalunya. Though of no use to the king, the count, still considered a threat, was taken back to Siurana. Josep and Bru were instructed to take a detour with the news to Castellbò, the town belonging to the Foix family inside Catalunya.

Josep was horrified to see Bertrán de Solsona among the members of the count's entourage there to receive the message. Far from greeting each other, it was clear from the way they looked at each other that their mutual hatred had not lessened. Josep crossed back over the bridge from Castellbó towards La Seu d'Urgell and as he did so, looked back to see if he could see the Count of Foix's daughter. He could not but instead caught sight of a tall, stooped, hooded figure coming out of the castle door and surreptitiously rejoining the group. It could have been Guillaume de Nogaret.

†

Christmas was coming within a week and Josep headed back to Ribes to see his mother, Clara and Habiba.

"You won't mind if I travel with you at least, will you? Bru asked pitifully.

"How can I stop you Bru?" Josep replied as kindly as he could but it was clear between them that Bru wouldn't be welcome at Can Baró.

"I wish she would talk to me Josep, set my mind at ease, then I'd happily go my way and be parted from her for good but we were such good friends, me, her and her brothers, my cousins. We were such good friends for years before you and your mother arrived. Not that I blame you, young master, in anyway, there was a time when you were small when all went on as before but then it all changed and I don't know why."

"I'll try to intercede on your behalf," Josep said. "I'll leave you here."

"Yes, I'm fine here. There's a small hut around the hill. You can find me there."

There was much sorrow and anger when Josep made his request on behalf of Bru. Habiba immediately withdrew to her room and Josep's mother's eyes filled with unaccustomed tears.

"We don't see you for months, then you return and put his feelings before ours?" Catarina said.

It was Christmas Eve again. Clara had decided that the time had come when old ghosts had to be laid to rest. Josep of course was not there to witness Clara's meeting with Bru but couldn't help overhearing her when she returned.

"We were lovers, Catarina. Then I was like a mother to you and Josep and it didn't feel right any more. His violent rough way of life had appealed to me but it hasn't for some years," she paused, "...since we were seen one night by Josep."

"But what did he see that was so terrible? Catarina asked. "Two people loving one another?"

"Our lovemaking was physical and... vocal," she said.

"You mean there was a lot of groaning and sighing?" Catarina asked.

"Oh yes, he was like a wild animal foraging." Clara paused. "It was exciting."

"And Josep was always so fixated on Bru's prowess as a warrior." Catarina said. "Do you think he thought Bru was hurting you?" she asked as delicately as she could.

"That's exactly what I feared and how could I possibly reassure him it wasn't the case?" Clara said. "As my life developed you and Josep became more important to me than Bru. He was a connection with my brothers and father, the Crusade against Granada and all those things that happened in the reign of the last king."

They paused. This was probably the most intimate conversation Clara and Catarina had ever had and Clara was clearly beginning to feel much better about herself.

"Poor Bru," breathed Catarina, "Can't you get him back?"

"I fear it is too late," Clara said. "How can I? I told him never to return and he gave me his word he wouldn't. It would be foolish. We would both have to go back on our agreement."

"Do you believe he is innocent?"

"I have my doubts."

"But that's terrible, Clara. Whether he killed Habibas's husband or not, the poor man did nothing wrong other than fall in love with a woman he shouldn't have."

There was a moment's lull in the conversation.

"But isn't that the same as you, Catarina? Why didn't that relationship last?" Clara asked.

Josep was sure Clara didn't mean to be cruel but from the shadows his mother's silence was ominous. He peeped into the room and glimpsed his mother's face, shocked and frightened.

"Enough!" Catarina hissed. "We were talking about you and Bru."

Clara was silent. This is why she didn't enjoy talking about these things, Josep understood. It opened up the heart but it also made it vulnerable. Honesty is like water, Josep thought, open your heart and the truth seeps into every corner. Better to keep it shut.

Catarina had, by this time, withdrawn to her room, passing by the kitchen long enough to catch sight of Josep, who stood up from where he was sitting and took a step towards her as if to comfort her. But she looked bewildered and turned away from him too. From her room, Catarina darted back through the kitchen into the living room where she had been talking to Clara.

"Not a word of this shall you breathe to Josep, do I make myself understood?" she said, her voice as low as she possibly could. There was a crackle of burning wood in the hearth. Apart from that, total silence.

Josep couldn't fathom it at all. So Clara and Bru had been lovers but it did not mean much to him. He knew of cousins marrying. Yet what had been said between Clara and Catarina was to remain a mystery to Josep for the rest of Bru's life and assumed gravitas through silence. All this talking had achieved little, Josep concluded. People were prepared to go only so far. There always seemed to be a limit beyond which problems began.

"If I've lost Bru because you two can't have a simple conversation, I won't forgive you!" he shouted at his mother the following day.

"Josep, it's not like that!" Clara said. "You're still too young to..."

"Too young to what?" Josep replied. "Too young to feel sad and lonely and miss friends and family? It's not as if I have a lot. I work with Bru and he's like an uncle to me, whatever he may have been for you..."

Clara's eyes widened and the colour drained from her face.

"Get out of my house! How dare you talk to me like that. Go on! Get out!" she whispered hoarsely.

Catarina then came flying at Clara like a cat in water.

"You leave him alone, he's done nothing wrong, where else is he to go?"

Then Habiba rushed between them from her room, screaming in Mozarabe. The three women froze, breathing heavily, all in tears. Josep took a look at them, turned and left.

"Merry Christmas! I shall be in Tortosa." He murmured as he went out of the door.

"Josep, Josep! Come back! Josep, darling, please don't go like this!" His mother pleaded. But he had already sprung onto his horse and was gone, cantering down the path. It was not difficult to find Bru.

"Come on, Bru, we've always had each other. I'm happy to be with you," Josep said.

Bru's face, so unusually sullen for him, then brightened like a torch had been held to it.

"Are you, young master? Well, well, I am glad to hear that! I am happy to be with you, too!"

"Let's head down to Tortosa." Josep said. "Pere de Queralt and his party will be there in a few days."

It was magnificent countryside they were riding through. The low hills and sandy beaches of the Garraf gave way to the dramatic cliffs around Tarragona, a sheer drop down to the sea, which looked all the lovelier seen from a higher elevation. The pine forest here was dense and swept from the high hills down to the cliffs in thick swathes of green of different shades, offsetting the deep blue of the Mediterranean.

CHAPTER 12 THE ROAD TO TORTOSA

All around them on the road to Tortosa a multitude seemed to be travelling towards Tortosa, very few coming away from it. As Josep had seen further north some weeks before, farmers were busy transporting as much as they could. Nobody knew exactly why, either. In fact, they had been given different instructions depending on where they were. In the north, to head to Roses; or further down the coast on the Maresme to Sant Pol; or Barcelona; or south of Barcelona to Tortosa. Their produce would be brought at above average prices and as this was a royal decree, everyone scrambled, not only out of patriotism to King Pere but also on account of this great opportunity for themselves.

Farmers and farm workers streamed along the road driving flocks of sheep, goats and herds of cows before them and the air was loud with their cries, shouts and whistles and the animals' plaintive responses to a bewildering variety of calls and noises. Weaker animals were strapped to oxen-drawn carts or had their throats cut at the side of the road and were then loaded up, their blood left to drip from where they lay on the carts. The blood stained the dusty road, mingling with the droppings. The road seemed like a huge, crawling animal inching along through the glorious low hills on either side of the mighty Ebre River.

Stray animals wandered off the road to drink at the riverside, to be bundled up by the son or daughter of the farmer and brought back to the main road. Other animals lost their footing in the slippery mud next to the river or mistook the marshy land and thick reeds for solid ground and became embroiled in the shallow water, hooves sinking quickly into the river silt and becoming entwined in the reeds. By the riverside, bloated carcasses of animals lay rotting and everywhere there was the slow flapping of crows and majestic buzzards. Even the occasional vulture stooped surreptitiously to dine on a gash in the flesh of the dead animals.

"Looks like a monk helping himself to too much altar wine!" observed Bru sharply. It was true. The vulture had a bald head and a rough of feathers around the neck that together looked like a monk's tonsure.

"I'm tired of this noise and chaos," said Josep.

"We may be able to get off the road at Mora and take a boat down if you'd like that, though you'll have to pay for it as I don't have any money on me, not a cent to my name again," said Bru.

The river was streaming with boats of all sizes and descriptions. Gavarres, or barges, moved sluggishly, like driftwood in the water obeying more the general currents than the tillerman with his long-handled right-angled rudder. Some transported sacks of grain, cheese, legs of ham, and sat low in the water. Others were used to carry the livestock. The nervous cattle and flocks, horses, mules and donkeys, kept their heads up and rigidly looked forward as if willing the direction to be followed and complaining noisily when the barge drifted left or right and they had to adjust their footing. Tartanes, faster boats, with lateen sails and clinkers for several sets of oars, sped down or across the river. A steady stream of traffic was coming from upriver and passing the little jetty where Josep and Bru found themselves and Josep asked where they were coming from.

"Everything comes from Mequinensa," replied a boatman, eager to strike up a conversation if it meant two fares. "You've got goods arriving from the forests of the Aragonese Pyrenees by way of Monzón on the River Cinca."

"The Ebre swallows up the Noguera Ribagorçana at Fraga, doesn't it?" said Josep.

"Exactly, jove. Then from the Catalan Pyrenees, you've got the Noguera Pallaresa meeting the Segra at Balaguer. The two rivers that result, the Cinca and the Segre, both flow south of Lleida and thunder into the Ebre at Mequinensa. It's a world of water up there."

Josep was delighted. He loved the idea the waterways were so extensive and interlinked. For a moment, he realized he hadn't had his drowning dreams now for some time.

"Have they always used the Ebre as another road to the sea?" Josep asked fascinated.

"That is the way it has always been, for generations in my family, at least. You have to pay a good amount for the transport," he said, eyeing the two travellers again. "But there are fewer brigands on the waterways. The river is much quieter and there are normally fewer obstacles."

"You should see the Tortosa road," said Josep.

"Yes, they tell me it's busy. Everyone round here is heading there. King Pere has ordered twenty or so galleys to be built and the amount of wood they need is enormous. They're cutting down half the forest in the Aragón and Catalan Pyrenees. Can I take you anywhere?" the boatman asked, finally coming to the point.

"To Tortosa, I suppose!" Josep laughed.

"Will your servant be travelling with you, sir?" the boatman asked, referring to Bru. "I'm not his servant but a free soldier in the employ of the king with the right to call myself an almogaver!" Bru growled back.

"Peace to you, sir. I meant no offence, sir!" the boat man said quickly in alarm. "You'll be in good company where you're headed. They say there's already a camp of one or two thousand in the Raval outside Tortosa. They've got Pere de Queralt and Eiximen d'Arenós to command them. They say that Count Arnau Roger of Pallars is expected any day."

"Atoning for his misdemeanors in the siege of Balaguer, no doubt," replied Josep.

"They say like a man re-baptised in the faith, never a more loyal subject to the king," said the boatman.

"May God bless and preserve him and all who serve him," said Bru, calm again. The boat man mopped his brow. He had been unnerved by Bru. Money changed hands and Josep and Bru boarded a fast lleny while their horses were led onto a small barge or bot.

They left the tumult of the quayside of Mora behind them. Its great castle disappeared from view as the broad Ebre River looped back to the west and the distances between the various vessels grew and Josep and Bru scudded along in relative peace and quiet for some time.

"Word has it, all sorts of mishaps and accidents have been occurring further north," said the boatman. "Carts laden with hay with split wheels and shattered axles and no apparent reason for it at all."

"I've seen such things near Lleida," said Josep.

"Not that it makes that much difference, the king pays for everything at a good price and the longer the farmer's on the road, the higher the price he can demand and the king's men pay it but it's all being stockpiled at the harbours under a strict guard," the boat man explained.

"I guess there are some who would like to get their hands on it to sell for their own profit," said Josep.

"Indeed, young sir, well said, that may well be. But the price rises don't affect everyone equally. If you are well-off, a couple of pennies per pound extra daily is neither here nor there. But if you're living from hand to mouth, it can make a difference over a week between eating seven days a week and going hungry for a day, so there are hungry people out there desperate to get their hands on all that stockpiled food."

Josep wondered at this and realised he'd rarely been in a situation of such need in his life. He imagined how it must be not to know from where your next meal is to come and what that kind of desperation could force you to do.

"There's been a lot of unrest in Barcelona, for example," the boat man continued. "That's where there's been the most mishaps."

"I suppose the problem is worst there because it has the most people and therefore more hungry mouths to feed than most places, " said Josep.

"The king does his best to maintain a supply for the needy but there's always a limit and someone's always left empty-handed and underfed," he said.

Josep imagined the filthy desperate faces in the glow of torchlight waiting and restless, light-headed with hunger, ready to go to any lengths in order to eat.

"You need to have a strong garrison to protect a city in those cases," the boatman said and Josep nodded grimly.

The river was beautiful all the way down from Mora d'Ebre, dotted with islets on which stalks, cranes and flamingos fed in flocks. The gently undulating valley was lined on both sides of the river with reeds tipped with their sheaf-like heads the size and shape of spades waving in the breeze. Beyond that, there were outcrops of holm oak and pine.

Coming round a bend in the river, the currents swept them more quickly than usual and the boat man went silent as he concentrated on his task.

"A good deal deeper here. It takes a bit of work to hold the course," he said, pointing the boat south downstream. The water changed colour from light brown to black and the foam created by the craft glittered around the prow all the whiter for the contrast. On either side of their vessel, the mighty river valley now rose to form cliffs, the height of cathedral towers. The mountain slopes were dotted with giant beech trees and cypresses and everywhere you looked there was a craggy fastness where the great birds of prey could make their eyries. On the west bank, crowning a high cliff with views north and south over the river stood a mighty castle, its stones hewn from the rock around it, glowing yellow in the heat of midday.

"That's Miravet!" Bru shouted, "the great Templar castle."

The Beausant, the red cross on the white background of the Templar order was flying. Next to it was the flag of St George, the Patron Saint of Catalunya and next to that, the vertical red-and gold-stripes of Catalunya Aragón, the Royal Ensign, or Senyera.
"Either the king or the princes are here, then," concluded Josep.
"It wouldn't surprise me," the boatman said. "Yesterday they were flying the Senyera at Mora."

Beyond the rocky summit of the castle of Miravet, they passed another dramatic bend in the river. Majestic beeches and oaks, pines, cypresses and yew trees, all pressed in on one another down the slopes, covering the mountain sides with an indescribable depth and variety of shades and hues of green.

The almogaver camp was located about a mile upriver from the town of Tortosa and La Suda, the beautiful Moorish castle which stands above the city. You could smell the camp before you could see it. For a start, it was vast and as Josep discovered as he explored later, it was bound by small rivulets and sandbanks. He had the impression that the almogavers would have spread out endlessly unless contained in some way. The stench of human waste and rotting food was awful. There was one enormous trench in full view of everyone to the right-hand side, where everyone went to relieve themselves. This waste was washed away by a stream but its action was sluggish and the filth was beyond description. Josep decided he and Bru would stay as far away from that part of the camp as possible.

"But it's the most convenient side, young Master!" argued Bru. We'll be next to the camp entrance if we stay there."

"I couldn't survive even a day there, Bru!" Josep shouted through his hand attempting to keep the contagion from his mouth and nose.

"Oh, young Master, you're going to have to toughen up. It gets worse than this, believe me."

Apart from this waste channel, there was no order to the camp. The tents were pitched wherever it suited their owners so there was little order or convenience as the occupants scrambled in and out knocking into each other.

No privacy existed and the general hubbub of several thousand voices was often punctuated by the shouts of the women who accompanied their men on campaign. The infants that abounded in the camps terrorised each other with games involving running and catching each other, kicking up endless dust and their squealing only added to the din. Among the detritus of discarded food, shattered pottery and unidentifiable bones was all the waste produced by the various animals that were kept in domestication by the almogaver families. Dogs were highly prized. Cats were occasionally kept by women for company. Hens in wooden cages provided meat and eggs.

Better organised families to the edge of the camp had a goat or cow and a few families a transportable smallholding, complete with several animals and a donkey. These almogaver families, generally older with several adolescent children were not interfered with, Josep noticed. The tents of these people were more robust and easy to take down and stow on the back of the donkey. Josep could imagine what an indefatigable force such a family could muster if required to protect its own. Mislaid items of value were returned. No thanks were given except for a tight smile and raised eyebrows in recognition that the owner had been careless.

However, for all the outward degradation, the evident uncouthness, the foul language, the insanitary conditions, the amoral cruelty and toughness, it was a self-regulating, vibrant community, a social phenomenon. Josep didn't care to think what would happen to an outsider who unwittingly broke the rules that bound the camp. He unconsciously quickened his step to get back to his own tent, deliberately as far from the entrance as possible. In so doing, he scattered a swarm of flies feasting on an unidentifiable mound of filth that he carefully sidestepped.

The following day, an hour-long boat trip down the Ebre from Tortosa took them to Port Fangós, the river estuary of the Ebre. At this time of the year, it was cool and peaceful around here. You could see for miles from atop any building as it was flat as far as the eye could see, a land of rice fields and rivulets. Flamingos in their thousands packed together in the ponds and lakes that the mighty Ebre created, as pink as the prawns they feasted on. It was extraordinarily peaceful and there was an air of wholesomeness and robust good health here.

That did not change the fact that the air was ringing with the rhythmic pounding of hammers on nails and securing bolts as carpenters and shipwrights worked together from dawn till after dusk painstakingly assembling what was the cutting edge of technology and warfare at the time: the galley. These huge structures were fifty metres long, had three decks, a castle at the front and rear and benches for thirty oars on both sides on each deck. This amounted to one hundred and eighty oarsmen per galley, plus the sixty almogavers that always accompanied the rowers and the twenty knights that always accompanied that number of almogavers at a ratio of three to one. Then there was the crew consisting of a Captain and Boatswain and the twenty sailors to put up, trim and take down its lateen mainsail and foresail. There were as many as three hundred souls on each galley, therefore, and the king had ordered twenty such galleys to be built and twenty teams were duly working on each ship. Each one was lined up carefully along the north-east facing beach of the Delta del Ebre occupying an area of a hundred metres of beach and had up to a hundred carpenters, carpenters' mates, apprentices and fitters working on it. A foreman and shipwright, answerable to the master Shipwright, who in turn was answerable to the chief engineer. Each team was like a hamlet with tents set up neatly next to the woodpile of ash and oak logs floated down from the length and breadth of the king's lands on the rivers that flowed into the Ebre. It was so unlike the almogavers camp; the air smelt of fish, woodfire and pine resin. It took Josep several hours to walk from one end of the shipyard to the other and he was struck by the wondrous order and efficiency of the teams at their task, not to mention his awe at the sight of these powerful sleek seagoing battering rams that rose from keel to top deck to a height of twenty metres or more. The air was full of the sound of sawing and shouted instructions marking a seriousness and intentness that Josep had not seen before. These were technicians working on the most advanced equipment west of Constantinople and they were taking pride in their Royal commission.

In the camp, Bru was pressed into service training the almogavers. Without frequent vigourous exercise, they were a danger to everyone: themselves, each other and all around them. Bru took them beyond the edge of the town where the algaroba or carob trees began growing in profusion and practised climbing and ambush techniques. There was no such thing as pain or physical discomfort to an almogaver and they were easily able to grapple the soft rubbery trunks of the algaroba trees and scramble into their upper branches. The idea was that they stayed up in the trees till told to jump down but if they fell before the order, which normally happened because a branch snapped under their weight, they plummeted five metres, sometimes more, and thought nothing of it. They picked themselves up, staggered a little if concussed then laughed or swore, according to their nature and the next moment, leapt back up into the tree. Bru told Josep that the only way to stop an almogaver was to cut his head off and then he'd still come at you but as he could no longer see you, you were safe. It made Josep laugh in nervous disbelief because these men seemed indestructible.

Days turned into weeks and Josep took messages on horseback to the shipyards, Les Drassanes de Tortosa as they were called, which stretched either side of the estuary at the Delta del Ebre between the beach north of Sant Jaume d'Envejà and Alfaca, a distance of about seven miles in total.

Josep became known to the Chief Engineer and Master Shipwright and several of the Shipwrights in charge of their own galleys. Some of the yards were more difficult to get to behind thick sabina bushes or high sandbanks and the Shipwrights were less communicative and the whole operation more secretive. There was a general air of secrecy. Everyone for miles around knew serious shipbuilding was happening but nobody knew anything more than that.

One evening a troubadour came to the almogaver camp at Tortosa and spent several hours singing songs about the good King Pere making an enormous fishing fleet that would so scare the fish into submission that they would swim peacefully into the nets. This caused much amusement when the almogavers realised the fishermen represented them. Another song was about a messenger from the papal legate who came in his best clothes to the king in Barcelona to ask what he intended to do with all these galleys. The king and the legate met on a galley being prepared at the Reals Drassanes de Barcelona and, so the story goes, when asked about where the scaffolding was for urgent repairs to Barcelona Cathedral, the king replied "Your worship is standing on it!" This dismissive quip on the part of the king inspired a song. The taverns rang to the singing of the shipbuilders, who knew the chorus.

So tarry not
Nor waste our time
We've a fleet of galleys
A Royal Line

and we'll do with it
What we think best
Our greetings to His Holiness!

Everyone was singing it in the camp too or whistling or humming the tune. It had become like an anthem. There were other songs all with the same theme, each one greeted with such enthusiasm and uproarious laughter that you would think the camp was about to erupt. These savage truculent guerilla fighters, filthy ragged and shaggy-haired were splitting their sides at these refined couplets that mocked the great and mighty, prelates, kings and the pope himself. Nobody was spared the satire and King Pere always came out on top. Yet still nobody knew what the king intended to do with his brand-new fleet of galleys that was depleting the royal coffers and oak forests and had the whole of the western Mediterranean in a state of trepidation.

CHAPTER 13 THE HAFSID DELEGATION

1282

The freezing mornings of February when the rice fields stood hard-ridged and glittering in the early morning frost endowed the hills around the Delta de l'Ebre with a limpid clarity that delighted the eye despite the freezing wind.

Josep was roughly wakened by Bru one such morning.

"Josep, it's your Lord Pedro to see you," was all he said.

As Josep stumbled out of the tent, rubbing his eyes, Lord Pedro de Ayerbe was awaiting him on his fine stallion, both horse and rider sending tendrils of warm air into the blue of the freezing crystal sky. Josep squinted up.

"Josep, come with me immediately!"

"My lord, I am barely dressed. Where are we going?"

"There's no time to tell you. Come."

Bru, attentive to Josep as always, had his horse to hand already and as soon as Josep had dressed and mounted his horse, threw up his warmest padded doublet and a chunk of bread against the cold. As the road wound out of Tortosa, Lord Pedro explained that they were to meet Pere de Queralt at Miravet Castle and make haste to Barcelona. They made their way up the Ebre River and were met at the gates of the mighty hill top castle by Ramón Saguardia, the Provincial Lieutenant of the Order of the Temple and commander of the castle.

"Enjoy a simple lunch inside," he said and they were taken through the five-metre-thick rock and sandstone walls into a long thin chamber on the second floor up a flight of wooden steps. The food was roast beef and bread and they drank strong red wine from the area. From up here, Josep could see through the different arrow slits with which the austere chamber was illuminated up and down the sweep and curves of the Ebre River and north over brows of tree-clad hills into the distance.

"Your patron Jacques de Molay admired this view," Saguardia said and sat next to Josep handing him a note.

"Please deliver this to the Temple headquarters in Barcelona and bring back any message they may have for me," he said.

"The king honours us by including us in his plans," Josep heard Pere de Queralt say.

"Whatever they may be!" someone replied, to which there was laughter.

"Let that be especially secret to all who serve King Philippe of France," said Lord Pedro.

"Rumour has it his agents have spread again through the kingdom causing accidents with provisions heading from the countryside to the coast," Saguardia said.

"That's what I…" Josep started to speak only to be silenced by a stern look from Lord Pedro.

"Carts overturned, wheels inexplicably smashed, everything done to maximise inconvenience and done in the maximum secrecy. They have apprehended one agent in Barcelona," Saguardia said.

"So that's what I kept seeing on the road. All that damage was deliberately caused," Josep thought but said nothing.

Lunch finished, Ramón Saguardia courteously but stiffly bade them farewell.

"Your horses have been fed and watered and the friars have packed provisions for you lest you must spend a night on the open road. The king expects you in two days' time."

One of the horses started to skitter and caused the other to do the same. Saguardia took the reigns of the first horse in his hand and pulled sharply down, uttering an incomprehensible word. His stiff form moved only as much as necessary and his words were as sparse as his castle was unyielding and the horse quietened immediately.

"Go with God and God speed you. You will always be welcome here!" Saguardia said as Josep and Lord Pedro left. Josep would remember those words.

They clattered down the steep cobbled castle approach and shortly were on the open road once again.

There was evidence of damage, disarray and destruction all around all the way from Miravet to Vilafranca. Whoever was causing this was not one or two but a whole company of agents who seemed to be everywhere. Where were they hiding? Where did they stay at night? How did they disguise themselves? They must be fluent in Catalan, Josep thought. The note was safely in his pocket. He kept patting it to check it was there.

They stayed the night at an inn near San Miquel d'Olerdola as they didn't want to stray too far from Vilafranca-Barcelona Road and set off early in the morning in bright sunshine. They passed frosty vineyards that covered the rolling open country of the plain of Penedès, the view of Montserrat bright and sharp ahead of them and made good time. They passed through the thick walls of Barcelona at the Porta dels Framenors in the early afternoon. They were to meet the king at the Reals Drassanes, the Royal Shipyards, built into the mighty walls at Porta Santa Madrona, next to the port.

It was Good Friday, the twenty-eighth of March, 1282. They attended the service in the Monastery of the Framenors next to the Drassanes at the third hour of the afternoon. Josep always disliked this as it was so solemn containing no Eucharist in commemoration of the crucifixion. Lord Pedro then immediately went to the Drassanes and into conference with the king who awaited him there. Meanwhile, Josep sat alone in the upper chambers of the vast, empty, echoing building, counting the bricks out of boredom in the intricate arches and tracing the lines of the vaults in the roof. He had had nothing to eat since early that morning as he hadn't had time when the horses were stabled to unpack the provisions.

It was all he could do to stay still. He was itching to know the contents of the note that he had been handed by Saguardia in Miravet. Why had he given it to him? Why had he mentioned Jacques de Molay to him? He knew he was a severe man, not given to small talk. Did the note he bore refer to Jacques? He could barely contain himself. It had been several years since he had had any communication with Jacques and he numbered him among the people he felt he was losing from his childhood. He had good memories of him connected with his boyhood, a trip to Sitges, his first days at Cavallers. He had been there to install him. He realised he thought of him as a father. The thought excited and frustrated him. He wanted to go and deliver his note, late though it was.

He couldn't contain himself any longer and stood up and started walking down to the ground floor of the shipyard. He started rehearsing excuses in his mind in case he was intercepted by his knight about tiredness or stomach cramp. The gnawing hunger he felt combined with the stench of the Caganell, the nearby city cesspit, was starting to make him feel nauseous. It was surprising people didn't get ill from the odour, he thought. He had to go. He could be back within the hour.

The shipyard was eerie at this time of the night. Hulks of nearly finished galleys lay in neat lines, disappearing into the distance, like sleeping giants lying on their sides. Nobody was around. Then he glimpsed something in the gloom. What looked like two figures crouching were hovering weirdly in the mid-distance. Josep blinked and realised he could see a lleny drawing near the dock of the Royal Drasssanes. The vessel was coming in at a strange angle as if approaching from Montjuic. The shipyard wall to Josep's left cast long shadows over the seafront at this point. No one the other side of the wall could possibly see the boat as it docked and the view from the mountain of Montjuic was obscured by the dense canopy of trees that cascaded down the hill. Besides, it was the night of Good Friday and the streets were empty.

A boat bearing two figures in North African dress was breaking into the Drassanes and he was the only person who could see it. He stifled the urge to shout as suddenly the figures of the king, Lord Pedro de Ayerbe and an older man appeared. They proceeded to tie the boat up and helped the two figures in the boat disembark. As his eyes grew accustomed to the light, Josep recognised the older man as Giovanni da Procida, whom he had first met years ago when organising the king's business in Aragón after the Ferran Sanchis incident and again the previous December accompanying the king to France. He didn't seem to age. To Josep who had an excellent memory for faces the strangeness of the situation struck him anew and he felt exposed and vulnerable. The king, Lord Pedro and Giovanni da Procida must have made their way down from the upper chamber outside which Josep had been sitting via another passage on the other side.

He felt alarm again at the precariousness of his situation. What he was watching was not for his eyes at all yet what could he do? Lord Pedro was so stern with him these days he could barely have explained away his absence from outside the chamber let alone account for his presence here at this most secret of meetings. He ducked under the rear of a galley between the uprights of the scaffolding. The Drassanes were so cavernous and high-ceilinged that echoes carried easily. There was no sound but the gentle lap of seawater, no light but the moonlight filtered through the palms in front of the north-east wall of the shipyard. Josep could hear every word.

"Bugron as we call him, your Majesty, or Ibn al Wazir, Lord of Constantine, wishes to come over to your Majesty," Giovanni da Procida was saying, translating for the two Moorish travellers who were dressed in the heavy dark one-piece over-garments worn in everyday life in North Africa.

"He is displeased with having to pay tribute to Charles of Anjou and wishes to consult with you about becoming a Christian and requests the Christian militia to protect him from his brother Mirabusecri, or as we call him, Abu Favis Ben Ibrahim, King of Bougie. They are the sons of Ibn Hasan, whom we call Miraboaps, the younger brother of the King of Tunis, King Ibrahim Abu Ishak, Mirabusac. We restored the king to his throne and he has paid us tribute since 1279," Procida continued.

The king turned to Giovanni da Procida, deferentially bowing in the direction of the two diplomats.

"Ask them if King Mirabusac of Tunis knows anything of these plans," he said.

Giovanni da Procida translated easily into the Tunisian language the two ambassadors spoke. One replied, then the other and they looked shocked. Giovanni da Procida translated.

"They remind you my Lord that this was our idea and that they have arrived from Collo, the port of Constantine, having received our proposal from our agents there. If there is a breach of secrecy, it is on our side. There has not been time for them to speak to anyone but Bugron, who would hardly be likely to divulge this secret and they have been at sea for the past three days since then."

The king's countenance was more mobile than usual. A look of relief crossed his face.

"Good, good!" said King Pere, nodding deeply, "You are most welcome here. I wish to escort you to your chamber where you will find every comfort at your disposal."

Giovanni da Procida translated, the two ambassadors visibly relaxed and there was even a flicker of a smile as they shook hands with the king, exchanged courtesies and made gestures which were clearly meant to show trust and gratitude.

The passage the party of three had used was now revealed to Josep. An unobtrusive wooden door Josep had not noticed in the wall opposite closed as Lord Pedro de Ayerbe made his way through it, as the last of the party of five to leave the workshop floor of the Royal Drassanes. Josep sprang to his feet, his heart in his mouth and scrambled the short distance across the shipyard floor and back up the stairs to the front of the chamber where he had been posted and resumed his position, panting with exertion, fear and exhilaration. By the time he heard any sound from the other side of the door he had had ample time to compose himself. It was impossible for Josep to see where he had been on the lower floor, as the stairs up which he had fled turned one hundred and eighty degrees thus obscuring any sight or sound. A clock struck midnight when Lord Pedro finally emerged.

"Young Josep, you are a stalwart lad! I imagined you would be asleep. Upon my word, you are made of strong stuff! Well done!" he laughed. Lord Pedro was so rarely complimentary to Josep these days that Josep smiled at him blearily. It was good to be praised and it was true: he had been there for hours and was exhausted and hungry.

"Let's get back. There's no urgent business to do till tomorrow midday," Lord Pedro said. He and Josep left via the main entrance. They had every reason to be in the Drassanes if they were on official business and within minutes they were passing through the inner city gate of Framenors. Their hostel was behind an enormous wooden door up a flight of well-polished marble stairs and Josep's chamber had views over the Passeig Maritim. In the meantime, the saddle bags had been placed on the table in their room and they feasted on the provisions the friars of Miravet had packed for them. Overcome with fatigue the knight and page fell into a deep sleep that lasted the whole night.

It was March the twenty-ninth, a day before Josep's twentieth birthday. Lord Pedro de Ayerbe had given Josep the next two days off so that Josep could celebrate his birthday properly but regretted he would not be able to stay until then. When Josep awoke it was already late morning. Lord Pedro was not around but had left a note for Josep wishing him a happy birthday in advance along with a copy of the latest songs they were singing in the taverns. He was delighted.

It was also Easter Saturday. Josep threw open his windows in his bedroom and had a spectacular view over the entire harbour from the Monastery of the Famenors and the Convent of Santa Madrona on his right to the Consolat de Mar and La Llotja on his left and the entire seafront between the two sets of buildings.

The shallow beach-lined harbour was teeming with life and the roar that came from it as he opened the shutters was deafening. The boats were harboured a good distance from the shore where it was deep enough for them not to get grounded and were connected with the shore via wooden jetties to which the ships and boats were tied at right angles. To his right, opposite Drassanes there were five newly finished galleys being tarred and having their sails fitted to their two masts. Ahead of him, there were transport vessels, tarrides, being loaded with livestock and horses. Smaller faster llenys darted around the harbour carrying smaller loads and galeres or lay at anchor the length and breadth of the harbour. The wind was fresh in their dart-shaped downward-pointing latine sails. Josep was excited about fulfilling his mission of delivering his note from Ramón Saguardia to the Headquarters of the Order of the Temple.

He slipped out into Carrer Carme and asked directions to Carrer dels Templars. He walked up Carrer Avinyó and then turned right and headed towards Plaça de Sant Jaume. The smell of freshly baked bread was irresistible and he had a delicious breakfast of hot bread and warm fresh milk served by a dairy maid on Plaça Sant Jaume. Street vendors went to and fro, merchants passed huddled in secretive discussion, carters and barrelmen clattered across the square, ladies of rank passed by in luxurious carriages. All life was represented here. He felt elated. Skirting round the Palau Real Menor on Plaça de Sant Miquel, he got onto Carrer dels Templars and on finding the cross pattée hewn into the stonework which announced all Templar possessions, next to an enormous wooden door, he found the heavy pewter knocker and let it fall and heard the thud reverberate cavernously through the entrance and courtyard of the Templar headquarters.

He was courteously escorted up the plain but spotless stone steps to an enormous vaulted room with views onto the plaça below and was shortly received by the master of Catalunya and Aragón, Pedro de Moncada. He had the same dignified bearing as all the senior Templar commanders Josep had known: sinewy, trim and athletic-looking, bearded but short-haired and despite his years, as he was a man approaching sixty and so older by twenty years than Berenguer de Belvís and Ramón de Saguardia, commanding in his minimal movements.

"I have heard you are twenty tomorrow, young man!" he began, grasping Josep's hand firmly and smiling faintly.

"Yes, Master," Josep replied.

"But I have heard mixed things about you from a variety of sources. Berenguer de Belvís tells me you are impetuous and foolhardy and apt to make enemies."

"My lord, Lord Belvís knows me well, but refers to events that happened when I was little more than a child five years ago," Josep countered as politely as he could. He couldn't believe he was being reprimanded.

"Do you mean to say that you are maturing well, like a good wine?" asked Moncada, with a twinkle in his eye. "Be seated. Let us have a glass of Tarragona red wine. Your patron, Jacques de Molay, is partial to it."

They tasted the wine. "I hope I have matured as well as this wine," Josep ventured, hoping to amuse the old soldier monk and take the chill out of the first minutes of their meeting.

"This is still a young wine and it will need attention to ensure its promise is fulfilled. It would be best if some of its potential could be used to develop a rounder personality, a deeper character, otherwise it could give someone a sore head."

"Yes, my lord," Josep agreed, noting inwardly he was being lectured and was not to respond.

"Your work in Lleida, Siurana and Tortosa has been noted, however. It seems your irritation and boredom with your knight Lord Pedro de Ayerbe decreases the longer you spend away from him. He has always tried to set a good example and fulfil the role of the father for you."

Josep felt himself flush, he was not sure if it was anger or frustration, but he felt embarrassed. He didn't want to be disloyal to his knight but he wanted to defend himself, too.

"You see, young man, how close to the surface you allow your feelings to be?" Moncada said quietly, looking calmly at Josep. "You might have known I would mention these things as Berenguer de Belvís did. You are still hot-headed and easily provoked. Is it pride or vanity?"

"I respect my knight enormously," Josep managed to utter.

"That is a good response Josep," the master said. "Don't be so easily roused to anger.

Am I not on your side? What is it that pricks you so within?"

Josep knew what it was but felt it more circumspect to treat Moncada's last question as rhetorical. He put his hand inside his tunic, reminding himself he was here to deliver a letter. Moncada then produced a letter for Josep, too.

Moncada invited Josep to stay but Josep could not control his urge to flee. Once outside, he saw the letter was not addressed to Saguardia but to himself. He tore it open.

"Malta, February, 1282.

My dear Josep

Happy birthday. I hope this finds you around the thirtieth of March. I have been away so long I hope you will not resent my wish to see you when I shortly arrive in Barcelona. I have heard that matters in Ribes need some attention. I feel responsible. I hope we can meet.

Your patron,

Jacques de Molay"

He had to read the letter several times to check there was no hidden meaning. Nevertheless, he was delighted his patron had remembered him on his birthday. That night, Josep and his knight were invited to dine at the court the king had called to be celebrated in Barcelona at his official residence, the Palau Real Major, the larger of the two palaces in the centre of Barcelona. The court coincided with the traditional Easter celebrations that would officially begin at midnight on Sunday, the thirtieth of March, Easter Sunday.

"His Majesty will be well advised to accede to the demands of the various collectives represented today," Giovanni da Procida was saying to Lord Pedro loud enough for Josep to overhear. He shot Josep a wary glance, which Josep pretended not to notice. Giovanni da Procida shifted uncomfortably and Lord Pedro leaned his head a little closer. Josep heard him mention "La Busca" or the lower orders and "La Biga" the bourgeoisie.

"But he'll have to be most careful if he wants stability with the counts, barons and lords in Catalunya" said Giovanni da Procida. "His frontier with Navarra is always problematic, we can't even trust his relatives," he said referring to Juan Núñez de Lara, Lord of Albarracín, related by marriage to Jaume de Xèrica, Pedro de Ayerbe's half-brother.

"If Navarra should go over to the French, Albarracín will become the new border!"

Giovanni da Procida said.

"There is little my brother Jaume de Xèrica can do to influence things, that is the truth of it," Lord Pedro said. "I've spent much of my military life patrolling those northern and western borders and I have capable people garrisoned all over in case of an incursion," Lord Pedro said. "Josep has joined me on many of these trips, haven't you, Josep?"

Josep nodded, eager to be involved and ignoring the notion he wasn't supposed to be listening.

"I know the roads, paths, horse trails and passes of Navarra and Aragón as well as anyone I know, my lord, on account of having had the privilege to serve with you," he said.

"Well said," whispered the old Neapolitan, Giovanni da Procida, in his husky accented Catalan.

"I'm sure there will be many uses for such skills in time to come. Where would you like to accompany your king?"

"Anywhere his Majesty can use me," Josep said to laughter and murmurs of approval from the two old soldiers next to him and those around who had happened to overhear him.

"But I should especially like to go overseas!" Josep finished. There was a momentary pause and a guarded exchange of glances between Lord Pedro and Giovanni da Procida.

"Josep has been working in Tortosa recently," Lord Pedro put in, "and has been a valuable messenger between the shipbuilding crews and the king's representatives in Port Fangós."

"Excellent, excellent!" said Giovanni da Procida visibly making a mental note of the information, "I am sure there will be plenty for you to do shortly," he said, eyeing Josep meaningfully.

The main business of the day was receiving Sancho el Bravo, King of Castilla who had come to court offering help in any sea mission the king might have. However, rumour had it he was more interested in checking that the king didn't have designs on Castilla. The Queen was keen for her sons Alfons and Jaume to entertain the two Cerda brothers, Ferran, twelve, and his brother Alfons, seven, who had come from their safe house in Xàtiva, south Valencia, "to meet their uncle." So long as King Pere had the true heir to the throne of Castilla, Sancho would protect Catalunya Aragón's interests.

Josep's head span as he was told this rather rapidly by Crown Prince Alfons, also Josep's age and Josep readily agreed to help look after the two younger lads.

"I'm grateful to you for that," Prince Alfons said. "It has allowed my mother to absent herself and avoid meeting the man who has actually brought them here." Josep felt again that he was out of his depth.

"Who has brought them here your Highness?" he asked. Prince Alfons looked at him in surprise before he replied.

"Jaume Pere de Sogorb," he answered.

"Your Highness, please forgive my ignorance but I do not know who he is," Josep said.

"I mean to say before the king met my mother, he was in love with a girl called Maria and Jaume Pere was the result. Four years later, he married my mother. It hurts her to speak about or to the king's love child."

Josep nodded but inwardly admired the young prince's resilience and thought it was similar to his own situation. Nobody wanted to talk to him about the fact he was a "love child" himself.

"At least he knows who his father is! I wish I knew, especially around my birthday!" Josep thought to himself.

There was magnificent feasting during the afternoon and as the evening came on one final ceremony was performed. Jaume Pere de Sogorb was vested admiral and commanded to name the three vice admirals. He named Ramón Marquet, Berenguer de Mallol and Roger de Llúria and everyone marvelled at what good hands their navy was in. History would prove them right.

The second announcement was that all ships were to assemble at Port Fangós on May the first no matter where they were harboured or presently being built. It was extraordinary to Josep to see a man of his own age, as Jaume Pere was, commanding men twice his age.

"He trusts his family," Josep thought to himself. "Keep your enemies close and your family even closer!"

CHAPTER 14 THE SICILIAN VESPERS

Lord Pedro de Ayerbe and Josep were invited to the Palau Real Major for the Easter Sunday and Monday festivities, Easter Monday or La Mona. No sooner were they ushered through the castle doors into the Great Hall than who should come out of the Royal Chapel of Sant Agatha but Jacques de Molay himself. He and Josep collided with each other and Josep was knocked to the floor, banging his nose accidentally in the process. It started to bleed profusely and he was so surprised, he let out a gasp, part astonishment, part pain and he was aware that his eyes were watering.

Jacques de Molay was concerned, but then noticing the crowd forming around them, he stood back. "You great sissy, you're crying!" he said, holding Josep at arms length. "Let me take a look at that! Josep you do get into some scrapes but what a fuss over nothing."

When he stopped, he was greeted with whoops of laughter as everyone started pointing and laughing at Josep. Josep couldn't believe it. He hadn't seen Jacques for years yet at the instant they met Jacques had not only injured him but then mocked him in public. He went off to clean himself up.

All he could think of was what a catastrophic reunion but he was still so delighted to see Jacques that he literally swallowed his pride, gathered his wits and went back into the Palace from the gardens, thanking the servants who had helped him clean up. He realised he sounded strange, his nose must still have been full of blood. He finally spotted Molay with Lord Pedro de Ayerbe and Pere de Queralt, Guillabert de Cruïlles, Bernat de Peratallada and various other high-ranking courtiers, all enthralled by Jacques de Molay, standing, his chest thrust out, a large goblet of red wine in his left hand. He was gesticulating wildly and delivered what must have been the punchline of his story as all those around him broke into uproarious laughter. For the rest of his life, Josep remembered the prickle of embarrassment as he approached and the laughter ceased. Jacques had been laughing about him.

"Molt bé, jove!" Jacques said meaninglessly and finally managed to put an arm limply round his shoulder. "Deu n'hi do that wine is strong."

Josep couldn't believe his ears. Was this all his beloved benefactor could say after all these years? There was something false about the Catalan expressions he was using.

"Jacques I've been looking forward to seeing you, I couldn't believe it when I got your letter, it was the best birthday present I could ever get, thank you ever so much!" he said.

"Don't use that expression, Josep!" replied Jacques acidly. "It sounds so unbecoming in a young squire. Do you not know the company you are in?"

Josep was mortified. He was thanking him as warmly as he could and Jacques was correcting his expression. He looked Jacques in the eye and was startled to find a blankness there. Jacques quickly looked away and muttered something Josep couldn't hear but it sounded horribly like "sissy" again.

Thankfully they were shortly rescued from a stiff conversation about what Josep had been doing recently by the arrival of the queen, who needed to speak urgently to Jacques but cast Josep a sidelong look as if to say "What on earth has happened between you?"

Josep wanted to be by himself and found a quiet corner. He felt somewhere between lost and betrayed. Memories started rushing back to him, snatches of different moments of his childhood when he had felt close to Jacques. He measured up the present with the past and none of it made sense.

After waiting some time for Jacques and Queen Constança to return, Josep thought he didn't want to see anyone. He put his hands to his nose and found that it was swollen. How could he explain that to the others? He couldn't laugh it off. He had to be alone.

He left the Palau Major and within minutes was walking down Carrer Lledó. He came to the old city gate that led from Plaça Regomir to the Palau Menor. It was of course locked at this time of night.

On the other side of the gate was the Templar headquarters opposite the Palau Menor. The gate connected the Templar house to the Palau Menor, where the Queen and her entourage sometimes stayed. The gate was never manned as being opposite the Templar headquarters was considered protection enough. There were palm trees growing beside the gate which always shaded the gate from the sun and masked it further at night. As Josep passed on the other side of it, he heard voices. Two whispered voices. Obviously as his patron and the queen had disappeared from the Palau Major at the same time and both had a connection with the Palau Menor and the Templar house, Josep's mind conjured wildly with the idea that it was the Queen and Jacques de Molay.

"Palermo was to fall today at Vespers, then messengers were to be sent from Palermo to Trapani in the west and Messina in the east. Messina will be the most difficult to take as there is more access there for Charles of Anjou's fleet in Calabria," the male voice was saying.

"But what is the delay?" It was definitely the queen's voice. He could recognise the accent in her Catalan and she even said some words to Jacques in French, Jacques' first language. There was no doubt about it. It was Jacques' voice, his particular accent in Catalan. There was no slurring from drink. Josep's mind span. Was Jacques informing the queen about a coup against King Charles and the Angevins in Sicily? But why Jacques? If the king knew, presumably he would tell his queen, the most interested party. Perhaps the king didn't know. That must be it! Jacques was explaining the planned coup but no message had come to confirm it. Josep's mind raced as he remembered Friday night at Drassanes. If a message were to have come from Africa and had arrived at the Drassanes, surely the same would be true of a message from Sicily. Exactly the same procedure, presumably, he rapidly surmised and of course it would come here to Barcelona as the king was here at present. People were busy celebrating Easter, they were off their guard for a few days, it was perfect timing, even the seas at the beginning of spring were calmer. How long would it take the fastest boat, Josep asked himself rapidly, to get from Trapani, the nearest Sicilian port, to Barcelona? An unarmed lleny and a dozen or so men on either side and with a good wind could make it in four days, three days perhaps.

"I'm afraid your Majesty must be patient," Jacques said, as if in answer to Josep's question. "News will be here either way in three days. They will wait until nightfall to come ashore."

"Thursday at nightfall," the Queen muttered.

Josep realised he hadn't seen Giovanni da Procida the whole evening yet he had been the one to meet the Tunisian deputation on Friday night at the Drassanes. Josep was certain that Giovanni da Procida was anxiously waiting for news if he wasn't actually there himself. Josep felt the hairs of the back of his neck stand up. He felt vulnerable. The queen seemed to have a sixth sense with him. He therefore quietly but quickly withdrew. As he did so, he trod on a cat behind him. There was a high-pitched miaow and a "Who goes there?" from Jacques.

Josep fled as quietly as he could down Carrer de la Ciutat not stopping till he got to Carrer de la Mercè right down in front of the harbour walls. He didn't dare cut across and take a shortcut in case Jacques managed to head him off by chance.

When he returned to his room, he put himself to bed having first quickly ministered as best he could to his battered nose. He saw from his reflection in the pewter washbasin in the flickering candlelight it was still bloody.

Josep was awoken the next day not by his knight but by Jacques himself at nine o'clock. He was most solicitous and concerned about which way Josep had returned last night.

"The same way I arrived," Josep replied rather unconvincingly in his own mind.

"I went up to Plaça Sant Jaume, then down Avinyó. Why do you ask?" he bluffed.

"No matter, a possible security problem, you should be careful on those streets at night, they can be dangerous," Jacques replied. "Let's see that nose! The Queen tells me it was swollen and bloodied," he blustered.

"I'm sure she didn't tell you to come round and play nursemaid to me," joked Josep, desperately trying to appeal to the soldier monk's sense of humour.

"Ha ha!" laughed Jacques. "That's a good one, Josep!"

Unfortunately, it all felt forced and was but a passing moment.

"I don't talk to the Queen that much, young Josep," he said, "but she's most concerned about you. She seems to have a soft spot for you!"

"Or so it seemed from what she said last night when you left her!" Josep heard himself say too late to stop, unable to push the thought of the overheard conversation between Jacques and the queen from his mind.

Jacques cast Josep a wary glance. He knew he'd gone too far.

"When you left her at the Palace," Josep said.

"Exactly!" Jacques harrumphed uncomfortably. "She was most concerned. Let me see that nose." He made as if to put his great clumsy thumb and forefinger around Josep's nose but Josep pulled back and leapt to his feet.

"Tell her Majesty, if you please, it's fine. I'm fine. How does it look?" he said holding his head back far enough away from Jacques' soldierly grasp.

"Good, fine, a little bulbous, a little purple but…acceptable, fine!" said Jacques conclusively to Josep's relief but also irritation, as he had been the cause of it, which he seemed to have forgotten. It seemed any kind of apology or explanation was out of the question.

"Well, jove, to business!" he said bluffly, moving on.

"I should like to visit your mother in your company. Would you be prepared to accompany me? In her last letter to me she was keen to stress how much she would like to see us together"

"And if I refuse, which part of my anatomy will you rearrange?" Josep found himself saying to himself. "How can I refuse, my lord?" he said.

"Ha, ha ha, indeed, jove, well said! The problem is that I'll be delayed for a few days here."

"I wonder why," Josep again said to himself.

"So I'd suggest you went down on your own, say, tomorrow first thing?"

"So that you can receive your Sicilian messengers untroubled no doubt!" Josep mused inwardly, one ear listening as Jacques finished.

"And I'll follow you down as soon as I can," he said with a check in his intonation.

"I appreciate how deeply you obviously value your relationship with my mother but I must remind you that I wouldn't contemplate going to visit my mother if it weren't for you and therefore I politely request that as I don't often see you and had been looking forward to the journey to Ribes with you, that I wait for you until you are ready to depart."

Josep said this so calmly that Jacques was actually taken aback and it was he who could hardly refuse. Jacques left Josep shortly afterwards with the distinct but pleasant feeling that he had been able to outsmart and outwit Jacques de Molay, whom he now knew to be a spy in the queen's service. A little information was a useful thing. That combined with courtesy and careful flattery was a winning combination, Josep thought.

He thought about the scene of the Tunisian deputation and realized something similar could well be repeated in a couple of nights' time, this time with the Sicilian messengers. Unlike last time, however, when this occasion occurred, Josep knew exactly what he would do, where he would hide and he was determined to do so. The messengers would come to the king and presumably Giovanni da Procida too first. How Jacques de Molay would receive the information was less clear, perhaps the queen would let him know as he had been her agent in the affair and his work was done.

The following Thursday three days later Josep was instructed by Pedro de Ayerbe to take up position on the draughty stairs and wait so long as he was in conference in the upper chamber at the Drassanes. Josep wasted no time in finding a good position to spy on whatever might ensue at the entrance to the high-arched shipyard. The night was similar to the previous Friday and all was quiet around midnight. From the position he had taken, Josep could see everything that happened and he could still easily and quickly retreat to his post if needs be. His prediction was correct. Lord Pedro, King Pere and Giovanni da Procida came through the back door as before but Josep could barely control himself when he saw the great form of Jacques de Molay join them moments later.

A lleny shortly afterwards docked and the exhausted oarsmen lay on the floor as soon as they got out of the boat. The captain of the boat appeared as water was given to the crew.

"Greetings Roger, you are welcome. You must be exhausted. Chambers have been prepared for you within the Drassanes," Lord Pedro said to the captain of the ship, whom Josep did not recognise. "Let the king talk to them first and let him dismiss them," Roger replied.

Josep realised the captain was the famous Sicilian sailor, Roger de Llúria, as he spoke what Josep could only assume was Sicilian to the oarsmen and sailors of whom Josep counted twenty-four. They responded by asking for things Josep couldn't understand but sat up now groaning and stretching and looking utterly miserable. Josep could barely contain his curiosity and wondered if they were free men. He found it hard to believe anyone would volunteer for such a task as these men had obviously carried out. In pairs, they were helping each other with olive oil, tending to sores and blisters on every part of the body that been in contact with the bench. Strips of material used to bind hands, knees and ankles were black with dried blood. One rower started to convulse on the deck uncontrollably. His condition worsened when he was given water and he was wailing between coughs and thrashing about wildly. His back arched agonisingly one more time and then he was still. His bulging eyes were closed by Roger de Llúria.

"We have two more dead on-board," he said without emotion.

"The family of this man and the other two will be rewarded generously!" King Pere said. "What was their salary?"

"Ten sous each man, your Majesty, or half a pound of silver."

"Double it and triple it for the family of these who have died."

"That is most generous, your Majesty," said de Llúria, translating for the crew who struggled feebly to find words for their gratitude.

"If they are to be my navy in future, I shall have to make a good start. Three dead is not inspiring," the king said. "You are still not married, are you?"

"Your Majesty arranged for my marriage to Margarida de Lancia whom I met at your court ten years ago, your Majesty. My mother is Bella d'Amichi, maid of Queen Constança from her infancy."

"Of course, how forgetful of me," said the king smiling. "Sometimes my happiest moments and best decisions escape my memory. However, this is not the moment for reminiscence. We must tend to the crew!"

Lord Pedro then led the crew through the back door to the rooms Josep supposed were on the other side of the secret door, through which the envoys from Tunis had been taken.

"Be quick, Lord Pedro. I need your expertise here, too!" the king said. Josep knew he would be safe where he was for a while. Yet he thought he hadn't seen Jacques and Giovanni da Procida for some time. He then saw them seated at a nearby table, to which the king led Roger de Llúria and seated him.

"When did you set out?" was the first question Jacques de Molay asked him.

"We were dispatched from Trapani at sunset on Sunday. There was a strong southeasterly wind so we were able to make good time and the sea was with us all the way but we have not stopped. Each man has slept one hour in twelve. Before we left, we knew Palermo and Trapani were in Sicilian hands and there was a rumour Corleone in the centre of the island had also fallen but we know nothing of Messina in the east and Catania in the south-east. Yet we know it was a well coordinated revolt, everyone involved was waiting for the instructions: "Moranu li Franchiski! Death to the French!" in Sicilian. Unfortunately, women and children were put to the sword!" he said and at this his head dropped.

"We had urged mercy for the women and children but of course as always happens they got in the way of looting or barricaded themselves in their houses and so provoked suspicion of harbouring menfolk so were slaughtered. There is so much anti-French feeling that if anyone so much as uttered a word of French, they were branded French and were killed, too. Of course, the rebellion has also been used to settle old scores among the Sicilians and many Sicilians have met their end as the result of ancient family feuds."

"Have the local commanders been able to get supplies of food, drink and weapons?" asked Giovanni da Procida.

"As far as I know, there was no problem with that, as all provisions from the garrisons were requisitioned but of course that will run out soon and as no taxes will be paid for some time, the coffers will empty quickly and buying and selling food will become a problem. Order needs to be restored and salaries of new officials will have to be paid quickly to ensure stability."

"There was more money due to come from Constantinople over the next few days, wasn't there Jacques?" asked Giovanni da Procida.

"That's right, and there are more funds from the Emperor Michael in the Templar headquarters in Malta, here in Barcelona and at Miravet," Jacques de Molay said. "I will organise letters of credit and have them sent to the island so that trade can be re-established with the Templar houses acting as bankers. I shall also dispatch a messenger to the Emperor informing him that King Pere has been informed."

"Thank you, Jacques," said the king. "Once a new regime is in place, we can start to think of pursuing a naval policy against Charles of Anjou between Messina and Amalfi. Do you believe that the Sicilians are willing to request me to be their king, Roger?" he asked.

"It is difficult to know at the moment, your Majesty, you have invested heavily in this rebellion but so too has Constantinople and the Sicilian nobles know this. It depends on whom these nobles feel can represent and protect them best. Sicily has been a papal fief since 1266 so therefore a request may be made to be ruled directly from Rome but as Pope Martin is himself French, he would probably declare the rebellion unholy and excommunicate anyone involved in it. In that case, the Sicilians can turn either to your Majesty or to the Emperor Michael but Michael has no interest in adding Sicily to his burdens. His aim was always to distract Charles of Anjou from attacking him in Constantinople. So the Sicilians will eventually be forced to request you as their king," Roger was clearly exhausted but straining every nerve to be as clear but diplomatic as possible.

"But this will take time, will it not?" King Pere said rather emphatically. "Charles of Anjou will of course have to rethink his plans to restore the Latin Emperor in Constantinople and will have to deal with the Sicilian problem but will be impatient and therefore will devote the best of his resources to the task," said the king, brooding over the problem.

"Then it suits your Majesty that there should be as long a delay as possible before a request is made for you to be king: the longer the process takes, the more Charles of Anjou's resources will be worn down," interjected Jacques de Molay. "In any case, your Majesty will need a base from which to conduct his operations. Majorca is too sympathetic to the French cause; Minorca is a vassal but is untrustworthy and too distant; Malta is too small and they are still firmly pro-Angevin. The ideal bridgehead to invade Sicily would be somewhere in North Africa, Tunis, Constantine or Gerba," he mused.

"A mission to Constantine as we have been planning would therefore serve many purposes," Giovanni da Procida said. "Your Majesty can move his troops and navy near his objective but cloak his intentions by claiming he is merely leading the Holy Church in her crusade against Islam. If you had Papal support for this crusade, the disguise would be perfect. You would also give your military a real exercise to rehearse the invasion."

"That is true, Giovanni," said the king, "but what if I should meet King Charles' fleet between here and Trapani? How much damage will he be able to inflict if I set out straight away?"

"There is no hurry, your Majesty," said Giovanni da Procida. "Charles will coordinate his counter-rebellion from Naples and the Calabrian coast. He will deal with it as a local problem and delegate the task to his son Charles of Salerno but there is no harm in your biding your time for the moment and letting matters take their course. Let us see how much the Sicilians can do for themselves. Then if they need help to conquer the eastern part of the island, you can be in position to help once they make their request."

"Exactly, exactly!" agreed the king. "Roger you will be the one privy to this information. Do not even inform my son, Jaume Pere de Sogorb. All present must swear the utmost secrecy in this matter."

"We swear!" they all said with one voice.

Josep's heart was thundering in his chest. So this is what Berenguer de Belvís had been hinting about when he had last spoken to him how many years ago was it at Monzón? The Templars were in fact involved in a clandestine pre-emptive action backed by Constantinople to prevent King Charles of Sicily from putting a pro-French emperor on the throne of the Roman Empire of the East. King Pere wanted Sicily, his wife's legitimate inheritance. But the queen was in fact one step ahead of the king in this objective.

Later that night, Jacques and Lord Pedro were not surprised to find Josep asleep on his chair outside the upper chamber and there was good-natured banter as Jacques accompanied them to their inn. He then continued up to the Templar headquarters.

CHAPTER 15 FATHER FIGURE

On the way down to Ribes, Josep could draw nothing out of Jacques.

"I won't say a word Josep until I have your mother's permission!" he said, so they left it at that. Yet he was at his most charming the evening they arrived and everyone was laughing.

"Some things never change," Josep thought to himself "and some things can never be the same again!" he told himself, too. He didn't think he could ever forgive Jacques his tipsy indiscretion. He had made him a laughing stock in the Royal Palace. Josep remembered the night they had found the man dying in the cave. He considered that night had changed the course of his life and been the end of his childhood. He thought Jacques had clearly forgotten this incident and felt betrayed and angry. He asked himself if he loved Jacques less as a result and realised that regrettably that was the case.

At one point in the evening, Jacques and Catarina went out into the garden together and Josep saw his mother nodding several times at what Jacques said. He made a mental note to ask Jacques what agreement he'd managed to wrestle from her. In his own mind, he knew Jacques couldn't know for sure the true identity of his father until Catarina revealed it to him but he must have a good idea. It was more a matter of confirmation of what he suspected.

"Your father would be proud of you," was all Catarina would say when she heard Jacques de Molay's summary of events in Barcelona and the general high regard everyone including the king and queen had for Josep. Yet no subtle coaxing could make her reveal any more about the identity of Josep's father.

"He was a good man," she said once again. Then she said: "He himself told me he was a bon homme but I didn't understand what he meant."

"Mother, a bon homme is what the Cathars call their leaders. Was he involved with the Cathars?"

Jacques looked as if he was going to burst with the tension but Catarina didn't reply.

"So I am called Goodman because he was a bon homme?" Josep asked, with a note of excitement in his voice.

Catarina's colour rose and she turned away.

"Mother, what is it that you cannot say? You are among friends!"

"Josep, I can't!"

Seeing Josep was annoyed by this reply, as a means of getting him on his own, Catarina asked him to come and help her with something in her room.

"Josep, I can't tell you who your father was because I never knew who he was. That makes me feel so ashamed that I can't say to you, "This man was your father, he was called such and such." He used to tease me telling me he would tell me in good time. I didn't think anything of it, I thought we had all the time in the world but then it came to an end."

"Did he leave you, mother, when he found out that you were with child?" Josep asked.

"No Josep, absolutely not! He was the happiest man in the world when I told him. He held me and put his hand on my belly and he felt you move." She started weeping and Josep's immediate instinct was to comfort her.

"Josep, he would have made such a good father." Josep held her close. He felt she had never been able to weep before.

"I was scared at first, then lonely. Luckily, Jacques knew Clara, she had delivered many children in the area and he pointed me in her direction, giving me a note of introduction to hand to her."

"But Mother she must have asked who the father was or at least if you knew who the father was. How could you conceal that from her?"

"I concealed nothing from her, Josep. What I am trying to tell you is that your father's identity was a mystery to me, too." She paused, dried her tears and then took a deep breath as if steeling herself for a monumental task.

"He used the name Goodman because it sounded like Bon Homme and Guzmán but he told me to be careful to whom I told this as Guzmán is an important noble Spanish name and he was not from that Guzmán family. I haven't told you for this reason and I still don't understand what danger it could do you if you say you are a Guzmán."

"I suppose people could claim I was an imposter and was using a false name," Josep replied.

Catarina looked at him meekly, red-eyed.

"I didn't want any harm to come to you, Josep. I've lost him, I don't want to lose you, too."

"No, mother, of course not," he said. "I thank you for telling me. I do feel better about things," Josep said to console her.

Catarina smiled through her tears.

"You would have loved him as I did. He loved riding and travelling and being in good company."

"Then what happened to him, Mother?"

"Josep, I don't know. He disappeared from one moment to the next, one day he was with me, the next he was gone."

Josep noticed she had been playing with a ring he had always known her to have, which she wore around her neck, not on her finger. He considered asking her about it, thinking this would calm her and comfort her. Perhaps, he thought, it would prompt her to add a few more details to what was an unsatisfactory account of who his father had been. Yet he didn't feel he could ask her any more direct questions as she was already upset enough. It wasn't supposed to be an interrogation.

"I've always loved that ring!" he said, smiling gently and looking into her eyes, then back at the ring around her neck.

"Oh this?" she said almost absent-mindedly. "This is not a ring!"

"Oh, isn't it? What is it then?"

"It is one of two things that I still have from your father." She took the necklace holding the ring off from around her neck and slipped the small silver loop off and into the palm of her hand. When Josep looked at it more closely, he could see it was silver but also encrusted with tiny gems.

"He said the diamonds were too small to be of any value but the brooch itself was from Granada. That's where he was from, you see, even though he used the name Guzmán."

She looked uncomfortable and cast a wary glance at Josep. Josep had been expecting this so covered up the emotions that gripped him as the truth began to come out.

"Granada?" he asked smiling, keeping his expression calm and open. She took a breath and then continued, clearing her throat. She was still on the verge of tears, Josep knew, as if telling the story was breaking her heart. Something in Josep's expression must have reassured her as she looked again into her son's eyes.

"Josep, I feel such a fool telling you these things, they make so little sense and cannot help you in answering the questions I know you wish me to answer."

"Mother, in your own time. There's no hurry, is there?" he heard himself say.

She looked him in the eye again for a moment then shaking her head, smiled.

"You're more grown up than I give you credit for, son," she said. "I love you for it." She took a deep breath.

"This is half of a brooch he gave me, the other half he kept," Catarina said. "It was a lover's gift he made days before I last saw him. The idea was when we were reunited the two parts of the broach could be linked together again."

"That's beautiful," Josep said, taking the half brooch in the palm of his hand and raising it to eye level. There were grooves at the top and bottom and on either side of the piece of jewellery worn smooth by the action of the other half as it had slid over it and the two halves had held each other in a compact and snug figure of eight.

"By turning the two halves in a certain way, it comes apart but when they are linked, they pull against each other and the link cannot be broken."

"What a fitting piece of jewellery to give you!" Josep said smiling. "He must have thought carefully about what to give you. It's perfect, both beautiful and appropriate."

"That's what I thought, too, Josep and looked forward to the day when the two parts would once again come together. But it wasn't to be..." There was a pause.

"So you take it as a keepsake of your father!" she said.

"But what about you?"

"Oh, I have the other thing he gave me, which I have never taken off."

She pushed back her hair to reveal a pair of simple golden earrings, each one inset with a glittering large gem.

"Diamonds!" she said. "From Africa, he told me, from where the best quality ones come."

"They're beautiful, too" Josep said.

"He was a wonderful man and he had exquisite taste, Josep," she said.

Josep felt as she said it that he knew as much about his father as he needed to know. And over the years, often when confronted with others who had known their father all their lives and took him for granted, he treasured this information about him, which, though not much, was valuable to him beyond measure. He kissed her goodnight and said he and Jacques would leave first thing the following morning.

"I feel I know at least a little about my father," Josep confided the next day to Jacques when Catarina had retired. "And what I know is valuable to me."

"I am glad to hear that, Josep but remember, unless your mother gives me permission to tell you any more, I am beholden to say nothing!" he said. Josep thought it brutal and unnecessary. He wondered at the man and decided at that moment that Jacques was in love with his mother and that he, Josep, meant little to him.

"In that case the secret will probably go with her to the grave," Josep replied.

"But didn't she look lovely, Josep? You're a lucky boy to have such a beautiful mother!"

It was a non-sequitur and felt like a cold rebuke more than anything.

"I suppose so," Josep said, deciding to confide no longer in Jacques de Molay.

"I'm awfully relieved you are more comfortable in your home again. Aren't you?" Jacques said.

"Yes, of course!" he said but thought the opposite. "Thanks for trying, Jacques," he said, smiling deliberately a bit shyly. He knew it would drive Jacques away. Jacques couldn't handle Josep's earnest side at all, he thought to himself.

Jacques sniffed and a shadow crossed his face. Josep looked way and nodded sardonically to himself.

They said goodbye to Catarina, Clara and Habiba and left.

"I shall return soon!" Josep said.

"Let us press on ahead full speed for Port Fangós and Miravet," Jacques said and the two spurred their horses to a canter and left the little town of Ribes behind them. Little did Josep know then that it would be some years before he would return.

†

The icy mornings of February gave way to the ruinous blasts of March and much damage was caused to the galleys. There were days when it was so stormy that the shipbuilders could not work and the sea was so rough that the huts on the shore had to be abandoned. At that point, the order was given for all the shipbuilding teams to find accommodation in Tortosa.

"That is just what the town needs," said the mayor.

The extra two thousand people were accommodated in temporary wooden huts at different locations around Tortosa. The town was so cramped that carriages and carts were not allowed in through the city gates and had to stay outside. The stench of human waste was all too familiar to Josep as the trenches designed to carry away the waste struggled with the extra demand. Thankfully, the winds dispelled most of the bad odour but more people kept arriving in the city.

Wheat, barley and oats arrived by the boatload so special huts had to be constructed to store it all. This meant that there was no shortage of staples: bread and vegetables were in plentiful supply and there was roast meat for dinner for everyone in the king's employment.

Equipment was being brought in too, whole cart loads of crossbows and crossbow bolts, lances and short spears or dards, breastplates, helmets, greaves for the shins, cuisses for the thighs, paresses and mangonells or warship-mounted catapults, small and large. Great carts appeared with enormous wooden wheels bearing groaning consignments of stones for the different catapults. It was clear the town was on a war footing but nobody knew where they were going. Then one day in mid April, the king himself arrived in their midst unannounced.

"Nobody can catch the king as not even his close friends and family know where they're going to be the next day," the joke went round. Jacques left with the king.

La Senyera flew from Miravet Castle and King Pere, Queen Constança, the seventeen-year-old Crown Prince Alfons, and the younger princes and princesses, Jaume, fifteen, Elisabet, thirteen, Frederick, twelve, Iolanda, nine, and Pere, seven, were taken on a tour of the town on horseback. The king gave a short speech, urging the shipbuilders to redouble their labour and asking anyone who could to help move the goods to Port Fangós or to bake. The navy needed biscuits for its expedition, so "Bake for Victory" was a phrase the king used repeatedly. From one day to the next, the city went from smelling like a cesspit to a bakery and the mouthwatering scent of sugar, fat and flour scented the skies for miles around.

We're fitting out the galley

We're toiling on the shore

We'll hunt the foe at sea

If not the alley

And beat him down with milk and flour.

So went a song Josep kept hearing and it made him laugh.

"Town is like a catapult ready to go off!" Josep heard an almogaten comment one day in one of the crowded taverns.

At that moment an earthenware mug came flying through the air, smashing an almogaver in the face and a ferocious fight ensued. Nobody knew who was fighting whom but chairs were smashed over backs, mugs were jabbed into faces and across throats. Tables were overturned, their legs ripped off and used as clubs. Luckily, there were enough people outside the tavern to bring the situation under control quickly so there were no fatalities or serious injuries, some bad cuts, many bruises and everyone emerged from the incident as if from a dream. It was a sign of the times: Tortosa was a tinderbox.

"Your Majesty must move, wherever it is that he wishes to go!" said Bernat de Cruïlles, one of the king's most trusted advisers.

"I await the blessing of the Virgin Mother of God!" was his reply, widely reported as a sign of the king's piety. He wanted Mary's approval hence he waited till May, the month sacred to the Virgin Mary, Stella Maris, Star of the Sea, patron saint of sailors.

CHAPTER 16 A FLEET FIT FOR A KING

In the last week of April news started circulating that the king was in two places at once and the fact is that he rode so tirelessly between all the key ports in his kingdom that he was often in three ports in the space of twenty-four hours. Thus, on Sunday, the twenty-third of April, he heard Mass at daybreak on the beach closest to the church in Torruela, had a brief lunch in Palamós and stayed the night in Sant Pol de Maresme. In each place, he was urging on the completion and repair of the galleys at the Drassanes. On Monday, he sent the vice admirals to each port that had a shipyard with instructions that all ships were to assemble in Port Fangós immediately. He himself went to inspect the Drassanes next to Montjuic in Barcelona. Repelled by the smell of the Caganell, Barcelona's cesspit, next to the Drassanes, he travelled south the same day to Tarragona, passing through Sitges, and had Mass said in the early hours of the morning in Tortosa, where he met his admiral, Jaume Pere de Sogorb.

The fleet was magnificent and once it had been reviewed thoroughly by King Pere and all the Captains received by their sovereign Lord, a great feast was held to celebrate. Josep was amazed when the king saw him dismount and came surrounded by his closest advisers and friends to speak to him.

"Do you like my fleet, young man?" he asked and those around roared with laughter. How was Josep supposed to answer? He did what came naturally. He dropped on one knee and bowed his head.

"Look at me when you address your king!" King Pere said.

"Stand, squire!" he then said more kindly. "Don't you know I have come to give you thanks?" Josep took a deep breath and looked the king square in the eye.

"Your Majesty has done everything in his power to assemble this mighty fleet. I hope it serves his purpose well."

There was a momentary flicker of displeasure at this comment. Then, widening his eyes, the king let out a great guffaw.

"Well said, young squire!" bellowed the king raising Josep with one arm under his elbow, the other cuffing him around the top of the head. Peter of Queralt moved forward so that Josep could see him and he flashed Josep a glance as if to say, "Hold your nerve!"

All the king's courtiers crowded round Josep, Guillem Moliner, Pere de Palau, Galcerán de Pinós and Dalmau Rocabertí, Ramón Muntaner's knight, together with

Arnau Roger, Count of Pallars.

"I have again had excellent reports about you," continued King Pere. "Guillem Pellicer, my trusted emissary, has heard nothing but excellent reports from the master Shipwright and Ramón Saguardia, the commander of the Castle of Miravet."

"Your Majesty pays me the compliment of my life!" Josep managed to find breath enough to utter. There were cheers and the king beamed around him. He took off his crown and swept back the mop of thick brown hair from over his eyes, readjusted the crown on his head and looked around him.

"I would like all young squires of your age to be like you," the king said. "Devoted, tough, modest. In one word: reliable. I name you squire, young man, to Lord Pedro de Ayerbe."

There was another mighty cheer and Josep was raised up on the shoulders of the king's closest courtiers and paraded around from table to table. Even his own knight Pedro de Ayerbe looked pleased. This made all the more impact on Josep because he was used to being reproached these days rather than praised by his knight. When the minstrels and troubadours finally came out, Josep was put down. He quickly made his way over to Bru Miret, who grappled him so close to his chest Josep thought he was going to pass out from asphyxiation, as well as the stench of unwashed brute that emanated from this filthy warrior. Surrounding Bru were hundreds and thousands of others like him. The entire camp from Tortosa as well as from all the other more distant camps, each under an almogaten, had made one enormous single camp to accommodate all the mountain and border shock troops that the king had summoned to his mission, secret though its purpose was.

As Josep stepped away to relieve his bursting bladder in privacy, he surveyed the surroundings from a raised knoll covered in a sabina thicket. As far the eye could see, from north-west to south-east of the delta de l'Ebre were the resting keels of the newly launched ships built at the drassanes of Port Fangós. One hundred or so new vessels lay like the scattered belongings and dismembered limbs of giants waiting to be reassembled into monstrous action. There were full-sized galleys, smaller boats, or llaguts, larger tarrides, huge flat-bottomed boats larger than barques called huissiers specifically for horses, as well as others Josep didn't even know the name of they were so specific to a purpose. The air was chilly at this time of night but not as cold as it had been last month Josep noted and the camp fires that were scattered everywhere seemed to go on for as far as the eye could see. The stench of the army camp was also on the air, the tar and tallow of the endless torches, not to mention the remnant odour of charring beef from the feast.

Josep couldn't believe the praise he'd received from the king. He had called him one word, reliable, and breathing deeply so his chest swelled out, he felt the prick of a tear and wondered if he'd ever be able to tell his mother all this. He relished the moment, thought of Jacques, experienced that curious deflating weight in the pit of his stomach whenever he thought of Jacques and wished he could tell his father.

Then on the faintest of breezes, he smelt it for the first time: burning wood timbers, a smell he had not smelt for some weeks since the galleys had been finished. There was a boat burning somewhere, he didn't even know he was bellowing when he realised he was running full tilt at the crowd.

"Fire! Fire!" he shouted at the top of his lungs. He had time to reach his horse when there was a sudden hush from the thousands of almogavers, archers, crossbowmen, sailors, shipwrights, nobles, cooks, whores, camp followers, women and children.

Then he heard a roar. To the southeast of Port Fangós, one of the galleys was ablaze and as the wind was fresh, if it wasn't put out immediately, it would set fire to the other ships. There was a sudden commotion, then the terrifying sound of several thousand feet pounding behind Josep who kept abreast of the throng as he was on his horse.

He was the first to reach the burning boat and saw a hooded man fleeing on horseback to a vessel beached two-hundred metres from the burning ship. He threw himself out of the saddle, went into a roll to break his fall and shield himself from the fierce heat he could feel from the blaze.

"I have to get him," he said to the first person who arrived. "I have to get him before he escapes, he knows what has happened here!"

So saying he sprinted off along the shore trying to head off the man who seemed strangely familiar to him. He could see him untying his llagut and readying his manoeuvrable sail for departure and he threw himself into the surf. The boat started to gain speed as it caught the fresh wind. He had never known so much strength in his body, he was upon that boat within seconds, could see the whites of the eyes wide in disbelief from behind the hood as he grappled with the gunnel which was all he had to haul himself over the side of the small yacht.

"Of all the wicked treachery, to arrive under cover of night with so many other boats to cover him up, what treachery treachery treachery!" the words thundered in Josep's mind as he went over the side blows raining down on him from the hooded man who fought with all his might as if his life depended on it. Josep caught the oar before it was brought crashing down on his head with both hands. Twisting it out of the hands of his assailant, he rotated it like a mace above his head, catching his would-be assailant on the side of the head and knocking him off balance. Diving to his left, he landed with splayed hands on his chest and aimed a powerful swinging kick at the man's side. He caught him full force and the next second the man was pounding the water next to the boat swimming away. But Josep dived in and in one long underwater pull, was underneath him, clawing at his face as he fought for air.

Josep had him, his assailant was clearly concussed and coughing uncontrollably. Josep threw back the hood and twisted it at the man's neck to use it to half throttle him, then he struck out for the beach pounding the water with long powerful strokes with his free arm. Within minutes he was on the beach, the gasping body of his victim utterly powerless face-down next to him. Not wanting to take chances and with a relish for revenge quickly taken, he aimed a crushing blow at the man's temple and knocked him out.

Bru was the first to find Josep and the enemy spy. The damage he'd done took many forms. Not only was a galley burned to cinders but two boats, a small llagut and an armed lleny, had also been damaged, as had several others left in the panic to control the fire. In the wind, these boats had been blown into the surf and in the moonlight looked the like dead sea creatures stuck in the sand at impossible angles. It was unclear how long repairs were going to take and the delay clearly angered the king.

"Get the teams working at once!" he ordered. In this atmosphere of frustration and suspicion, arguments started to break out among the different shipbuilding crews. Rumour was rife and therefore the other main source of damage. The galley that had been set alight had belonged to the Tortosa crew.

"You men of Amposta have always envied us as we are the main city in these parts and had first choice of where to pitch our yard and materials coming down the Ebre. Why did you not make an appointment with the shipwright and he'd have shown you around? There was no need to burn our galley out of spite!" screamed a stooped, hook-nosed man.

"You are liars and braggarts but that is nothing new or surprising. What need did we have to burn your galley when it would have sunk under its own weight anyway? You used far too much wood in the upper body and your ship was top-heavy, so you may have the choice of materials but you use them the worst!" came the reply from a man from Amposta. There was a roar as the men of Tortosa then threw themselves at the men of Amposta and at their boats tossing anything they could get their hands on at them amid the beached craft. Luckily, there were no weapons to hand as they were all still locked up in Tortosa, a good league away, otherwise there would have been much blood spilled.

The rumour spread like wildfire and similar scenes were re-enacted between the teams of Llançà and Roses, Torruela and Palamós, Sant Feliu and Sant Pol, Casteldefels and Sitges, Vilanova and Calafell, Tarragona and Cambrils. Although from the outside these men had accents that were similar, for those on the inside it was the small differences that were infuriating. These were the crucial details that egged them on in this internal bloodletting. The almogavers kept themselves apart from all this. They spoke a Catalan that was from the deep south of the Kingdom of Aragón, from the south reaches of Gandia and the Xuquer river, where they saw most of their work these days on the borders of Valencia and the kingdom of

Granada, a difficult dialect full of Spanish sounds and vocabulary but impossible for the Castillians to understand. It was devilishly difficult for a Catalan; it was basically their own language. They stayed aloof from the arguments between the shipyards though there were internal squabbles amongst them as always.

Under interrogation, the spy revealed little other than that he was clearly French, clearly working for the French, but for whom specifically remained a mystery. Josep had thought he recognised him when fighting with him but realised it was more that he reminded him of many figures he associated with danger in recent times

"It goes back further than that, Josep!" Lord Pedro said to him. "Do you not remember the hooded man we saw with Fray Domènec at Cavallers together with the lad from there?"

It took Josep a while to recall. He had a dim recollection of the mysterious man in a hood talking to Bertrán de Solsona, his arch enemy from childhood, and that memory led him to Amaury in the Pyrenees, killed by another hooded man whom they couldn't capture.

"The hood is something I associate with danger, my Lord," Josep said.

"And now that I think about it, I seem to have seen more and more of them around recently. It is a French monastic fashion, is it not?"

"Yes, it is," replied Lord Pedro.

"I somehow associate it with someone else who I can't seem to remember."

The excitement and enthusiasm had turned sour in a matter of days. The prisoner was held but would not speak. Without ceremony and to assuage the frustration and growing bitterness of the crowd, he was hanged from an improvised gibbet. He died slowly, his convulsions swinging him back and forth. When dead, he continued swinging in the wind, which seemed to bode ill.

It was at this inopportune moment that the king decided to address the army.

"Once our boats are repaired and the weather permits, we will set sail!" he said.

At that point, the noble Arnold Roger Count of Pallars, spoke to the king.

"Your Majesty, we have great pleasure in the words you have spoken to us but we beseech and humbly beg you tell us to where we shall set sail!"

"Count, I wish you and all others here present to be sure that if we knew that our left-hand knows what the right-hand intends to do, we would cut it off!" the king replied and when the count and the others heard these strong words, they ceased asking.

"Lord give your orders and we will carry them out," the count replied.

And yet, day followed night and night followed day and still they did not leave.

One night, Josep happened to be near the king's tent as Queen Constança had requested his help with Prince Frederick. While they were talking and playing, the king exploded at Queen Constança.

"Woman, how can I sail if I don't have the assurance of our agents in Sicily that we will be welcome. This is deliverance not an invasion!"

Under cover of darkness, another embassy was dispatched to Sicily to check on the situation. Josep was in daily contact with Prince Alfons who confided in him what he heard his mother and father discuss.

Two weeks after it had been dispatched, the boat bearing the embassy returned with news that the rebel Sicilian army had taken Messina and Charles of Anjou's fleet was poised to attack it and launch a counter-attack.

"You could use Alcoll, the port of Constantine in the kingdom of Tunis, as a bridgehead to attack Sicily, my Lord, now that we know that Charles' attention is focused on Messina. We can at least set sail for North Africa without fear of being intercepted. This is the moment we have been waiting for," Bernat de Cruïlles, one of the king's closest counsellors said within earshot of Josep.

"We have waited this long, I shall make my decision in my own time!" the king growled back.

That night, as Josep settled down to sleep next to Prince Alfons, he overheard the king and Queen Constança one last time.

"My love, the time has come, we shall leave with the full moon as early in June as possible. I cannot reveal to you the final details or the mission could easily be undone. We must guarantee a good reception in Constantine, so that we can make the preparations for saving Sicily as secure as possible," Josep heard the king say.

"A fleet of more than a hundred galleys is an excessive force for a friendly visit," said Queen Constança.

"I know, I know!" the king said irritably. "There is no way to disguise it but disguise it we must. Yet if Charles of Anjou chooses to attack us, he will come off the worse for it. Or Mirabusac's brother Miraboaps or his family for that matter."

Josep began having dreams of drowning again. He always had them when he was tired and stressed and try as he might he couldn't put them out of his mind on waking. The sea for him was a vast blue creature with a constantly changing form. Constantly hungry though without limbs to grip its prey, it depended on its infinite shape-shifting to confuse its victims and draw them down with invisible but certain power to the depths, where they were devoured. Josep always awoke from these dreams in abject terror. He'd been on the sea once or twice in his life, both times with Jacques and had found it truly thrilling but there was something else left in his mind, out of reach. Why was he still so terrified of drowning?

The order was given in the last days of May to prepare the boats for departure and the sight was magnificent. There was an unequivocal nature to the king these days as he strode through the moorings and inspected the goings-on. He was like a royal architect asking the most minute details about each and every vessel in his fleet storing away information, ceaselessly checking names of boats and galleys, captains of ships, boatswains, recording the numbers of sailors on each vessel. Josep accompanied him on these fact finding sessions. From the twenty-ninth until the thirty-first of May, the king slept for three hours. He was up all night on the thirty-first making final checks but the shipyards were silenced, the crews were spending their first night aboard the ships, the first of many. On the express instructions of the king, nobody was allowed to disembark and movement was to be kept to an absolute minimum. In the moonlight at four in the morning of June the first, 1282, Josep marvelled at the mighty fleet laid out like a town. Sawn planks had been laid along the shoreline to enable the king to access the smaller vessels there drawn up on the beach. Had it not been for the vast wooden jetty laid out like trestle tables for a giant's banquet, you could have imagined the smaller boats with their characteristic forward sloping triangular rigging were a fleet of fishing boats resting between harvest shifts on the sea. But the great looming shapes of battleships lay beyond about a stone's throw from the shore, creaking in the early-morning swell, high at their moorings with the tide, their sheets, halyards and rigging moaning in the light wind, beating against the masts, clapping rhythmically in their anticipation of departure, slumbering Behemoths ready to rise up on the shifting back of the sea to do battle.

"The sun beckons us to join it where it rises! Head for the sun!" was the king's instruction after Mass was said on the beach to the still-embarked crews.

"East, east, chasing the sun! All boats prepare to depart!" the king shouted, jumping down from his horse. He embraced Queen Constança and Frederick.

"Your Majesty, the fleet is ready to depart. We await your signal," called Admiral Jaume Pere de Sogorb, from the king's galley. Josep from the galley next to the king's under the command of Vice Admiral Ramón Marquet saw the king pull away from the Queen and bound up the jetty, up the gangplank. He leapt nimbly over the side of the royal galley landing firmly on deck. A cheer went up and down the shoreline as everyone marvelled at the king's high spirits.

"El Rei! El Rei! Aur! Aur! The King! The King! Hurrah! Hurrah!" they continued to shout for what seemed an age. Then, without warning, on an unheard signal to the oarsmen, below decks, the oars were plunged into the still waters of daybreak. The king's galley was the first to pick up the light breeze at the head of his fleet.

Rosy-fingered dawn lit up the glittering foam around the welcoming keels and the sails of one hundred and fifty craft gladly filled. Josep looked back after half an hour and could still see the queen and the infant Frederick watching from the beach, could see the smoke rising from scores of camp fires among the tents between the jetties and the scrubby bush behind, where the stallholders, camp followers and non-martial elements of the enormous camp were starting to disassemble the camp and move on. The king's galley, being lighter and captained by Roger de Llúria, the vice admiral, considered the best sailor of his time, made light work of keeping ahead of the fleet and an hour after departure, the coastline was but a smudge on the horizon. Around him, Josep could see the fleet both sides and fore and aft but apart from that could see nothing but the sea. He thought about his mother, his last words to her and how long it would be before he saw her again. He had spoken to her about his father and was sure he would find out more when he next saw her. It seemed a new page had been turned. He felt optimistic. He looked at the huge ball of the sun as it rose in the east, gold above red clouds on the horizon, and it reminded him of the Catalan shield. He welcomed the beauty and warmth of the sun, its power, beauty and splendour and knew he was where he had to be.

End of Book One

GLOSSARY

Aljama (Catalan from Arabic): Muslim community in a city under the protection and jurisdiction of the king.

Almogaten (Catalan): almogaver commander, often mounted

Almogàver (Catalan): Catalan shock troop infantry, descended from Pyrenean fighting shepherds, expert in guerrilla warfare

Barraca (plural barraques) (Catalan): simple hemispherical stone-built shepherd refuges

Cavallers (Catalan): "Knights," the name of the academy of pages and knights

Cinturó (Catalan): belt

Coltell (Catalan): long pointed cleaver-like knife carried by the almogavers

Cova Negra (Catalan): The Black Cave, a geographical feature in Sant Pere de Ribes

Deu n'hi do (Catalan): my God!

Drassanes (Catalan): shipyards. Where capitalised, this denotes a port area of the city

Espardenyes (Catalan): espadrilles with sewn in cotton bindings to tie around the ankles

Garriga (Catalan): scrub or moorland

Gonella (Catalan): simple cotton short-sleeved outer upper garment

Infant (Catalan): Crown Prince

Infante (Castilian): Crown Prince

Jove (Catalan): young man

Llagut (Catalan): small rowing boat or one-masted yacht

Lleny (Catalan): a small fast galley

Matxo (Catalan): hybrid mule for pulling carriages

Morisc (Catalan): descendant of Muslims in Iberia after the reconquest

Molt bé (Catalan): very good, well done

Mudèjar (Catalan): architecture: a Moorish style developed after the reconquest

Nen (Catalan): lad

Rei (Catalan): king

Refugi (Catalan): mountain shelter

Riera (Catalan): (normally) dry river bed

Sageta (Catalan): arrow sheath

Sou (Catalan): Catalan gold coin

Tarrida (Catalan): small, two-masted commercial galley, with seventy-five oars on both sides, sometimes used for transporting horses

Veguer (Catalan): the most senior legal official in medieval Barcelona. The Casa del Veguer, the residence of this official in Barcelona, is next to the Royal Palace on Plaça del Rei (King's Square) in Barcelona.

Zurdo (Castilian): left-hande

ALSO AVAILABLE

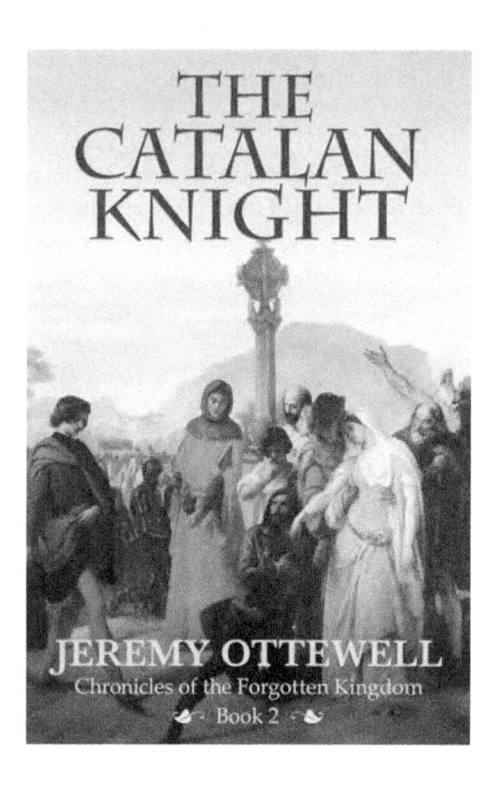

Book 2 of the Chronicles of the Forgotten Kingdom

Can the starving, bloodthirsty Catalan Almogaver warriors defeat the unholy alliance between France and the Vatican, and bring down the French knights in all their glory and hubris?

Unbeknown to Josep, he is a marked man already, and he must survive ruthless intrigue and spine-chilling cruelty to find his roots, serve his king and win the heart of the woman he loves.

Book 3 of the Chronicles of the Forgotten Kingdom

Josep Goodman has survived the war in Sicily and returned to the woman he loves, but soon toxic infighting plunges the Catalan - Aragonese Crown into civil war.

Loyalties switch, friends become foes, kings and princes marry their enemies. Swept up in the storm, Josep eyes one last campaign that – if he survives it – could bring wealth beyond his imagination.

The Chronicles of The Forgotten Kingdom reach a heart-stopping, bloody climax in this third and final chapter, The Curse of Constantinople.

Printed in Great Britain
by Amazon